INSIDE TRACK

John**PLIMMER**&Bob**LONG**

**HOUSE OF
STRATUS**

First published in 2000 by The House Of Stratus

The House of Stratus, an imprint of
Stratus Holdings plc, Lumley Close, Thirsk Industrial Park, Thirsk, North Yorkshire, YO7 3BX. UK

www.hosbooks.com

Typeset, printed and bound by The House of Stratus.

A catalogue record for this book is available from the British Library.

ISBN 1-84232-172-2

PART ONE

1

"It would appear that Mr Blade doesn't want to talk to us," the detective said, pacing steadily around the interview room. He came to rest by the door, his back to it. He was slightly behind Blade, so that he had to turn awkwardly to look at him. "That's probably because he doesn't yet know what a nasty temper you've got, Jonesy," he said, addressing the man on his right. He sat down on the chair on the opposite side of the table and stared at Blade.

Blade was slumped in his seat. His eyes were still watering. He knew this solid, thick-set little shit packed a punch. His nose still throbbed from the detective's violent idea of an introduction. Whatever happened to, "I am DC Nightmare and I'm commencing this interview at ten thirty two?" Whatever happened to a citizen's rights? Whatever happened to the bloody police in this bloody country? Blade asked the question anyway. "What about a solicitor?"

Warm, tobacco-scented breath hit his right ear as one of the other goons snarled, "Funny how you don't know a bee from a bull's arse isn't it. Now you're a QC in your spare time. You'll get your solicitor, sunshine, when we're ready. Right?" It was the answer Blade expected.

"You see, Mr Blade," the short man started, back on his feet again, leaning across the table, his face just a few inches from Blade's own. "It's not just this little caper. We're making enquiries into a dozen or so other blaggings and they've all got your name on them."

Blade risked another question. "Who are you?"

There was a chuckle; from in front, behind, from both sides. "I'm Nemesis, sonny, god of vengeance and retribution. And if that's too complicated for you, I'm the long arm of the law. But more central to your current predicament, matey, is the fact that I'm the bloke asking the questions." He took his weight on both hands, resting heavily on the table. "You know, it always amazes me how many of you sad bastards come in here and sit there thinking 'Bollocks'. Sooner or later you all crack, you know." Blade looked at him. "I mean," Shorty stood upright again and, folding his arms, he leant back against the window, "even a retard like you's got to realise you're well and truly in the shit long term for this little charade. A sawn-off shotgun? They're going to throw away the key. Picking on poor old duffers in one of Her Majesty's post office vans … you're not what you might call a hero, are you son? You're going to need all the help you can get."

Blade just looked at him. This arsehole wasn't going to offer him that ciggie, let alone invite him to talk about his childhood.

"So," Shorty unfolded his arms and leant across the table again, "how about some cooperation? A bit of mutual back scratching shall we say?" Blade said nothing. The copper stood up and shrugged. "Okay," he said. "We'll do it your way."

The lights flicked out and Blade felt his hair being tugged from behind. His head was pulled back and his arms were pinioned to his sides. His boots clattered against the woodwork on the underside of the table as his legs shot up and out as his body's reflexes fought to keep his balance. There was cursing and fumbling in the darkness. Then a plastic bag slid over his head and was tightened around his neck. Shock made him breathe in sharply and a plastic wall filled his mouth. Instinctively he tried to breathe again, but the ligature was already too tight and he felt the sweating, clammy plastic hard against his skin.

"Are you going to start talking now, you bastard?" Blade twisted and writhed like a man on the gallows. His throat was tight with terror. This wasn't Hitler's Germany. It wasn't Stalin's Russia. It was nice John Major's England.

* * * * *

"Christ Almighty, get a move on lads. We haven't got all bloody day." Harry Ventnor was trying to be casual about the afternoon's job. It wasn't his first and it probably wouldn't be his last. Even so, there was something about the way he held his fag. Something about the tightness in his voice. It was like that for all of them. Nerves. Fear. The build up of tension inside. Like a knot growing inside your belly. Steve Blade noticed it. So did Mike Stanley. Malcy Wilcox wouldn't notice anything unless it kicked him up the arse.

"Where's the car?" Blade asked.

The jerk of Ventnor's head said it all. "Over there, outside the launderette."

Blade looked across the street. The rain they'd promised on last night's weather was driving steadily out of a leaden sky. The Sierra Cosworth was navy blue. Not too new, not too old. Nothing flash so no envious bastards would notice it. Nothing beat up so no nosy copper would wonder why it was still on the road. And the colour was good. The best that dozy old Joe Public would come up with would be 'dark'. Perfect.

Ventnor had stolen it the night before and changed the registration plates to match an identical Cosworth that he'd seen parked up shortly beforehand. He was a meticulous man who didn't believe in taking unnecessary risks. That's why he was such a good wheelsman. One of the best in the business. He'd only come unstuck with the law on a couple of occasions. His main strength was his bottle. He'd stay on a job, standing his ground until every member of the team had been checked back into the car, no matter what was happening around them. Taking out a post office van was just another day at the office for a man like Ventnor. Okay, so he couldn't perform on the pavement, but behind the wheel of a car no one could touch him for his nerve. Not round here anyway. He'd spent most of the night carefully checking the ringer over – going over the engine and the vulnerable parts of the transmission to ensure everything was in perfect working order. He'd filled the tank with petrol and cleaned everything down so that there wasn't a single mark or fingerprint that could give them away. He'd taken similar precautions with the back-up car which was parked in a lock-up about a mile away from the job. He wasn't too chuffed about the weather: for a getaway driver heavy rain was the worst possible weather, unless of course there was snow and ice around. He preferred a dry road. One which the tyres could grip when he was chasing his arsehole away from the scene of a blagging. Worse, because of a recent dry spell, the rain would be mixed with oil, petrol and diesel; which would turn the road surface into an ice rink. He would have to be on top form today. Still, Ventnor told himself, this job would be a piece of piss for a man of his calibre. He just had to keep those nerves in check. Use them to his advantage. To sharpen his reactions. Sharpen his wits.

"Okay," Blade checked his watch, "four thirty. We've got half an hour. Everybody fit?" They all nodded. Four mates in donkey jackets and overalls, knocking off early. Ventnor unlocked the Cosworth and they were in; Blade and Ventnor in the front, Stanley and Malcy in the back.

"Remember, tosspot," Stanley couldn't resist ragging Malcy. "All you've got to do is grab the bags and shove them in the car. Right?"

Quick as a flash there was a knife in the lad's hand, glinting at Stanley's throat. "Shut your scumbag mouth, grandad. I know what to do." He barely had time to finish the sentence before Blade's hand snaked around the headrest and snatched the blade away. "Are you mad, you little shit? We're supposed to be a team, all right? A team with a job to do."

The fire died in Malcy's eyes as his boss faced him down. Blade pocketed the knife and studied the pair in the back. Malcy Wilcox was a cocky little bastard, a shoplifter at eight and an arsonist at ten. He belonged to the I-won't-get-caught-because-I'm-clever school. But Blade knew he would because he wasn't. Just don't let getting caught happen this time, sunshine. Not this time. Mike Stanley was ten years older and ten years saner. But he didn't suffer fools gladly and young ones not at all. All the way through planning this caper the two of them had been needling each other. "Now's not the time," Blade said, turning back to the windscreen and staring ahead at the traffic and the rain. "You two can kill each other after the job's done, okay?"

Ventnor drove slowly. No cutting corners. No jumping red lights. He didn't even cross his hands. Luck was with him too. He slipped the Cosworth into the space outside the post office, with a clear run behind and in front. The timing was perfect. Five minutes to go.

It was the longest five minutes of Malcy Wilcox's life. It wasn't his first time either, but he didn't know the team and the bastard in the back with him was on borrowed time. They all knew they'd do a stretch if they were caught, just because they were sitting in a stolen car with the engine running. Plus there was the small matter of the gun. He didn't want to go down with Mike Stanley. Didn't even want to stand next to him in the dock. "What about this pissing rain, Bladey?" The incessant noise it made, drumming on the car roof, was grating on his nerves.

"It'll only help." Blade still stared ahead, searching through the gathering dusk and rain for the first sight of the van. "Joe Public'll be in a hurry to get inside. Less time to notice us, know what I mean?"

Mike Stanley couldn't leave it alone. "Any prat knows that."

Ventnor caught the kid's reaction in the driving mirror. His jaw flexed and his eyes grew sullen. But he said, "I hope you're not including us in that Bladey. Getting inside, I

7

mean." No one laughed but it broke the ice and the tension inside the car subsided for a moment.

"Mike, don't forget." Blade's mind was running over the action to come. "Malcy and I've got to get into the back of the van before the bastard closes the door. There'll only be ten grand in the guard's hand when he comes out of the post office. It's the rest we want." Stanley nodded, cradling the newspaper-wrapped package in his lap, the one that held the sawn-off twelve bore. They'd been over it so many times, he could recite it in his sleep.

Mike Stanley was exactly the kind of man you needed on the pavement to cover your back. Solid and dependable, he was the best backer Blade had ever worked with. At six foot three he was an awesome sight behind a sawn-off and it would take a volcanic eruption to rip out his arse before he would loose his grip. But he needed this one to work. He'd already been locked up seven times and knew he couldn't take any more bird. He'd made a solemn vow when he last walked out through prison gates never to go back. One more heavy stretch and his life would be finished. He planned to retire on today's takings and head for the extreme north of Scotland. Perhaps even to one of those little islands. To a small farm where he would be left alone to live in harmony with nature. And go fishing whenever he wanted. Sitting there in the Cosworth, nervously fingering the sawn-off, he wondered if he should take his portion of the money and catch a train up north straight away. Stash the cash, wait a few days, then come back when things had quietened down and the police had stopped sniffing around. He could always say he'd been away on a fishing trip somewhere.

Ventnor swept the wipers across the windscreen now and then, peering through the sheet of water cascading down the glass. It was almost dark now and the reflection of the lights through the rain made it hard to see. He had the car's heater running full blast so the windows didn't steam up. Now he flicked on the rear heater so the visibility would be better through the rear windscreen. His main concern was the law, snooping around and wanting to know what four blokes were doing waiting in a car while the shops closed. And especially why one of them was carrying a shotgun. Given the situation, the merest glint of a helmet in the driving rain would probably have Ventnor's foot through the floor and they'd be out of there.

"Why don't you leave the wipers on?" Malcy wanted to know.

"Don't tell me my job, son," came Ventnor's terse reply.

Blade saw it as his job to defuse and calm. They had to focus on, concentrate on, the job ahead. "Ever seen a car parked at the kerb with its wipers going, Malcy? You'd ask yourself, what's he waiting for? What's he up to? What we don't need just now is anyone noticing us, okay?"

The kid nodded and shrugged his shoulders. He tucked his hands under his armpits and sat there like a coiled spring. "How much longer then?"

"Shut it!" Blade hissed. Bringing the kid along might have been the biggest mistake of his career. "Let's all just relax."

"Now there's something I wouldn't mind relaxing with," Stanley nodded in the direction of a piece of skirt scurrying through the rain, splashing along on wedge heels and duelling with other people's umbrellas. Her own was an unmistakable bright pink. After this job, maybe he'd himself find somebody just like that to replace the bitch who'd pissed off the other week with his kids. "Shit!" His eyes had focused beyond the girl. "Over there." The newspaper was off and the barrels shone dully in the shoplight reflections. Ventnor had seen him too. His hand hovered over the indicator, ready to pull out and get going.

"Calm down." Blade's heart was pounding. In his ears it sounded louder than the engine. He heard the safety catch click off. "Put it back, Mikey. You and I can't count far enough for the number of years we'll do if you off a copper." The busy was walking towards them, the shoulders of his dark blue overcoat silver with the rain. It bounced off his helmet and ran in rivulets from the rim. A rare sight. Mr Plod on his beat.

"We off, Steve?" Ventnor needed the word.

"No, not yet." Blade licked his lips. They were suddenly achingly dry. "Mikey, Malcy. Down on the floor."

Ventnor watched their heads vanish from his driving mirror. When he looked forward again, the officer had stopped in a shop doorway. He was talking to the shopkeeper. "Bet they're chatting about the weather," he muttered.

"We'll move out when I say so, Harry. Slowly, right?" Ventnor nodded. "He isn't going to hang about in this weather." Blade was talking partly to calm them all, but mostly to convince himself. "Come on, give your mouth a rest and piss off home. Must be tea-up in the station by now." The seconds ticked slowly by, but eventually he waved to the shopkeeper and wandered away at the time-honoured pace. Two and a half miles an hour. And then he was gone, turning left down a side street.

In the car the tension lifted like a cloud. Blade snatched open the holdall by his feet and pulled out the black woollen balaclavas. Quickly they hauled off their donkey jackets, revealing drab blue overalls. It was Ventnor's job to collect the coats at the vehicle change-over and then get rid of them after they'd got the money back to the safe house.

Five o'clock. The van was late.

"We've shit out." Malcy's fingers had all but tied knots in the balaclava on his lap. "It isn't coming, Steve." He was wriggling about on the back seat as if he had ants in his pants. He felt sick. Ventnor noticed how pale he looked and understood exactly how he felt. They all felt the same. In his agitation, Stanley kept checking and rechecking the parcel in his lap, just to make sure it was still there.

One minute past five and Blade began to wonder if he'd made a mistake. They couldn't wait much longer.

"Here it is." Ventnor had caught the black bulk and the headlights first. "Get ready."

* * * * *

The lights flashed on and the bag came off. Blade's head bounced onto the desk as he fought for air, his tortured lungs screaming. His head felt ready to burst. His arms were still firmly locked to his sides.

"Now you know who we are, my son," Shorty snarled from somewhere behind him. "We're the people who don't piss about. Psychopaths-are-us, okay? You see, we're used to dealing with shit like you. Bully boys who shove shotguns up old men's arses."

*　*　*　*　*

The van flashed scarlet as it came towards them under the streetlights. Blade glanced right and left, ahead and behind, scanning the glistening pavements for the law. The Crown's vehicle crossed the street and pulled up in front of them. Just as they'd watched it do so many times before. Every Tuesday and every Thursday. Always at exactly five o'clock. Regular as clockwork. Today was the first time they'd been late. The guard, in crash-helmet and visor, opened the front passenger door and jumped to the ground. Off he went into the post office to make his pick-up. He'd be exactly 27 seconds. Meanwhile, the van's driver opened his evening paper – that tell-tale trait they'd watched for weeks. Stupid, unobservant, predictable bastard. Thank God for him. Nobody spoke. The tension was palpable as they watched and waited. Blade's left leg was shaking to the rhythm of the idling engine. He placed his hand on his knee and held it still.

"Now!" said Ventnor.

"Wait!" said Blade. Steadying them. Checking for the moment. Feeling for the edge.

There was the sharp rustle as the newspaper came off once more. Then the safety catch clicked again. The balaclavas went on at a signal from Blade. "Now, people." His voice was quiet, calm. "Now's the time."

Mike Stanley had the speed and got there first. As the guard came whistling round the rear of the van, he felt

Stanley's shotgun barrels cold upon his neck. The man's shoulders drooped and his mouth fell open in shock and surprise. Stanley's hand swiftly covered his mouth, smothering his cry, and his voice was like gravel through his balaclava as he whispered, "Don't be a hero, grandad. Just step aside. It's not your money and it's not worth dying for."

* * * * *

"Of course," Shorty yanked Blade's head up by his hair, "there's nothing personal in all this, you understand. But you play with fire, son, you're going to get burned. Am I right? And, to be honest, we're not going to be too upset if we manage to kill you. Okay?"

Blade tried to speak. It was more of a squawk. "No," he managed. "It's not okay."

They sniggered. "Well, you would say that, wouldn't you?" the short man said. "But you really should have thought of that before you decided to take out post office vans for a living."

* * * * *

The van driver came to the end of the article and folded his paper. Christ, Bill was taking his time. It was getting late and he wanted to get off down the pub. The darts team from The Prince Regent was coming in to his local tonight and it should be a good night. He'd better check the old geezer hadn't had a heart attack or something. It was against regulations for him to get out of the van but, unable to see anything in his mirrors, he opened his door and hurried round the back of the van. The van's back door was open. Where the hell was ... Stanley's shotgun looked him straight in the eye. "Please, mate," he gasped. "We're not going to cause trouble."

Blade and Malcy were in the back of the van, hauling at the heavy canvas bags. They ran back to the Cosworth, and flung the bags through the open back windows. Then went back for a second run, falling over one another as they clambered back inside the van. Ventnor's feet balanced the clutch and accelerator, the gear in, the brake off. Blade heard Stanley's boots crunching on the tarmac. He was getting nervous, shifting from foot to foot, his breath smoking out and upwards in the wet night air. On the other side of the road, homeward-bound commuters hurried along the shining pavement, umbrellas lifted, heads down. Thank Christ, Blade thought, for British weather.

"Third time," he grunted to Malcy Wilcox. "Let's have it all."

Harry Ventnor revved the engine impatiently, ready for the off. This wasn't the plan. It was supposed to be one hit and away. What was the matter with the greedy bastards? They were giving the old gits time to take in details, shortening the odds with every second.

"Take it easy." Stanley heard one of the guards mutter. He jabbed the barrels into the guy's throat.

* * * * *

"Now, let's start again, shall we? How many jobs have you done in the past twelve months?"

Blade looked at him. And he saw his old man of all people. His dear, dead old dad, smiling at him. "Stick it out, son," he was saying. "Stick it out." Someone at least was on Blade's side.

"Bollocks," he said.

This time the lights didn't go out. The plastic bag smelt appalling. He could read the inverted 'Tesco' as the pressure slammed down on him again. This time he tried to ride it, breathing gently, keeping the sweating plastic off his face. But this time there was a sharp thud on the back of his head. He gasped, his vision blurred and his ears started to ring.

"The man asked you a question, dipstick!" a voice growled to his left.

There was another sickening thud, this time against his temple. He would have fallen forward, but his legs were buckled under the chair, his arms were held fast and the hand holding the twisted bag at his throat kept him upright.

"Come on, big man," a voice taunted to his right. "Don't piss us about. You know you'll feel better if you get it all off your chest."

The voices were distant and Blade felt his mind closing down. The inside of the bag was running with spittle and sweat, and darkness was filling the opaque shadows of the room.

* * * * *

"That's it." Blade tossed the last bag into the car and young Malcy whooped with delight. Stupid little tosser. Stanley levelled the sawn-off suddenly, sending both guards diving for cover. Then they were all in the Cosworth and Ventnor's foot was through the floor, rubber burning on the rain-polished street.

They'd done it. The weeks of preparation. The checking and double-checking. Sorting out the lads. Keeping the lid on Stanley and Wilcox. All worth it. All over.

"Jesus, we did it!" Malcy was tugging off his balaclava, rolling around on the wet canvas under his arse.

"Yeah," murmured Stanley, slumped with relief in his corner. "Can't wait for the Crimewatch reconstruction."

Blade's face almost smashed on the dashboard. He felt a sharp jolt as Malcy Wilcox crashed into the back of his seat.

"Stop. Armed police. Turn off the engine and get out of the car." They could hear the loudspeaker over the screech of the Cosworth's brakes. The broad body of an unmarked police car was skewed sideways in the road ahead of them, lights flashing, siren blaring. Another was swerving to a halt behind them. They'd got three hundred yards from the van and they were already boxed in. Like a nightmare. Like a bloody nightmare.

"This isn't happening." Stanley opened his door and started to climb out of the car, shotgun in hand. Ventnor sat there, gunning the engine, knuckles white on the wheel. There was nowhere to go. Filth in front. Filth behind. Rows of parked cars on either side. And about five hundred grand to defend. Like the bloody Valley of Death. Ventnor ducked instinctively as he heard a rifle crack somewhere behind his head, two explosions, one after the other, like slow hand claps. He turned and saw Stanley lifted bodily by the impact of the bullets that had ploughed into his head and torso. The sawn-off sailed through the air and landed with a clanging sound on somebody's bonnet. Stanley's body collapsed, blood pumping from the mess that was once his head. The poor bastard hadn't even had time to groan.

Blade gritted his teeth. "Kill the engine." Ventnor did as he was told. For a moment they sat there in silence, while young Malcy Wilcox whimpered in the back, unbelieving, open mouthed, unable to look away from the corpse lying beside the car. Black figures were visible now in the half light, closing in on the Cosworth, pointing their guns. Blade could read the white letters on their glistening helmets – POLICE. There was a further screeching of brakes and Blade saw the car in front reversing, allowing a third car to swerve past it in a blaze of blinding light. It ploughed full tilt into the Cosworth in a tearing and rending of metal and a shattering of glass. Harry Ventnor had released his seat belt. So his body snapped back, then forward, his head thudding on the steering wheel as he took the full force of the impact. He slumped to his right, his face pale against the steamed up window.

"Armed police." Blade heard the loudhailer again. "Get out of the car with your hands in the air."

"Bladey." Malcy was almost incoherent, sobbing. "What'll we do? What're we gonna do, Steve?"

"Do what you're told." Malcy did. He kicked open the door. Bags of money flopped out with him and he lay face down on the road, his hands over his head, crying into the wet tarmac. Blade looked down at his hands, clasped together in his lap. He had a cut on his left thumb. Shards of glass lay all around him. Numbly, his uncomprehending mind wondered why. When he looked up again, there were police all around the car, barking orders at him, gesturing with their semi-automatics. "For Christ's sake," he said softly through his teeth. "Calm down." He unbuckled his seat belt and opened the door slowly. Another money bag slipped out and hit the road with a soft thud. His left foot trod gently beside it. How many guns were pointing at him? Six? Seven? He couldn't be sure. But he could hear the excited babble of a crowd gathering at either end of the street. What a balls up. Mr Plod couldn't be so trigger-happy now. Steam was hissing from the Cosworth's radiator grill. Haloes of red and blue light flashed in rotation and the crackle of radios punctuated the moment.

"Lie face down on the ground," came another order. "Place your hands behind your back."

Blade still had Malcy's knife in his pocket. One move for that, he knew, one move out of the ordinary at all, and he could kiss his arse goodbye. He'd finish up lying in the gutter with Mike, his blood trickling down the drain with the rainwater. There was still one gambit left though. A loophole in the law, so to speak. To his left was a dark alleyway between a newsagent and a greengrocer. It was narrow and bulging with scattered piles of rubbish, but to Steve Blade, it was heaven sent.

"Okay." He stood with his hands in the air. "Okay, I'll do whatever you say. Don't shoot. I'm unarmed." There was one man in his way, but he'd take his chance with him. He couldn't stand in the glare of the spotlight for long. He let his shoulders drop as if to comply with the order and join Malcy on the ground, then charged sideways, driving a shoulder into the hesitating copper, batting him aside. Then he was gone, away down the alleyway into the darkness.

He heard no shots. No ricocheting bullets. Only shouts of fury. The alleyway ended in a brick wall but someone had conveniently pushed a dumpster up against it. He jumped to his left, hauling himself up a slippery pile of wooden crates and onto the dumpster. Then he was over the wall, landing on a loose shale path on the other side. The rain was easing now, but there were puddles everywhere. He splashed through them, his lungs already at bursting point. In the semi-darkness he remembered to throw away the knife.

The path continued straight on, down to a busy-looking street that ran parallel to the one he'd just left. The street blazed with lights and late afternoon traffic. He ripped off his balaclava and threw that away too. Over a hedge, into someone's excuse for a garden. What should he do? Stroll casually into a newsagent and buy some ciggies. And ask innocently why all the police activity in the next street? Why not? A running man would attract attention. Best to slow it down, brazen it out. He steadied himself, fighting for breath. Right. Now. Round the corner.

It felt like walking into a wall. As he turned the corner, he went down, thrown backwards by the force and suddenness of the punch. He looked up to see a tall, dark-haired man standing over him. Plainclothes. He knew the build, the attitude. Blade raised both hands in a gesture of surrender – the same trick he'd pulled just now – then closed his left hand tightly in the man's groin. He dragged himself up and kneed the groaning officer to the ground. Then he was hurtling back up the pathway. He skidded to a halt. Two uniforms were clambering over the wall, cutting off his escape. He spun round to see more silhouettes pounding down the path from the other direction. He raised his hands in the air and clapped them on the top of his head. Oh bollocks, bollocks, bollocks.

"Try running now, rabbit," he heard one of the silhouettes sneer before knocking him to the ground and roughly cuffing his wrists.

* * * * *

"Bladey? Bladey? Is that you?" It was Malcy Wilcox, his distant voice calling down the passageway, through the white-painted breeze-blocks. Steve Blade sat on the hard wooden bench, cradling his head in his hands. What had happened? What the hell had gone wrong?

"I haven't told 'em nothing, Bladey, honest." Malcy called out again, trying to find a friend in the silence. "Any idea where Harry is? Stanley's dead." This wasn't a game any more. They weren't throwing bricks from vehicle to vehicle as practice, checking times, watching faces. Now it was for real. The kid was terrified, but it was time for Steve Blade to cut loose. He lifted his head and growled, "Shut up, you loud-mouthed scumbag. I don't know you. Understand? I don't know you."

Blade knew the score. The Old Bill would have the cells bugged, they'd be taping every word. They were both in enough shit as it was. No point in giving it to the bastards on a plate. Silence. The kid was scared, but he was no mug. He'd got the message.

What had gone wrong? All the planning. All the preparation. How did the law know they'd be there? From one solitary copper to a whole bloody SWAT team armed to the teeth? Where was Harry? Malcy Wilcox was down the corridor, fearful, uncomprehending. Harry couldn't have got away. When Blade saw him last, he was slumped behind the wheel, out like a bloody light. For a moment … but no, Blade shook himself free of the thought. Not Harry. Straight as a bloody die, Harry was. What about Stanley? No, never Mike Stanley. Or Malcy? Too stupid. Jacky Benson? No way. Jacky'd never do a thing like that. Besides he didn't know enough. He only knew the time. But not the place.

So how did they know? How the fuck did they know. This was supposed to be an easy job. He'd spent months planning it. Getting the team together. Rehearsing. Preparing. This was supposed to be his last job. The final one. He'd told Sammy that this was going to be it. That failure wasn't an option. This was the one that was going to make her dreams come true. She had always been there. Loving. Loyal. Beautiful. This had been the job that was supposed to provide enough money to feather their nest for the rest of their lives. Enough to get them out of the tiny corporation flat they shared – a living room, a box for a kitchen, and a tiny bedroom – and into somewhere bigger. Somewhere warmer. South America or the Continent. They hadn't decided. But somewhere where they could start a family. Where their kids could grow up safe. Out of trouble. Somewhere where half the bloody neighbourhood weren't ex-cons.

He stood up in the cell. Above him was a small, barred window, the night sky beyond. No moon. No stars. Just black emptiness. His eyes trailed down the white shiny wall and his heart and hopes dropped with them. He couldn't see her. Silly. It had only been a few hours, but he couldn't remember what Sammy looked like. Not exactly. But he could hear her voice as she said what she always said when he went out on a job. "Don't get run over now, Steve." He never told her where he was going or why. He didn't have to. She had that sixth sense and she knew.

"I'll be back later," he heard himself say. "Then we'll pack our bags shall we? And hop on a plane." She smiled at him as he closed the bedroom door.

He heard the clatter of boots on the polished corridor floor and the rattle of keys. Blade turned to see a lanky, balding sergeant standing in the open door. "Come on, son, we'd like a word."

* * * * *

The sergeant left him in Interview Room Number Three. It was as cold and empty as the cell he'd just left. There were more bars on the windows, this time fuzzy behind reinforced frosted glass. There was a rectangular table and three chairs, hard and upright. He sat in one of them, his back to the window. He knew the drill. They'd be in in a minute. Two of them, possibly three. One of them would introduce himself as DI So-and-So. The other would be Sergeant Shit-Hole. If there was a third, he'd station himself by the door, just in case. Depending on what happened with the other two, the third man would be deaf, blind and dumb. Three bloody wise monkeys. They would have tossed a coin outside the door. One of them, maybe the DI, would be the nice policeman. He'd offer Blade a fag, call him Steve, and whinge about the state of the nation. The sergeant would be the nasty policeman, badgering, needling, shouting. Always in your face. You couldn't give them just the one job. That wouldn't satisfy them. You'd have to sit there and listen to torrents of bullshit, hour after hour, until tempers frayed and nerves snapped. In the end you'd tell them you were Jack-the-fucking-Ripper just to get the bastards off your back. Just for peace and quiet.

The door opened. Four plainclothes men. Two of them were big outside lavatories with attitude, one was about average height and build, and the last was a ginger-haired little runt who looked like he'd been squeezed in a vice and spread sideways. Well, well. Four of them. This was preferential treatment. The thick-set short-arse asked Blade to move to another chair, the one on the other side of the table. Then he sat down in the chair Blade had just vacated. Shorty stared at him, his fingers drumming on the table top.

All four of them, Blade noted, as the other three took up positions around him like the points of a compass, wore dark suits and ties. Like they were going to a funeral. There was silence for a moment; the drumming stopped as suddenly as it started. The short-arse, Blade reckoned, would be the nice policeman. He didn't look like he'd have the bottle for anything else.

Blade struck first. He'd work quickly. Catch them off their guard. "Look, gents," he spread his hands as though in supplication, "I'm going to do you all a favour and save you some time. You don't get a dicky bird out of me until my brief arrives, okay?" He smiled, sat back and folded his arms. He knew the body language. This said, "I'm waiting for the fag, for the first kind word." He guessed it would be 'Steve'.

Instead, he felt a fist, fired fast and hard, straight into his face. Shorty's greeting. His head whipped back and he felt tears well in his eyes. Blood spurted down his overalls and soaked into the shirt Sammy had bought him two Christmases ago. Blade felt his nose. Not broken, but bloody painful. The ginger bastard grinned at him, like a vicar who'd just passed him a cucumber sandwich.

"Don't be a cheeky bastard, son," the detective said. "Speak when you're spoken to, all right? Can you follow that?" Blade could, but his attention was devoted to stopping the bleeding. "Pinch the top of your nose," came the friendly advice. "Thumb and forefinger. See, I learnt that in first aid. That should do the trick." One of the others reached over and passed a cold wet rag to Blade. They'd come prepared.

"Tell me." Shorty was leaning back, relishing the moment. "What's it feel like to have made such a balls-up of such a simple job, then?" Blade said nothing. Merely asserting his rights had got him a bloody nose. Anything he said now would lead to another smacking. "You must have worked it out by now that we've been watching you people for some time. Where did the sawn-off come from? Somebody's Christmas cracker?"

Blade said nothing. He recognised the lie. If Mr Plod had been watching them for some time, they'd have seen Mike Stanley buy the gun from that scrubber in the Rose and Crown.

Shorty stood and began pacing steadily around the interview room. "It would appear that Mr Blade doesn't want to talk to us …"

2

Jack Priestley rubbed his hands together and closed his office door to shut out any would-be intruders. He needed a little time to himself to concentrate on how he was going to run the operation. The usual concerns came flooding into his mind. What if the job didn't go down? What if the job went down and they lost them? What if somebody got shot? What if … ? What if … ? Priestley had experienced the same collection of thoughts many times before and knew that each and every operation would be different from all the others. As long as he remained mindful and aware of the dangers he was exposing himself and his people to, the chances of success would always be in his corner. His biggest concern was Steve Blade. What if he had to make the arrest? Would he do it? Or would he allow his old friend to walk? No contest. He'd lock him up. A lot of water had passed under the bridge since they'd last met. At least, he hoped it had.

"You doing the briefing, Jack?" Priestley's period of quiet contemplation was abruptly interrupted as George Nicholls' large frame appeared in his doorway. The detective superintendent's voice matched his stature; loud and booming, audible for miles around. He had a big, protruding belly; proof of numerous pints consumed over many years. And hands like battered shovels; proof of his ability to handle himself.

"Yes, Boss." Priestley stood up and welcomed Nicholls into his hideaway with a courteous smile. "Good weather for it."

"Jack, the forecast's terrible."

"That's what I mean. If we don't shoot them, the bastards will drown or catch the pneumonia." They both laughed while Nicholls made himself comfortable in one of the chairs opposite Jack's desk.

"How good is it really, Jack?" he asked.

"Good enough. This guy's never let me down before and I think it sounds right. We're due for another blagging on this pitch anyway. We've only got half the story but I think this one will turn up trumps."

"Okay, Jack, it's all yours. You don't mind if I come along for the ride?" Nicholls didn't expect an answer. They were expecting the bandits to be armed, so the firearms mob had been called in. Protocol therefore decreed that Nicholls had to oversee the action. So whether he came or not wasn't up to Jack. And in any case, Nicholls' attention was already diverted to a photograph hanging on the wall – the young Detective Constable Priestley sitting in the middle of forty other fresh-faced wankers on their CID course. Taken in happier days five years ago. "You've certainly changed since that was taken, Jack. Bit of a mess now, aren't you." Priestley wasn't sure how to take that remark, so said nothing. "Come on then," said Nicholls. "Let's go and put them all in the picture."

*   *   *   *   *

The briefing took about half an hour and when they were done the team scrambled to their respective positions. For Priestley and Nicholls, that meant the command vehicle – a bullet proof Range Rover. On their way across the yard to the waiting car, Nicholls asked apprehensively, "What about Stanley and Wilcox, Jack? Have they got the guts for this?"

"Absolutely. They've got the bottle all right. Young Wilcox has been well known to us since he was a kid. Nicking cars, breaking and entering, you name it. And you must remember Stanley? He was the joker who blew away the doorman's legs at La Dolca Vita a few years ago."

"I remember. I dealt with him for that one. What about Blade?"

"The word is that Blade's into everything these days."

* * * * *

Minutes later, their driver parked the Range Rover well away from the post office and out of sight. Peter Morgan, the firearms inspector, joined them in the back of the car. "Okay, Peter?" said Priestley. "Your boys all set?"

"Sure, Jack. Ready and waiting."

Priestley checked his watch. Four thirty. Time to test the radio and check in with Geordie Tomkins, his roof spotter. "Geordie, can you see all right from where you are?"

"Affirmative, Boss. The rain doesn't help, but I won't miss much from up here."

"Make sure you don't miss a thing. You're our eyes and I need to know everything you see." Mind you, it was pissing down, and that was the last thing you needed when there was the possibility of bullets flying about all over the place. He glanced worriedly at Morgan who nodded his agreement. The weather was certainly not good news. But Morgan's team was one of the best available and the least likely to get carried away when everything let rip.

"How's life in the flat, Jack? Gets a bit lonely at times I suppose?" Priestley knew that Nicholls was trying to be kind, and that he was sincerely concerned about Priestley's domestic predicament. But there was no way Priestley wanted to discuss his private life in front of Morgan and the driver. He missed Brenda more than he knew how to admit. He'd got used to their husband-and-wife life together. And it had taken him some time to get used to life without her.

He'd never forget the day he got home and found her note. It seemed so sudden. So unexpected. She just disappeared. Walked out one day and never looked back. It had taken ages to find her. And by then she was shacked up with some building society manager and had filed for divorce. He hadn't really been able to take it all in until he held the divorce papers in his hand. That had been six months ago. He had immediately put the house they'd shared on the market and moved into a small flat in the city centre. Nowadays he was rediscovering the bachelor life he'd never really had, and discovering it wasn't so bad. But he wished his boss could be a little more tactful. "You want to get out more, Jack," Nicholls continued. He was nothing if not persistent. "Come to one or two of the functions and spread your wings a bit." But one of Priestley's pet hates was police functions. He'd always avoided them like the plague. Even when he and Brenda were still together. The conversation was always about work and Priestley had better things to do in his spare time than talk about policing. He muttered a non-committal response, his eyes all the time searching the street for signs of trouble. Darkness had fallen, and the street lights were shining bright through the rain.

"Problem, Jack?" asked Nicholls.

"I don't think so," he said cautiously. "But there are too many people about. We could have done without so many of the Great British Public crowding in on us."

"Well, son," Nicholls coughed, "at the end of the day, there's not much we can do about that is there?" Fortunately, Nicholls' rather foolish remark was drowned out by a sudden screeching of tyres and only Priestley heard him. In the Rover, all four heads turned in the direction of the noise. The stray dog had almost seen its last lamp post. Thankfully the driver had missed him, but not by much. "Shit," gasped Nicholls. "That was a close one." What they really didn't need right now was a group of people milling around an RSPCA van.

The radio crackled to life once more. "Suspect car has just pulled up about ten yards from the post office. It's a dark blue Ford Sierra Cosworth with four up. Two in the front and two in the back. I can't see the number yet."

Priestley called to Anna Beecham, who was positioned covertly in a nearby side road. "Go have a look Anna and come back to me."

"Two minutes, Boss," came the reply and Anna slipped into the street and joined the crowd of hurrying pedestrians, her pink umbrella swooping up and down.

"The registration number is D32NPJ. Two in the front and two in the back confirmed, Boss. One in the back has a parcel on his lap. Could be the sawn-off."

"I'll check the number, Gaffer." This was DC Adrian Butcher, back in the control room at HQ.

Tomkins' voice came back on. "Hang on, team. We've got a problem. One of the local bobbies is on the plot." Priestley winced and glanced at Nicholls.

"Didn't we tell the uniforms, Jack?"

"No, Boss. I'm sorry, we didn't." Jack knew he'd made a cock up, and it showed all over his face.

"Well, son. There's a lesson to be learned. We should have done."

"Okay, team, he's walking away. He's passing the suspect car now. Looks as though he hasn't noticed it. Okay, he's going up Ralph Road. Okay, all clear."

"Do you want me to have the local controller informed, Boss?" said Priestley, trying to make amends.

"No, not now, Jack. It's too late. If we told them now we'd look even more like a bunch of plonkers." Priestley could only nod in agreement. Sod it! How could he have overlooked something so simple?

Butcher came on again. "Nothing on the car, Boss. Could be a ringer."

"I'm aware of that, sunshine." Priestley's voice was sharp and full of irritation.

"The van is approaching." Geordie Tomkins had the pulse again. "It's now stationary outside the post office and facing the Sierra. One man out of the van and going into the post office. Standby everybody."

Priestley interrupted. "Calm everybody. Wait, wait, wait. Back to you, Geordie."

"Okay, he's coming out of the post office and going to the rear of the van. Three men are out of the Sierra. The one with the shotgun is now with the post office man. The other two are in the back of the van. Okay, they're making their first run. They're going back to the van." There was a pause. Then Geordie continued, "Both post office men are on the pavement. One bandit, armed and with them. Two others in the van." The young, rain-drenched spotter thought it best to repeat his guvnor's orders, "Wait, everybody, wait." Then, "Two with bags out of the van." Another pause. "Christ, they're going back. Wait, everybody. They're making a third run."

Nicholls glanced nervously at Priestley, beads of sweat were forming on his forehead. The tension was almost unbearable. "For fuck's sake, Jack. Call it." But Priestley had been down this road before and ignored his senior officer. He knew exactly when to call it.

"They're making the third run." Geordie repeated.

Nicholls' mouth started to twitch. The pressure was getting to him. He had to say something. Anything. "What've they done with the bags?" he said.

"What're they doing with the bags, Geordie?" Priestley asked.

"They're throwing them on the back seat of the Cosworth, Boss." He paused. It seemed like forever. Nobody knew what was happening. Then, "Okay, there's movement on the car. All in the car. They're off."

"Jack?" Nicholls couldn't stand much more. He shouted, "Jack?"

"Okay team, let's take them." Priestley shouted into the radio. "Strike, strike, strike."

Adrenaline levels were on the ceiling and pulse rates through the roof. Heart rates soared as Priestley's team converged on the criminals as they attempted to make their escape. With loud screechings of brakes, flashing lights, and wailing sirens, they brought the bandit car to a standstill. All hell let loose. Nicholls buried his head in his hands as shots were fired. "Christ Almighty," he whispered. Another police car ploughed into the Sierra. "Fuck," he whispered. The command vehicle crept closer to obtain a better view of the ambush. The bandit car was blocked in at both ends. There was nowhere for it to go. For a moment there was silence, then the loudhailer blared again. One of the bandits hit the floor. Another climbed out of the car more slowly. Christ, thought Priestley. Steve Blade. He watched him stop, hands in the air, ready to hit the floor. But then he darted away suddenly to his left. Up an alleyway between two shops. Shit. Shit. Shit.

"One's gone up the alley, Boss," yelled the driver.

"Yeah, I saw him."

"Don't let him get away, Jack," urged Nicholls. "There'll be hell to play if he does."

"Back up, Charlie," Priestley ordered the driver. "Take that right and get us round the back." Priestley knew the area well. So did Charlie. The Range Rover skidded as it took off. A right and then a left brought the vehicle to the corner of the next street along.

Priestley jumped from the vehicle and ran towards the other end of the alleyway. He stood there for a moment, his back pressed up hard against a wall. He heard the running footsteps on the shale track. He heard the heavy breathing. Steve was coming towards him. A woman walked past, almost stabbing him in the face with the pointed end of her umbrella. The footsteps stopped. He listened to Steve struggling to catch his breath. He knew that Steve was only feet away. Just around the corner. He waited, clenching his fist, ready to strike. When Steve Blade moved, the punch landed smack in the middle of his face.

3

The glare in his eyes when he got home had been enough to make Valerie Butcher tremble. And now, the stony silence. The way he chewed his food. And threw the cutlery down on his plate. How much more could her feeble mind and body take? She stood in the kitchen, staring out of the window, watching a group of kids playing football in the flood-lit car park below. The council had recently installed the lights in a vain attempt to stop car theft. Not that it was having much effect. She thought of better days. She'd been attractive. Full of bounce and confidence. She'd enjoyed life to the full. And then along came Mr Right. Six foot tall, dark haired and handsome, Adrian had been impressive in his constable's uniform, serving Queen and country. A young girl's dream. A hero. They'd had the most beautiful wedding in the world. But now her dreams were shattered, just like the glass that once covered the photograph of the happy couple that used to stand so proudly on the sideboard. Her thoughts were disturbed by the sound of smashing plates as the table in the living room was overturned. Tears flooded her eyes as he entered the kitchen.

* * * * *

Valerie Butcher's naked body crawled across the carpet towards the far end of the room. Tears streamed down her face. Petrified, she mumbled incoherently.

"That's it, crawl you mangy, worthless bitch."

"Don't. Please Adrian. Don't," she pleaded.

He stood behind her, legs slightly apart, arms folded across his broad chest. Like a bird of prey waiting to pounce. "You're nothing to me," he shouted. "You mangy slag." She screamed as he kicked her in the buttocks with all his might, causing her to leap forward and bang her head hard on the edge of the radiator, just below the window sill. The wretched woman turned on her knees to face him, blood flowing down her face and neck. She held up her puny arms in a vain attempt to deflect the next blow. He looked at her in disgust. With his final punch she rolled over and fell into a merciful pit of darkness. Adrian Butcher slammed the door as he left, late again for the evening shift.

He had no idea why he did it. But every so often he snapped. A violent rage exploded within him and unleashed horrendous and wicked acts of torture on his frail and helpless young wife. Perhaps tonight it had been the release of delayed tension after a heist he hadn't even really been involved in. Perhaps it was because he was angry that he wasn't there. Wasn't there to meet out his own form of punishment when he triumphantly made his arrest. Part of the team. A hero in his own eyes as well as everyone else's. Or maybe it was the sight of the old bruises on her face? Perhaps the nervous trembling of her hands when she placed his dinner on the table? Many would say he needed help. Some would say he needed hanging.

* * * * *

George Nicholls' joy and elation were self-evident. And his relief total. His face beamed and his voice was full of pride as he addressed the hero of the day. Priestley, for his part, sat back in his chair, his feet up on his desk, and smoked a cigar; his habitual reward for a job well done, or salve in times of crisis. He too was satisfied with the way the operation had gone. Apart, of course, from the death of Mike Stanley. That was unfortunate. But it could have been worse. It could have been one of his bobbies, or even Joe Public, lying in the gutter. And then there was Harry Ventnor under guard in the hospital, but the word was he would probably pull through.

"How're your bollocks now, Jack?" asked the detective superintendent with a wry smile.

"I'll live," Priestley assured him. He had a silly I'm-the-smartest-bastard-in-the-world look on his face.

And quite entitled to it too, thought his boss. "Well done, Jack." Nicholls' cheeks were rosy red. They'd be even more cherubic later, when he had a pint in his hand. "We could have done without Stanley's untimely death, but still, cracking job."

"Everything that has to be done about that, has been."

"Coroner informed?" Priestley nodded. Nicholls clapped his hands together and continued, "I've told them about it up town and the media's being directed to the press office. Let me know if there are any problems." Nicholls got up to leave. "What about your informant?"

"I'm going to give him a monkey later," said Priestley.

"What?" said Nicholls, surprised. "Five hundred quid? That's a bit cheap, Jack."

"Boss, the man's already had half. One thousand total. You signed it off, remember?"

"What? Oh, sure, sure," bumbled Nicholls. "Well, don't forget to get him to countersign the chit." He opened the office door, but before he left he turned and looked back at Priestley, his face suddenly serious. "And don't forget what I said earlier, Jack. Get yourself out and about more. Life's not all about this job you know. It's not the be-all and end-all," he said, closing the door firmly behind him.

Priestley smiled. He liked George Nicholls. Sincere, straightforward, occasionally forgetful. He looked upon him as a kind of father figure. One who wouldn't harm anybody – as long as you played it straight and didn't involve him in anything too risky. Mind you, his bottle wouldn't stand up to much of a test anyway. He'd almost shat himself when the gun went off. But then again, who did have much bottle these days? Still, Priestley admired his gaffer's honesty; he was straight as a die, a policeman of the old school and the best sort.

Priestley sat back in his chair and thought about his gaffer's closing remarks. Nicholls didn't know about Sonia Hall. Nobody did. Nobody could keep a secret in this place. Sonia Hall. A few more hours and he'd be with her. The beauty of the legal profession. The lovely Sonia Hall. The young, trim, learned counsel, who just happened to have invited him to dinner at her place tonight. She had a body that would send most men into orbit. And it would be his later on. Or so he hoped. All being well. He smiled in anticipation. The prospect was delicious. But for the moment there were things to be done. Time was getting on and he had all this crap to deal with before he could knock-off. He jumped up and made for the door, only to be intercepted by Anna Beecham. "Sorry, Sir, but I thought you should know. There are some men from the Force Crime Squad interviewing one of the prisoners." Priestley's good humour evaporated immediately and Anna was left standing in the doorway as her boss ran along the corridor and down the stairs.

* * * * *

"What the hell is going on, Oberon?" Priestley didn't bother to try to hide his anger. "What on earth are you lot doing here?" Bernard Oberon as a detective inspector in the Force Crime Squad and his people had no business interfering with CID affairs.

"Blade, Jack, Steve Blade. You've captured him. Congratulations." Oberon was quietly spoken and always well mannered, characteristics which tended to make the unwary drop their guard. "You're a hero, Jack. We've been investigating him and Mike Stanley for months."

32

"So? That doesn't explain why you're here. Where is he?"

"He's just having a quick chat with a couple of my lads. They'll be done in a minute. Don't worry. They'll get everything out of him."

Priestley was furious. "And what gives you the right to interview a prisoner who's been arrested by my people! Call your animals off, Bernard. You're treading on my toes."

"Don't need to," he said quietly. "Here they come now."

And there they were. Not two, but a gang of four. Swaggering along the corridor towards him. Devious bastards. Priestley met them halfway and glared at them. They stared insolently back. To his surprise he recognised one of them. Detective Sergeant Colin Boyle. A slime-ball of the highest order so far as Priestley was concerned. Short and stout, solid as they come, Boyle had a grin on his face from ear to ear. And aftershave that stank to high heaven. His minions followed closely behind. Two thick-looking thugs and a dark-haired man with a fag hanging off his bottom lip. Fag-man winked as he passed and Priestley had to fight the urge to punch the creep's lights out.

* * * * *

Blade wasn't sure if he was conscious or not. His face was pressed onto a wooden table top, but he wasn't certain he was breathing. He thought about it. Perhaps he was. There was a gurgling sound coming from somewhere and it occurred to him that perhaps it was him. Perhaps these were the death rattles he'd heard about as a child. The noise a body made just before it died. So, that was it. He wasn't dead. He was dying. Still in his body, but only just. He thought it best to keep still. And wait for Death to come along and take him to St Peter. Before he passed out again, he wondered what the Pearly Gates would look like.

Every intake of breath caused a piercing pain inside his windpipe. He supposed that was a good sign. Would a dying body feel pain? Cautiously, he tried opening his eyes. The room was a blur. He blinked. Even that hurt. There was a voice sounding off somewhere, but it seemed to be a long way away. Hard to tell. Slowly, like a beaten up camera lens, his eyes started to focus. There was a white enamel mug on the table in front of him. Fingers were wrapped around it. The burning sensation in his eyes was gradually subsiding. He blinked again. The fingers belonged to a hand. The hand to an arm. His eyes slowly followed the arm upwards. A face and ... "Oh bollocks," he heard himself croak.

"They're fine," said the face. "No thanks to you." Sitting on the opposite side of the table was the geezer who'd smacked him in the mouth. Whose testicles he'd used as leverage. No doubt he was waiting to take his turn in the torture chamber, in revenge for the belting he'd given his balls. Blade felt himself begin to shake like a newly landed fish, and slowly he pulled himself away from the table. Sitting upright in his chair, his eyes still burned and his head was pounding. How much more would he have to take? How much more could he take? If this one started on him, he'd admit to anything. Anything he wanted. Blade had never felt so exposed or so vulnerable. His mind was confused and cloudy. He couldn't think. He desperately tried to gather his thoughts but his head was spinning.

The mug moved towards him. "Drink this. You'll feel better." The face smiled. Blade's shaking hands fumbled their way around the mug. His arms shivered crazily as he lifted it to his mouth. But the cool water soothed his aching lips as he drank.

"You look terrible," said the face. Blade didn't bother to try to reply. "I don't expect you to tell me what happened in here," the face continued softly. "I've a bloody good idea anyway. It won't happen again." Priestley wasn't sure whether or not Blade would find his words reassuring. "Not while I'm in charge anyway. Do you want a doctor?"

Blade looked hard at the face. There was something familiar about it. His eyes needed more time. He didn't trust any filth, but at least this one wasn't knocking him about.

34

Not at the moment at any rate. He didn't reply. His eyes slid away from the face, towards one of the far corners of the room.

Priestley studied Blade closely and cursed under his breath. He got up suddenly and went to the door. "I'll be back," he said. It was then that the voice gave Blade an idea. No, it couldn't be. Never. Not Jack. Not his old mate Jack Priestley. He turned his gaze to the door as the latch clicked shut and stared at it in amazement. Who'd have thought it? Jack Priestley, a copper!

He listened to Priestley's footsteps until they had faded away into the distance. His mind flooded with memories. Swept back to see two grubby kids playing marbles in the dust. He heard his young self saying, "You ain't having me glarney, Jack Priestley, 'cos you cheated." He could see the innocent face staring at him in silence, wondering why Steve Blade had deliberately lied to him.

"I won your glarney fair and square, Stevie. If you want it back, you'll have to fight for it." That was how they settled most of their boyhood squabbles, and the scraps invariably ended up with bloody noses and grazed knuckles.

* * * * *

"You bunch of irresponsible morons." Priestley was outraged, his voice loud enough for everybody in the nick to hear as he yelled down the telephone at Bernard Oberon. "Have you any idea what those gorillas have done to him? I'm going to hang you and your psychopaths for this. The paper will be on Jim Nolan's desk by the morning."

"In that case, Jack, I'll have to get my lads back down there to make statements of complaint."

Priestley knew what was coming. "You bastard."

"Blade got violent and attacked my lads," continued Oberon calmly. "If push comes to shove, Jack, you know I'll have no other option."

"Yeah, and I suppose one of your scumbags will need stitches for a gash on his head. And then there'll be the bruising which I've no doubt will mysteriously appear on the same shithole's face?"

On the other end of the line, Oberon shrugged his shoulders, "You know the way it is, Jack."

* * * * *

There was a strange feeling in the pit of the policeman's stomach. He was sitting in front of a memory, a major part of his own history. The smell of pine disinfectant. Red Cardinal on doorsteps. Brass knockers on doors. Blue pavement bricks. Horse shit from the Co-op milkmen's drays. The sound of empty milk bottles being collected off front door steps. All were associated with the child this man had once been. Amazingly, after all this time, there was still a bond between them. He sensed it. He could feel it. Perhaps because they'd been so close as kids? Perhaps because of the hardships they'd shared all those years ago? Or perhaps because he felt such pity for a man who'd just been tortured half to death? Whatever, they sat together in silence. Both reflecting on the past. On the time when they'd been inseparable and a common feeling of loyalty still flickered between them. It came from the back streets of an inner city slum which they'd both survived, their pride and dignity more-or-less intact. Planning and scheming in the dust. Two heads together. One fair. The other dark.

"Ironic. We used to play cops and robbers together." Blade's eyes widened at the recollection. "Remember?"

"I remember. And cowboys and Indians." Priestley smiled at the memory and flicked cigar ash onto the floor, a habit his ex-wife had always admonished him for. "We go back a long way," he said, then paused. "Those others just now, Steve …"

"Forget it, Jack. I know it wasn't you. I don't want any explanations. I'll have my day, don't worry about that."

"I just want you to know, I'll be dealing with this case from now on. Me and my kids don't work like that. We don't have to."

"That's," Blade searched for a suitably non-committal answer, "comforting."

"There'll be a doctor here in a minute."

"I don't want one."

Priestley stood up. "You're having one. It's getting late, so one of my officers will charge you. Then you'll be taken back to your cell and the doctor will see you there. Make sure you're okay. We'll continue reminiscing in the morning."

* * * * *

The sky had cleared and the stars had come out by the time Priestley met Adrian Butcher as he was crossing the yard. "Working the late shift, Adrian?"

"Yeah. Need the cash, what with Christmas coming and all."

"How's the missus," Priestley asked conversationally.

"Fine. Why d'you ask?"

"Well I was wondering whether you two are still married, what with all the hours you've been working lately."

"You're not suggesting I take a few days off are you, Gaffer?" he quipped.

"You and me both, Adrian." Priestley looked at his watch. "Must dash. See you tomorrow." He ran towards his car, shouting back to Adrian, "Make sure Bladey gets some fags."

* * * * *

Priestley lay wide awake in Sonia Hall's bed. His arms were wrapped around her sleeping body and he inhaled the scent of her hair as he listened to her gentle breathing. He was exhausted but he couldn't sleep. His mind was in turmoil. He wished he'd talked to Sonia about what had happened but she'd made such an effort that he didn't want to spoil her

37

evening. The carefully prepared food. The wine. The candles. The firelight. He'd never been seduced by a woman before. He'd always thought he had to do all the running. But this was something he could easily get used to.

In his arms, Sonia's dreaming body quivered. He held her tighter and wondered what he was going to do. He ran through the incident again and again in his mind. After he'd left the station, he'd driven to a pub on the outskirts of the city: his and Jacky Benson's chosen meeting place for tonight's rendezvous. But what was bothering him had happened after he'd paid Jacky. He was sitting in his car, still smiling at Jacky's effrontery. The old bugger had had the cheek to ask for the bus fare home! He was half listening to a play on the radio while he waited the necessary fifteen minutes or so to give his informant time to clear the area, when he saw a woman scuttling – literally scuttling – across the car park. It was the way she moved, head down, body huddled, tiny little rapid steps, that caught his attention. It was so odd. As she passed his car he caught a glimpse of her face, half concealed by her scarf. And with a jolt he recognised her. Valerie Butcher. Adrian Butcher's pretty young wife. She didn't look so pretty now. She looked like an old woman. Hunched and worn. They'd been married in the spring in a great blaze of trumpets and celebration. He vividly remembered the pride with which Adrian had shown the wedding snaps round the office.

Instinct told him something wasn't right. In fact, something was very wrong. He sat in his car, his hand on the door latch, while he watched her shuffle the rest of the way across the car park and into the pub. He wondered what to do. This was very strange. Perhaps she was meeting somebody. Still. Odd. But whatever she was up to it was none of his business. What if she was having an affair? He knew Adrian was working the late shift. And who was he to break up a happy marriage? He turned the key in the ignition, depressed the clutch and flicked the gear lever into first. It was none of his business, he told himself again. But it wouldn't matter if he followed her in. Had a quick drink. Just to see what she was up to. He didn't actually need to do anything other than stand at the bar with his pint. His natural curiosity got the better of him and he turned off the engine and got out of the car. You'll have to be quick, he told himself as he hurried through the pub's ivy covered entrance. Time was pressing. Sonia was waiting for him.

She sat alone in a corner of the bar with a small glass of orange juice in front of her. She didn't see her husband's gaffer approaching. "Valerie?" Priestley's voice was quiet and soft and at first she didn't respond. He waited. Eventually his presence would penetrate her consciousness. When she did finally turn to look at him, a snapshot of those Muslim women who cover their faces flashed across his mind. She had hidden her face almost completely with her scarf and her shadowed eyes looked enormous. She blinked as the jolt of recognition passed through them. Unable to think of anything else to say, Priestley asked awkwardly, "Can I buy you a drink?"

"No. Thank you Mr Priestley." Her voice was quiet. Almost a whisper.

"Is everything all right?" he asked.

"Yes, of course," she replied, too quickly. "Why wouldn't it be?" But there is very little point in lying to a detective inspector well versed in the art of interview technique. A man who knew how to read a person's every reaction. A man who had been trained to spot a lie a mile off. The few seconds that Priestley had been with her were enough to tell him almost all he needed to know. The lady was terrified. That much was self-evident. She wasn't here to meet anyone. Precisely the reverse. She was here because she wanted to be on her own. She turned away. And Priestley took the opportunity to sit down on the stool adjacent to the bench she was sitting on. Now he could see the tears rolling down her cheeks. Each one glinted as it caught the reflection from the light above them.

"What on earth is wrong?" he asked. Of all things, he hadn't expected this. Another bloke, yes. But not this. He heard her gasp as she tried to speak. Priestley offered her the glass of orange, but she shook her head.

"Valerie, this is Jack Priestley, not some stranger. What on earth ..." She had turned fully towards him and allowed the scarf to slip away. In the dimness of the low-voltage ceiling light above them he saw the bruising. Saw the scars. Saw the flakes of dried blood. Now he knew everything. That was the final piece of the jigsaw. But he couldn't stop his eyes from turning to stone. The horrified expression that crept across his face as he took in her damaged features. There was a terrible gash on her left temple and livid bruising on her cheeks. Her lips were bruised and swollen too. He wondered what excuse she'd use. "What in hell's name has happened to you? How did you do this?"

"Car accident," she said gulping back sobs. "Yesterday. I'm all right. Honest," she lied, barely coherent. She fumbled in her sleeve, and pulled out a small, white handkerchief which she used to wipe her nose. Priestley allowed her time to pull herself together, then asked her to stay where she was while he went to fetch them a couple of drinks. The shock accompanied him to the bar. Car accident, my arse, he thought. Adrian Butcher more like. He turned, drinks in hand. It had only taken a matter of seconds but already she'd gone.

And now he couldn't get the image of Valerie Butcher's face out of his mind. When Sonia's alarm clock rang out the following morning, he hadn't had a wink of sleep and he still didn't know what to do. He had to do something. But what? Face Butcher down. Report him to the domestic abuse people? Ruin a fine young copper's career because of his own half-witted guess work. As the night passed, doubts had filled his mind about what he'd actually seen. And about what he actually knew. Perhaps he should try and find out more before he blabbed his mouth off to the powers that be. Perhaps in a couple of days he'd pay her a home visit. Perhaps.

4

Blade spent most of the night listening to some drunk in the next cell, screaming his head off. When he eventually saw the grey light on the other side of the tiny window, he accepted defeat. He tried to move. Every muscle in his body throbbed. He shuffled across to the cell door, and called, "Anybody there?" There was no answer. He raised his voice and called again, "Is anybody frigging well there?" Still no answer. "Christ, is anybody there?" This time he banged on the heavy metal door with both fists. Footsteps! Hooray!

There was a loud clang and the metal shutter dropped down. The pretty face of a young female sergeant peered through the gap. "Yes, Mr Blade?"

"Any chance of a fag," he asked, apologetically.

"Sure." She turned and walked away. She took her time, but eventually he heard her returning.

"There you are, Mr Blade." She handed him a full packet of twenty cigarettes and lit a match for him. "I can't give you the matches so just call me when you want one."

Unbelievable. A whole bloody packet. Like the Ritz. Had he dreamt what had happened the previous day? Had that all been in another place? "Where did these come from?" he asked, hoping that Sammy might have put in an appearance.

"Mr Priestley left them for you last night." The trap closed. Blade slouched against the door, listening to the young sergeant's retreating footsteps. He returned to his bench and, nursing his aching limbs, stared down at the cold concrete floor. He smoked his cigarette as though it was his last. The nicotine helped and slowly his muscles relaxed. He thought about Sammy. And he thought about Jack. He'd spent most of the night thinking about Jack. For the first time in years, he'd remembered the games they'd played and the trouble they'd caused. It was a shock to discover he'd joined the filth. But when he'd left school and joined the army, he'd quickly lost touch with the friends he'd grown up with in favour of the new friends he made in the regiment. He fell in love with the excitement and camaraderie of army life. Meanwhile, he remembered, Jack had stayed on at school to take his exams. He remembered telling Jack he was sissy the first time he came home on leave. They'd both changed. Jack had discovered learning. And he had discovered that learning frightened him. They hadn't seen each other since. Not until yesterday.

He shivered on his bench. He should be considering his position. Deciding what to do. Planning his next move. But it occurred to him that perhaps there was no next move. He knew that there was no way out of this particular spot of bother. And he knew he'd soon have all the time in the world to think about his memories.

* * * * *

Both copper and robber felt as if they were trapped in a time warp. Shared memories flowed across the table. Nostalgia had dulled the sharp edges of time and they spoke about events, now twenty years old, with fondness and humour. As a team, they decided, they'd been the best.

For a long time, both of them avoided questions about their more recent histories, preferring to remain in the safer territory that was their childhood, but eventually Jack asked, "Tell me about the army, Steve. I remember how excited you were about joining up when you left school."

Blade shrugged his shoulders. "There's nothing to tell. I joined as a boy soldier, as you know, then went into the Coldstream Guards."

"And?"

"It was a great life at first. I had it easy. I even finished up as the Imperial Boxing Champion."

"The what?"

"Imperial Boxing Champion. Champion of all the armed forces. The army, navy and air force."

"Christ, Steve. Sounds impressive."

"Yeah, I was pretty chuffed about it. But then my unit was posted to Germany. We all had some leave before the off. But by then I'd already done two stretches in Northern Ireland and Sammy reckoned she'd had enough. I was standing on the platform, waiting to catch the train back to the unit, when she laid down the law."

"Sammy?"

"My wife. Samantha Cullen. Remember?"

Priestley remembered very well. "Little Sammy! God. Yes. I remember. You were always sweet on her. I used to tease you about her!"

"What about you?"

"Divorced. Six months ago."

"Oh. Sorry to hear that."

"So was I. But I'm getting used to the bachelor life." A picture of Sonia, lying naked on her bed, flashed through his mind. "It's not so bad."

A tap on the interview room door disturbed them. A fresh-faced young detective looked in. "Sorry, Boss. But Mr Blade's solicitor is here."

Priestley nodded. "Thanks, Jamie. We'll be there in a minute." The door closed and he turned back to Blade. "So tell me, Bladey, what happened at the station?"

Blade shrugged. "Simple really. It was the army or Sammy. So I hooked it and went down as a deserter. I suppose that's when everything went wrong." He paused and looked down at his hands where they rested on the table. "I

44

didn't have any cards so I couldn't work. Except for a load of shit here and there for next to nothing."

"So that's when you started robbing post office vans for a living?"

"If you say so." His answer surprised him. He hadn't planned to submit so easily. But on second thoughts, perhaps this was confession time. "I'm not making any excuses. You asked."

"I know," Priestley's voice was quiet. "Are you still wanted by the army?"

"Am I bollocks. I did my bird in the army nick at Colchester Barracks. You know, they actually asked me to rejoin? But too much had happened."

"Some crossroads?"

"What was?" Blade was momentarily confused.

"Standing on that platform. What would have happened if you'd caught that train back to your unit?"

Blade spread his hands and shrugged his shoulders. "Who knows?" Suddenly he laughed out loud. "Remember Zorro, Jack?"

Priestley's eyes lit up and he joined in the laughter. "There wasn't a piece of washing left on the lines without a big 'Z' cut in it!"

Blade winked. "That was all down to you, mate!"

"You're still the same lying bastard," Priestley laughed. "I remember you with a pair of your sister's flannel draws wrapped around your head, slashing 'Z's all over the neighbourhood. And I took the blame and a smack on the head off the old man."

Blade could barely control his laughter. But it stopped almost as suddenly as it had started. "What happened to me glarney, Priestley?" Blade's eyes were piercing. "I used to sleep with that little gem, until you nicked it off me."

"Won it off you," Priestley corrected.

For an instant Blade looked almost sheepish. "Still got it, Jack?" Priestley slowly shook his head and both men burst once again into loud laughter. After a while silence returned to the interview room. They sat and looked at one another. Fading smiles replaced with more sombre expressions. "So, detective inspector is it now, Jack?"

Priestley raised his eyebrows. "And you've chosen armed robbery, Steve?"

Blade's gaze slipped off around the room. When he looked back, he said, "Who'd've thought it? You and me. Sitting here. Like this." They both knew Blade's future had been decided yesterday. There could only be one outcome. Priestley didn't say anything. He pushed his chair away from the table, stood up, and went to lean against the wall next to the door, both hands in his trouser pockets. The only thing that would alter the outcome was if Blade decided to cooperate. "So, do I get to see that solicitor?" he said.

"Whenever you're ready."

"I'm ready." Blade paused. "One question, though. Who dobbed us in Jack?"

"Mickey Mouse. Who'd you think?"

5

It was Harry Nesbitt who was responsible for getting Steve Blade into crime. As a boy, Harry used to climb across rooftops and drop through skylights into factories. By the time he was fifteen, he'd progressed to organised shoplifting. His gang would go into shops mob handed. Two of the team would distract the shopkeeper, whilst the others grabbed whatever they could. But Harry, unlike the rest of the kids he mixed with, had ambitions. And, as the years passed by, he worked his way into various groups of villains, making a living out of street snatches, burglaries and, eventually, armed robberies.

He'd always held a flame for Sammy Blade, since the very first time he'd met her when her husband was on the run from the army. At that time neither he nor Steve Blade had a light between them. It was no surprise to Sammy when Harry persuaded Blade to join forces with him. He had a scam in mind and Steve Blade was just the man to help him. Besides, he wanted to stay close to Sammy.

They'd pick a night, any night, but usually one towards the end of the week. Then Sammy would help them blacken their faces with burnt cork. They would dress themselves in dark overalls, then creep through back streets to the nearby parcel delivery company depot. There they would hide in the bushes and wait. Sammy used to joke that they reminded her of a couple of fishermen, dreaming of the big catch yet to be landed. If they waited long enough, eventually some prat would leave a trolley loaded with parcels just outside one of the loading bays. And when that happened, the fishermen would strike. Stealthily they would creep through the dark shadows cast by the overhead yard lights and net their catch, usually a couple of parcels each, before legging it back to Sammy like two excited kids.

The Blade flat was always the safe house where Sammy'd be waiting for their return. Her husband adored the sight of the thrill on her face as she waited to see what precious gifts would come out of the nicked parcels. Sometimes the contents induced fits of laughter. Other times bitter disappointment. Sometimes confusion. Like the time they found two hundred plastic butter dishes in one very large parcel. A parcel which her two cavaliers had struggled to carry because of its enormous size. Within a week, most of the neighbourhood had a new plastic butter dish on their table. Not many had butter inside, but they were sufficiently decorative to be worth paying a quid or two for.

But Blade was to remember for many years to come, the look of surprise on Sammy's face when the gamble eventually paid off, but not without a certain amount of heavy risk. He and Harry had grabbed two small parcels each but were seen by one of the loaders. They were chased for what seemed like miles before they eventually gave the slip to their pursuer inside a vast complex of Edwardian back-to-back houses. They were still gasping for breath when they presented their night's work to Sammy. All four parcels were addressed to a shop in Birmingham's jewellery quarter. When she opened them, the sparkle from dozens of diamonds, sapphires, emeralds and other precious stones reflected onto her face. The big catch had been landed.

But they all realised that was that. After such a successful expedition, to carry on their activities in the parcel delivery game would be folly. People would be looking out for them. So the two fishermen retired prematurely, and it wasn't long after that scam that they also decided to go their separate ways. But a friendship had been formed based on trust and cooperation. And a taste for adventure had Steve Blade in his grip. There was nothing to compare with the excitement, the adrenaline rush, when you were embarking on an audacious plot. He enjoyed the planning, the thinking, the scheming. Cunning came easily to him and his wits were sharpened on the knife-edge of risk. And the pay-off could be terrific. He and Sammy had lived the high life for a while after they'd shifted that jewellery, and there were other good times after that. But mostly life was lean. When you're earning your living on the street, life was either good or bad and there wasn't much in-between. Life was a rollercoaster. And Steve Blade loved it.

It was during one of the lean times, that he hooked up with Harry again. And witnessed the most spectacular and daring post office raid he'd ever been on.

* * * * *

It had always been Harry Nesbitt's party piece. To stand on a table in a pub and fling his arms out, mimicking a Spitfire, and humming the Dambusters March with everybody in the room taking great delight in throwing beer mats at the silly prat. And there, he was doing it again. Good old Harry. Celebrating his birthday in noisy, raucous style. Blade sometimes wondered if he was all there. Now, as he watched Harry flying round the pub, jumping from table to table to cheers and cries of jubilation, he was convinced that Harry was definitely short upstairs. Tears came to his eyes and he wept with laughter, just like everybody else, as he enjoyed the antics of the short, stocky, centre of attraction. Harry was only five foot four in his stockinged feet, but he'd always been broad and muscular. That night everyone reckoned he must have had a decent touch or something because he was paying for everything: the beer and food were free all night. And that was unusual for Harry. He wasn't exactly mean, but he wasn't exactly generous either. It was rare for Harry to put his hand in his pocket unless he was pushed into a corner. So whatever scam he'd just pulled, it must have been a good one to get him to unzip his wallet so far. So it was a good evening all round, and slowly but surely the whole crowd got pissed as newts. Sammy even got up and started to sing. Everybody joined in as she sang, Don't Laugh at Me, 'cos I'm a Fool.

Steve Blade looked up at her, his face red with beer but suffused with pride and adoration. It took him a while to realise that Harry had sidled up beside him. "Want to earn some dough, Bladey?" he slurred. He was half sitting, half lying, on the bench next to Blade, his arm wrapped around his shoulders – probably more to support himself than as a friendly gesture.

"Stupid question, Harry," Blade answered.

"Was, wasn't it! Be at Saltley Gate at half seven in the morning." Harry's eyes were bloodshot from the ale he'd sunk and from the smoke in the bar which was thicker than any fog in the cut. "We're one short. You can take it if you want it? Be worth your while, mate."

In those days, Blade was in no position to refuse anyone's offer. He'd have nicked an empty dustbin if he thought it would put dinner on the table. He'd been skint for a while now, so he nodded and accepted Harry's offer without a second thought. Sobered him up too. He looked at his watch. Only five hours to the rendezvous. "Sammy," he shouted, interrupting her song. "Time to piss off."

* * * * *

The following morning dawned bright and sunny. Blade stood on the corner at Saltley Gate and looked at his watch. He'd already been there for about fifteen minutes. It was quarter to eight and he wondered if the little rat had got so pissed up the night before that the job was off. Bollocks, he thought, he's not going to turn up. Should have known better. Time to get out of here, before he got picked up for loitering. Then he noticed the young woman, walking towards him. "Got a light, sailor?" she said. It was Nesbitt.

Blade was taken aback. "What the ... ?"

"Don't you dare use any foul language, young man. In front of a lady as well." The little man grinned from beneath his wig. The guy certainly has bottle, thought Blade. "You want to watch your manners, young man." The voice changed, dropped back down to its usual register. "Don't worry, Bladey. All you've got to do is stand over there, opposite the post office. When the van comes, leave it to us. It'll be here in a minute. Your job's to get me out of here if it turns to ratshit. Okay?" Blade eyed him up and down and couldn't help but be impressed. Harry looked the part all right. "The other two should be here soon," he continued. "Joe Pincher's driving the car. If it goes well just stay where you are and then piss off, quietly like." The voice changed again. "All right darling?"

Money for old rope, thought Blade. Nothing to do but stand and watch the action. Piece of cake. He appreciated the favour Harry was doing him. "Thanks H.," he said.

"Think nothing of it, Bladey. We all need a leg up now and then." And the unusual but well-disguised figure crossed the street and walked, or rather hobbled on her high-heeled shoes, into a nearby tobacconists.

Within minutes, a Capri with Joe Pincher behind the wheel pulled up and parked just around the corner from the post office. About five minutes later the post office van appeared and Blade, although given only a minor role to play, felt the familiar rush of adrenaline surge through his body.

The guard was only a young man. Perhaps, a stand-in for the regular guard. He obviously hadn't been on the job long and had clearly taken on board his manager's dire warnings about the danger of ambush as he went about his business – dropping off money boxes in the morning and collecting them in the afternoon. His apprehension was palpable as he nervously walked across the pavement towards the post office entrance. He was concentrating so much on getting his little arsehole into the premises where it would be safe and protected, that he didn't notice the young woman heading towards him. She walked straight into him and collapsed in a heap on the pavement with a cry of pain and surprise. The guard, already agitated and confused, immediately apologised and offered his help. With his eyes focused on the stocking tops and the young woman's bare white thighs, the youngster placed the metal cash container on the pavement and proffered his fallen victim a helping hand. Thank you very much, thought Harry. The guard was immediately kicked in the groin. He fell to the ground, paralysed and helpless, and the woman grabbed the container and ran to a car which appeared from nowhere with its back door open. Within seconds the car had disappeared, along with the woman and £30,000 in cash. Nice one Harry!

Now I've seen everything, thought Blade. He couldn't help but admire Nesbitt's effrontery and acting skills. That had been quite a performance. But more importantly, his own role was finished and it was time to disappear – quietly, as Harry had put it. As he slowly sauntered away, he could hear the alarms and sirens behind him and he knew he would never again earn money as easy as that.

6

The smell of disinfectant was all pervasive. He was almost choking with it. No wonder half these tosspots are sniffers, thought Priestley. With the amount of Jeyes Fluid they're using, they must all have the clap. He was following a screw towards the visiting rooms in the remand prison. He was a little nervous. This was an unannounced visit and he wasn't too sure how Blade would receive him. After all, he was the man planning to put Blade away for a long stretch.

"Well, Jack, this is an unexpected surprise. Come to give me bail?" As the door closed behind him, Priestley sat down. Bladey looked a lot better than he had the last time he'd seen him. But that wouldn't have been hard, given the beating he'd had off those evil bastards. He sounded better too. Chirpy. This was the Bladey he remembered from the old days. Never backward in coming forward. "Well?"

"Well what?"

"Have you come to give me bail?"

"You know it's not up to me." Priestley paused. Took a deep breath. "But I can drop the objections. Might give you the chance to get the domestics in order, before ..."

"You sound as though they're going to hang me up by the toenails, Jack."

Priestley wanted to finish his sentence. "... before you're sentenced. You're up the day after tomorrow. Put your application in and see what happens."

"Why would you do that?"

"Do what?"

"Jack Priestley, you are not Santa Claus. You are a slimy, devious, thinking copper. So stop flapping about. What's on your mind?"

Priestley grinned. This was easy. "Sentimentality, Bladey. Sentimentality. For old time's sake."

Blade wasn't buying it. "Jack Priestley, you couldn't give a shit about my welfare. They only give us quarter of an hour, so you'd better get on with it."

"Okay, Steve. You're right. I need to bounce something off somebody who hasn't got flat feet." He paused again. "One of my finest is knocking his missus about and I don't like it."

"So?"

"I don't ... I don't know." Priestley put both elbows on the table and rubbed his face. Images of Valerie Butcher flooded his mind. He'd paid her a visit the day before, having made sure that her shit-bag husband was well tied up at the station, and it had all come flooding out. He'd been pounding her from the very beginning. It had stared almost before they'd finished walking down the aisle as man and wife. The attacks were frequent, violent and vindictive. Adrian Butcher was a monster of the first order. Priestley knew he had to do something. And he had to do it fast. But he'd quickly crossed out going to the authorities. He'd spoken to Valerie at length, and to her mother as well, and he had some idea of what Butcher was capable of. The attacks were pathological. He was convinced he'd kill her if he was found out. So Priestley had reverted to type. To deal with this he was instinctively drawing on his past. So he'd come to see the one man who really understood who he was, what he was, and why he was. Steve Blade. And he was finding this was very, very difficult. Over the years, he'd managed to suppress his past behind a veneer of culture and education. He'd even managed to soften his inner-city accent, so that his consonants now had the polish of received pronunciation rather than the blurred edges of a Brummy slum. And all of this was difficult to scrape away, just so he could ask this favour off his old friend. He tried again. "I just … I don't know what I want. Except perhaps for you to listen to me."

"Why is it everybody wants me to listen to them?" asked the con, trying to make a joke. To lighten a situation that had suddenly become way too heavy. "But they don't want to listen to me?"

His question was ignored. "This one is a right bastard and if nothing's done about it …"

"Bad as that?"

"I'm pretty sure he'd blow her brains out if I used any formal channels. Follow?"

"Yeah. Any smokes, Jack?" Priestley fumbled in his jacket pocket and pulled out a packet of Hamlets. He took one and passed the packet to Blade, who also took one. Then the packet disappeared as if it'd been hit by a magician's wand. They both lit up. Blade stood up and leant against the wall before continuing. "So why don't you deal with him the same way as they used to?" All of a sudden he was a male Marjorie Proops. An agony uncle. "Remember? When it was okay for a bloke to belt his missus the once, but if he did it again he'd be paid a little visit?"

"It's unlawful."

The reply was as he expected. "Piss off, Priestley."

"Glad we agree."

"So you've come here to ask me to deal with this shithole. In return for some out of jail?" Priestley sat back in his chair. He'd done it. It was his turn to smile.

* * * * *

The night was murky. Daytime rain had been followed by a sudden drop in temperature at dusk. Now rolling mist seemed to stop and gather around each street corner. The residential street was almost silent except for a pair of hurrying feet, heading home at the end of the evening shift.

"Mr Butcher?" The voice was quiet. Muffled.

The detective constable stopped dead in his tracks and turned his head in the direction of the sound. "Yes," he replied.

There was no one there. Silence fell back. Then something struck him across the back of his knees. His legs buckled. He fell forward onto the wet pavement. The left-hand side of his rib cage felt a crushing blow from a well-directed boot. A sharp blow struck the back of his head. Hands grabbed his ankles and he was dragged into a nearby alley. His face scraping over the pavement and through icy puddles.

A metal bar reigned down blows upon his back, his sides, his head. Pain streaked through him. He was turned over. A hooded man leant over him. The front of his trousers was cut open with a knife. His dick exposed. Words reached his ears. "If it happens again, you'll lose this." The knife stabbed at his penis. He would have screamed, but for the gloved hand covering his mouth.

His blood mixed with the rain in the puddles. All his nightmares had come at once. Butcher couldn't feel the knife blade now pressing against his Adam's Apple. But he knew it was there. "Life is so precious." The voice was quiet. Measured. "Don't you agree? If you touch your wife one more time, you bastard, your precious life will finish. Do you understand?"

Butcher groaned. A hand grabbed his hair. His head was banged against the pavement behind him. Knock. Knock. Knock. The voice was louder this time. "Do you understand?"

Butcher was unable to answer. Numbly he watched the gloved fist growing before his eyes. It smashed into his face. Flattening his nose. He slumped to one side and wished that death would come to take away the pain.

* * * * *

Steve Blade walked out of the alleyway into the silent street. He stopped. Looked left. Looked right. When he saw the

56

parked car, he jerked his thumb skywards. Then he disappeared into the night. Inside the car, Jack Priestley picked up his mobile phone and reluctantly dialled 999.

* * * * *

The attack was swift, effective, and perfectly executed. Adrian Butcher would remember the agony for the rest of his life. But he'd never feel pain like it again. When his attacker left him bleeding into a puddle there was still a chance he would walk again. But by the time the ambulance men had finished, armed with inexperience and only a few weeks' training, Adrian Butcher was paralysed from the neck down.

7

Jack Priestley was in court three months later to see Steve Blade sent down. The moment Blade was taken from the dock and down the steps, Priestley left the court room. He wanted a word with Sammy Blade before she left. To offer his condolences, if she'd have them. To offer is help, if she'd take it. Whatever she needed. Priestley always liked to keep an eye on the men he sent to prison, and their families. He always visited the con from time to time while he was banged up and made sure his wife and kids were okay. He wasn't unusual in this. It made sense to keep in touch. That way you gained the con's trust and maybe that would be useful in the future. But on this occasion he changed his mind when he saw Sammy with Harry Nesbitt. Standing at the top of the court house steps, Priestley watched as Sammy Blade climbed into the back of Harry Nesbitt's shiny new Jag. She'd left the court room even faster than he had.

* * * * *

When Blade was shown into his cell at the holding prison that evening, he knew he should be well satisfied. He knew he'd done well from the deal his barrister had worked in return for the guilty plea. By rights it should have been double figures. So he couldn't realistically complain. But that didn't stop him feeling depressed. The judge had given him nine years. Just nine. That meant the most he'd have to do, before he got parole, was three and a half. Provided he kept his nose clean.

From his vantage point on the bunk, Blade examined his new home. The grey-white wall tiles were interrupted only by a few small panes of strengthened glass that made up a window, set high in the wall towards the ceiling. Lights out had been called ages ago. This was the time when it was hard not to think about curtains on windows. Carpets on floors. Bright red gas fires. And space.

He had to keep reminding himself that it could have been worse. And without Priestley's helping hand he'd never have got bail. At least he'd had a couple of months to sort things out on the domestic front. Sammy'd be okay. They'd had a good Christmas together and the neighbours had all turned up trumps. They'd made all the usual promises to support Sammy while he was doing his penance to society. But, Christ, how many times had he shelled out to feed a mate's missus and kids on a monthly basis?

He sighed and turned over on the bunk. He wouldn't be getting any sleep tonight. He would give anything to find out who'd nailed them. The bastard. The scumbag had probably been sitting there today, amongst all the other spectators, watching him go down behind Harry and Malcy. He could see the gathering in the public gallery. Toads and goblins, every one of them. Staring down from God's landing. Planning his future for him. Which one of them had turned Judas? The young pretender, Wilcox, had screamed like a baby when he was given three years. And Harry Ventnor had smiled at the judge as he was given his good news – a three stretch too. And in a nice, comfortable open prison to boot. Blade had stood alone, expressionless, listening to the fading echoes of Ventnor's footsteps, as he waited for the verdict.

The judge was a grim-faced git, high on his perch in red robes and a grey wig. Mr Supercilious as he said, "The public need to be protected from the likes of you. You are a cold and calculating professional criminal, who has shown no regard for the safety of other people or their property. You have been before these courts twice before and on both occasions received custodial sentences and yet you still persist …" And so on and so on. At least he'd managed to catch a glimpse of Sammy before they took him down. He could see she was blinking back the tears as she mouthed, "I'll wait." He was missing her already. He wondered what she was doing right now. Sleeping? Dreaming? Alone in their bed. Crying? He knew he had to try not to torment himself with thoughts of others trying to get their leg over. With wondering if she could remain loyal to him, when every dirty bastard in the neighbourhood was willing to help her through her ordeal.

Blade's thoughts were interrupted by sudden anguished cries. From a cell on the landing above it sounded like. He heard running feet and then a screw's voice; remonstrating with the imbecile. Some kid missing his mum. He pulled himself off the bed and stood for a while, trying to make out what the weather was doing outside. But it was three in the morning and all he could see through the small panes of reinforced glass was darkness. This was it. This Mr Blade, he told himself, is your immediate future. Get used to it. No mates. No pubs. No Sammy. No shagging. No nothing. He was facing the longest month of his life. The introduction to prison for Category A prisoners was a four week period of isolation. He'd done prison before. But never as a Category A. The cloud of depression was heavy on his shoulders. Prison was an institutionalised game and it sorted the men from the boys. There were many who entered the system as men and came out as boys. But not him. He'd been there before and survived. He'd survive again. But he needed to rid himself of this gnawing depression. It was like walking into a rain-filled head wind that wouldn't let up.

8

Sunlight was already streaming thought his cell window when the sound of his fellow prisoners making their way towards breakfast clattered into Steve Blade's cell. He'd been moved out of the holding prison and into HMP Gartree in the middle of the night. This morning, he had decided he would take things easy. Tread carefully. Tread very carefully indeed until he'd found his feet. Worked out how this place worked. When you are the new boy on the block it is always wise to be cautious – in prison, toes can easily be trampled on by the unwary.

When he eventually stepped out onto the landing, he felt like it was his first day at work. Not that he could remember what that actually felt like. It was nine o'clock and the place had fallen silent. As silent as a prison ever got. His steps echoed on the patterned iron walkways as he took his first, discrete, look around. In his book, one prison was much the same as any other. But there was a big difference here. And he spotted it immediately. Everybody knew what everybody else was in for. Each cell had a plaque on the door and what he read that morning made him giddy. A number had 'life' printed on them. Others said 'life; recommended 15 years'. Or 'recommended 20 years'. These were the business. Heavy, heavy stretches. According to the names inscribed on the plaques, half the criminal underworld was here. His sentence was nothing compared to some of these. 'Steve

Blade' said his, '9 years' and underneath that 'armed robbery'.

Appalled, fascinated, he stopped to read the inscriptions outside every cell. There were train robbers. Rapists. Murderers. Perverts of every kind. There were names he recognised from newspaper articles and the telly. There were members of notorious gangs from London, the Midlands and the North. This was a bastion of professional and hardened criminals. This was to be his home for at least three and a half years.

Most of the cell doors were closed, but halfway along the landing above his own he came across an open door. Inside a foreign-looking bloke was sitting on his bed, concentrating on a model of a gypsy caravan made out of matchsticks. In his hand was a tiny shard of wood, clearly destined for the model, though it was hard to see where. Blade stood and watched as the man's hand moved slowly towards the caravan roof. "First day?" the man asked, without looking up. As if Blade was expected. It occurred to Blade that perhaps he was. Blade remained silent. He stood and waited for the intricate manoeuvre to be completed. The matchstick approached the roof, and then with great care and precision, it was slotted into position. Success. God knows how long he'd been trying to do that. The man sat back and breathed a heavy sigh. "Finished," he said, and turned towards Blade, eyebrows raised, ready now for an answer to his question.

"Yeah." Blade wanted to appear as if he were a hard, couldn't-give-a-shit type. But the way he said 'yeah' didn't really come across like that. As it was, he felt as relieved as the man appeared to be. He stood up. No prison uniform for this lad. Sweater. Jeans. And a pair of slippers!

"Tony Lambesi. From London," he said, proffering his hand. Blade knew the name well and hoped that the flash of recognition he knew had flickered across his face wasn't too obvious.

"Blade. Steve Blade from Birmingham," he responded, shaking Lambesi's hand. Blade looked around Lambesi's cell, taking in the carpet on the floor. The duvet on the bed. The pictures on the walls. There were even a couple of table lamps complete with matching shades. It was like a five star hotel. Well, not quite. But by far the best Blade had ever seen in a prison of all places.

Lambesi grinned at the newcomer's surprise. "You like the set up?" Blade replied with a nod of his head. "You can bring anything in here," Lambesi continued. "Carpets, curtains, bedspreads, pictures. Trainers, sweatshirts. Educational things, if you're into that." He spoke quickly, as though he had a lot to say and thought his next words might be his last. "Cane for bird cages. Matchsticks," he continued, indicating his caravan. "You name it. You can have it. Anything except French letters, that is. Although you could probably manage to get some if you're into that kind of thing."

"Is that just for you or for everybody?" Blade's head was tilted slightly to one side, like a child wondering what Christmas was all about.

"All of us. The screws don't like problems here so they stand for anything. Within reason. You play up, they take you apart. So you don't play up, savvy?"

"Savvy." Blade nodded again, bewildered. "I take it there's some sort of pecking order?"

" 'Course there is. Frankie Richardson's here. You know Frankie?" Everybody had heard of Frankie. He'd run a mob in the East End in the seventies. Drugs, protection, porn. You name it. He'd had a finger in every sleazy pie going. Blade also remembered that he'd given evidence at his trial against some of the filth for taking bribes off him. There'd been a public outcry at the time because Frankie wasn't given life. In exchange for dishing the dirt on the crooked cops he'd only been given 20 years. Must have nearly done his time by now, Blade realised.

"I've never had the pleasure, but I know of him."

" 'Course you do. Well, my friend, he looks after everybody. He's the man. Follow? I used to work with Frankie in the old days. There's about half a dozen of the old school in here with us. You'll get to meet them sooner or later."

"Where is he now?"

"Don't ask." Lambesi's voice was suddenly sharp. Tinged with threat. Blade's face fell. He didn't think the question was all that loaded. "You don't ask the questions in here. Frankie asks the questions. And Frankie decides if you have it cushy or if you have it hard. You know? He'll get around to you in good time, so don't you worry."

Worry! Blade was having a tough time digesting all of this. All he'd done was rob a post office van! This was heavy, heavy going. Frankie Richardson. Tony Lambesi. Christ! Lambesi was the crazy knifeman who'd chopped people up for Frankie all those years ago. And now here he was. All pally. Offering him a cup of tea! Naturally, Blade felt compelled to accept. Foolish not to. In the circumstances.

* * * * *

Blade sat in Lambesi's cell for about an hour, listening carefully to all that the more experienced con had to say. Lambesi was a tall, thin man, clean shaven with greasy, black hair combed neatly back, receding at the front, tied into a ponytail at the back. He had pointed features and spoke with one of the broadest cockney accents Blade had ever heard. At length, Lambesi explained the Gartree prisoners' code and the layout of the prison.

"The canteen shop is opened three times a week. You can buy most things from there. It's like the old corner shop, you know?" Blade nodded and smiled at the way in which Lambesi always seemed to finish a sentence with a question. "We're on first names with the screws in here. That's the way they want it, so that's the way it is. Lights go out at ten o'clock every night, but it don't mean a thing because you can keep your own lights on inside your cell if you want, follow? Everybody is banged up at nine o'clock though. You get up at seven in the morning when they open the doors and get your breakfast at half seven, if you want it. I don't bother, but you get it from the ground floor canteen and take it back to your cell. If you don't want to work, they don't force you. It's up to you, follow?" Blade nodded again. Jesus, he was beginning to feel like one of those stupid toy dogs you see nodding away in the back of cars.

"Come on," said Lambesi suddenly. "I think I'll show you around." Blade found himself nodding again, but was glad of the offer and a chance to stretch his legs. Uncle Tony led the way.

There wasn't a sign of a screw. In the last prison in which Blade had been resident, there were screws every two feet. Or that was the way it seemed at the time. You could easily be forgiven for wondering which one was the top security prison. As they walked, Lambesi continued his monologue.

"For those who go to work, they start at eight thirty in the morning and break for lunch at twelve o'clock. Then they work from half past one to four o'clock." They were strolling along the iron walkway as though along a seaside prom, taking in the sea air. "Obviously you'll have to wait to see what Frankie gives you, but if he offers you the laundry, take it. That's the best you can get and I know there's a vacancy there at the moment, so keep your fingers crossed. The laundry does the washing for three other prisons, but it's the easiest touch going, follow?"

"What do you mean, Frankie gives you the work?"

"I told you, you don't ask the questions. Frankie tells you where he wants you to work. We're a team and he's the head man, follow?"

Blade didn't. He was confused about just about everything. "What if I don't want to work?"

"Sort it out with Frankie. But if he wants you in a particular place, it's because it would be in the best interests of the team, savvy? So it's best to do what he wants. We might need certain bits and pieces for whatever, right?" Blade thought it best not to say anything and replied with the customary nod.

Lambesi came to a sudden halt and turned towards him. "Tell you what, let's go and see if he's in." Blade nodded again. He couldn't wait.

Frankie's cell was in another wing, so it took them some time to walk over there. Like all prisons, the decor at Gartree was the same wherever you went. But that was where the similarities seemed to end. It was going to take Blade longer than he thought to find his feet. Or maybe it wouldn't. All he had to do was get used to teamwork. Mob rule. Whatever.

Suddenly Lambesi stopped again, placed an arm across Blade's shoulders, turned him, and said, "Frankie, how's things?"

A middle-aged man sat in an armchair inside a cell. Well, it might have been a cell. More likely it was another suite at the Grand. The penthouse suite, in fact. Frankie must have been carrying at least 20 stone. He had greying, curly hair and a fat face. A small cigar protruded from his large mouth, the top lip of which supported an enormous, greying, nicotine-stained moustache. Blade recognised Frankie's face immediately; the vestiges of the younger versions he'd seen in newspapers as an impressionable youth were still just about evident. He had to stop himself from smiling. Frankie looked ridiculous. A parody of himself. Just like in the gangster movies Blade had watched with Jack Priestley as a kid. Saturday mornings down the picture house. Frankie wore a silk gown. Behind him stood two toughs dressed in white shirts and grey flannels. Arms crossed. Legs apart. The cell walls were crammed with paintings and mirrors. All in ornate gold frames. A plush fitted carpet lined the floor. Over-the-top furnishings filled the stuffy room. Frankie had made himself comfortable. He might have been sitting in a room in a villa in Sicily. At last the big man spoke. A little dismissively he addressed Lambesi, "New?"

"Yeah. Steve Blade from Birmingham. Nine years for armed robbery." Blade blinked in surprise and glanced quickly at Lambesi. He must remember not to underestimate this man. Clearly he was well informed. How did Lambesi know that much? Blade hadn't told him anything. And they hadn't walked past Blade's cell. Then he remembered the impression he'd had that Tony Lambesi was waiting for him when he found him in his cell earlier.

Richardson waved his hand, inviting them to enter his abode. "So. You're a Brummie? We did all right with the Brummies. How're my friends the Fenguellos doing?"

Blade knew the Fenguellos only vaguely. They were nightclub owners and into the drug and prostitution scene in Birmingham. Way out of his league. He'd dealt with them on a couple of jobs but didn't really know them other than by reputation. Still, he answered, "Okay, I think. I haven't seen them in a while. I think they're doing all right."

Frankie's laugh was a loud bark. Followed by a short coughing fit. When the gangster regained his composure he continued, "When have the Fenguellos ever not been doing all right?" Frankie looked sharply at Blade. He stared. Looked him over. Finally he nodded. Blade hoped it was approval. Then he waved his visitors away. Introductions had obviously been concluded. The newcomer hoped he'd passed the initiation test. Only time would tell. Lambesi tugged Blade's sleeve and pulled him away. Not that he needed much encouragement.

As they made their way back to their own cells, Blade couldn't resist questioning Lambesi. "So, when will I get to know?"

"What?" asked Lambesi, his mind already on other matters.

"What job I'll be given?" Blade knew he might be pushing his luck a bit here, but he persisted. "When will Frankie let me know?"

Lambesi was curt. "Don't know. Wait and see. Everything is done according to what Frankie thinks is best for the team, savvy?"

* * * * *

As the afternoon drew to a close, Blade listened to the other prisoners returning to their cells after work. He was surprised to be visited by three of them, but relieved to see that they were all dressed in prison clothes. He'd begun to wonder whether he was the only inmate wearing prison overalls. They each handed him a package, like he was some sort of gangland chieftain to whom they were paying homage. The packages contained tobacco, some smokes, and some groceries. Nice. But Lambesi put him straight the following morning. This was accepted practice when a new boy arrived at Gartree. Frankie's instructions. Still, Steve Blade was impressed by the warmth with which he seemed to have been received into the fold. It wasn't what he'd expected. Especially after he'd discovered what most of his fellow inmates were there for. It was nice to be welcomed like a long lost brother. Maybe working as part of a team was going to be easier than he thought.

9

Carol Guardia watched him pushing his food around his plate. She was a slim, attractive young woman. Always the smartly dressed girl-about-town. He'd been distracted from the moment they'd met in the faded and shabby grandeur of the hotel dining room. "Fish off, Jack?"

He looked up and apologised. "No, Carol. I'm sorry." He put his knife and fork down. "My mind's elsewhere." On his argument with Sonia that morning. So silly. Such a waste of time. And ridiculous to hurt one another so badly over a matter as inconsequential as whether or not he would accompany her to one of her work functions. She knew he hated any kind of formal event. Standing in a room full of people you'd never otherwise give the time of day to and having to make small talk. He'd have to telephone her later and apologise. Tell her he was sorry. Of course he'd go with her. He'd be delighted. He knew that her upset had less to do with the party and more to do with the fact that she thought he was avoiding coupledom. Which he wasn't. After all, they'd been together now for more than three years. And as far as he was concerned that constituted commitment. But she was a woman. She saw things differently. And Priestley knew that it was he who was going to have to have the grace to back down.

"Well that's very nice," said Carol. "Thank you very much. I'm buying you lunch. Remember? The least you can do is keep your mind on me."

"Sorry. I'm sorry. I'll try to do better! It's just that something happened this morning …"

"I know. You put some more scumbags in jail and made the city streets a bit safer."

He sighed. "Yeah. Yeah, I guess so."

"You guess so. Jack! What's the problem."

"Nothing. Nothing I can't handle. I'm sorry. Don't worry about it."

"I'm not. I'm just wondering whether it's something I should know about."

"It's nothing you should know about."

"Fine." She paused. Jack waited. She was buying lunch. This was when she'd ask for payment. "So what's new in the world of cops and robbers, Maigret?"

"You're asking me?" he countered. "You're the reporter. You tell me." This was the usual routine. But today it went a bit differently. Usually they played for a while, then Jack would feed Carol a story which she'd publish in the local rag she worked on. Something about a case the police needed the public's help with. But today Carol sat back from the table. Today, there was something she wanted to share with him.

She spoke in almost a whisper. "Well now. Let me see … There is something I wanted to bounce off you."

Priestley waited. "Paul Meade," she said, watching closely for his response.

"Not him again? Carol, you've got a fixation with Meade. What is it this time?"

"Shit, Jack. Just because he's the leader of the council that doesn't make him totally immune from justice."

"Okay Miss Newspaper-Reporter-of-the-Year." He smiled. "You have my undivided attention."

"This is confidential, Jack." She leaned towards him. "And off the record."

"Of course it is."

"Don't piss me about, Jack."

Jack held his hands up in a gesture of submission. "Okay. Okay." All of a sudden she was deadly serious.

"My editor asked me to look into a piece of land out at Aldridge, near to the quarry."

"I think I know where you mean." Priestley raised his eyebrows. "And?"

"Well, Ernie couldn't figure it out, Jack. You see, he couldn't understand how, after so many previous applications for permission to build on that land had been refused, all of a sudden permission's been granted on the first application by the new owners."

"So?"

She smiled. "It's only recently been acquired by Cheapside Surveyors."

"And?"

"The council bought the land a couple of years back. And sold it on to Cheapside before Christmas. Paul Meade is a non-exec on the Cheapside board," she whispered triumphantly. "And just happens to have the chair on the Town and Country Planning Committee. Has had for the last three years." She paused. "And on top of that, he's also on the Police Authority. But you already know that."

Priestley sat back in his chair and for a moment stared pensively at two swans flying over a lake in a picture on the opposite wall of the restaurant. His eyes returned to Carol. "Evidence?"

"You're joking. He's in the shit, Jack. It's illegal for him to be on the board of any company purchasing council-owned land or property."

"Who says?" Priestley knew the answer, but it was fun to wind Carol up. In this kind of mood she was always easily tormented.

"Christ, Jack, local government legislation!" she exclaimed, exasperated at his imagined stupidity.

He grinned, just to let her know he was only teasing. "So? What do you want me to do about it?"

"I want you to do your job, Mr Policeman. Investigate him." As an afterthought she added, "But only after you've promised me I'll get the scoop."

"My love," said Priestley, grinning like the Cheshire cat. "You can have your scoop."

* * * * *

Paul Meade. Big time local dignitary. Highly regarded. Except for the small mishap a few years back when he was found with his pants down in a local brothel. But that had all been forgotten. Water under the bridge. Just about. The great British public had got used to the sleazy behaviour of the powers that be. Nevertheless, any kind of inquiry into this particular can of worms would have to be sensitive and kept low key. The guy was a powerful man with friends in high places. Still, if the bastard had had his hand in the till, he deserved whatever was coming to him.

10

It was a beautiful sunny morning. Unseasonably warm for early spring. There were no clouds, just bright blue sky and a feeling inside of how good it was to be alive. If it hadn't been for his immediate surroundings, Blade could quite easily have imagined himself in somebody's back garden, listening to the birds twittering in the trees. He flicked the frayed end of a piece of grass with his tongue. He'd been chewing it for God only knows how long. He replaced it with a fresh stalk and he hummed that song which begins with the words, "There's a bright golden haze on the meadow ..."

There were more pouring out of the building on his right for their morning stroll around the circle inside the exercise yard. From his vantage point on the bank by the fence, overlooking the circle, Blade watched the men go round. Round and round. Like Roman chariots on parade. Or sheep on a carousel. All going in the same direction. Following the leader. Talking bollocks. Planning and scheming through their arses. He could see Frankie Richardson holding court; his two minders close behind. Tony Lambesi was nowhere to be seen but some other poor little shit was having his ears filled with the usual garbage. He preferred to sit here in the sun. Quietly. Next to nature. Philosophising on the grassy bank. With a pang he thought of Sammy. She hadn't been in for weeks now and just recently he'd been missing her more than normal. He remembered her letter. He knew he shouldn't feel too concerned. Her explanation had been clear enough. Good girl. She'd explained all about her visit to see his probation officer. He pictured her working hard, checking out every opportunity, visiting everyone able to assist, protesting, spreading the gospel, trying to convince those who mattered that his confinement was a waste of tax payers' money. Working unselfishly to secure his early release. But there again, he was still missing her.

"Okay, Croaker?" asked the gruff voice as the entourage waddled past. This was Big Frankie's nickname for Blade. He had no idea why. But he knew it would stick with him now for the remainder of his sentence. However long that would be. He'd done nearly three years in Gartree now. Was an old hand.

Part of the scenery. He'd toed the line throughout. Done what he was told. Obeyed Frankie's rules. Done his bit for the team. "Sure, Frankie," he answered. Frankie nodded and went on his way. Blade smiled to himself. During the next minute and a half, he was called upon to acknowledge three other lords of the manor as they greeted him in exactly the same way as Frankie had just done. Each had their entourage of minders and hangers-on escorting them. Following in Richardson's footsteps. Where Frankie went, everyone else was sure to follow. Bunch of copy-cats. If Frankie were to do a zigzag, diagonally across the grass in the middle of the exercise yard, they'd all follow.

Blade's eyes carelessly scanned the view as he enjoyed the sensation of warm sun on his back. He noticed two boarders he hadn't seen before. Must be new. They'd attached themselves to the rear of the convoy. They were nasty looking bastards. Both in their early twenties he guessed. One tall and lanky. The other of a more average height and build. Must have come in during the night. He watched as they began to quicken their stride, gradually overtaking the cons in front of them.

Bemused, Blade followed their progress. They'd got all the time in the world. Why chase it? By the time the two new boys were passing Blade, they were practically running in their haste to get to the head of the queue. He could see that the one nearest him, the lanky one, had something hidden in his hand. Odd, he thought. Very odd. You don't hide anything in the nick unless it's of use to you or it's been ordered by another con. Puzzled as to what they were up to, he stood up to get a better view of the two heroes. By now they looked like they had rockets up their arses, so Blade took off after them. He had a peculiar feeling about these particular cavaliers. He sensed in his gut that there was grief in the air. Like a cloud had passed over the sun. He knew that the beautiful morning was about to be dramatically disturbed.

As he drew closer to the two hoodlums he realised they were closing in on Frankie. Right! Now he had the picture. No wonder Lanky had it hidden. It was a shiv, giving off a quick glint in the sunlight as it was turned upwards in the boy's hand. Ready to strike. Frankie was the target all right. These two bastards were setting themselves up as pretenders to his throne.

"Watch it, Frankie!" Blade cried, darting forward to grab the knifeman round the throat. Thank fuck for Laurel and Hardy. Frankie's minders spun round and demolished Lanky's mate with swift, savage blows to his head and balls. All delivered within a second. Lanky was a bit more of a problem though. Strong kid. And he wouldn't drop the knife. "Fucking Hell!" Blade gasped, as the kid's elbow pushed his insides back against his spine. As quick as a fiddler's elbow, Lanky slashed out. Equally quick, Blade managed to catch his wrist before the damage could be done. The number two was on the floor as Laurel and Hardy concentrated their efforts on him. It must have felt good. First time they'd had to do anything for months. Two strong, well-meaning lads. But both bungalows. Not so bright where it mattered most. Fortunately the screws were now also on board. Off the walls. And out of the buildings. Out of the bogs. Out of thin air. It was like the Governor's Ball.

* * * * *

Frankie greeted Blade with a big smacker on the cheek, accompanied by a wrestler's hug. Blade coughed and spluttered. He could hardly see the big man's face through the cloud of cigarette smoke. "Black Russian. The finest." Richardson held up his gold tipped cigarette as though it were a valuable jewel. He offered the box to Blade, who accepted the gift as a true hero should. "The trouble with young wankers like you, Croaker, is you've no idea what real living is about." Frankie chuckled. But Blade was still choking. That's right, he thought. Blowing your lungs up. That's living all right.

"Sit down, son." Frankie was in a good mood and Blade was the man of the moment. Blade sat down in the armchair Frankie had indicated and tried not to stare too obviously at the freakish tableau before him – Frankie in his satin robe flanked by his gormless minders, Tony Lambesi hovering in the background. "I owe you one, Croaker," the voice boomed. "And I always pay up." Nice one, thought Blade. How about getting me out of this place and fixing it so I never have to return. "But there's another favour I want you to do." That was typical of Frankie. You should always expect the unexpected from him. Just when Blade thought he was about to have his store cupboard filled with smokes and whisky, he had the rug pulled.

"There's a young kid coming in in a couple of days. I want you to look after him. Show him the ropes. Make sure he's okay. He's had a bad time ..." Richardson stopped and looked up at Lambesi for guidance. That's a good start, thought Blade. Very enlightening. Nothing like getting your act together. "What's the boy's name?" Lambesi whispered the necessary information. Frankie nodded. "That's it. Causer. Colin Causer. Known the family for years. He's yours, Croaker."

"You what, Frankie?" Blade was confused. "What do you mean, he's mine?"

"Have him for a while." The big man's arms were waving about. As if he were conducting an orchestra. "He's got problems, Croak. Look after him. You know, settle him down. Keep a watchful eye. Let me know in a couple of weeks how he is."

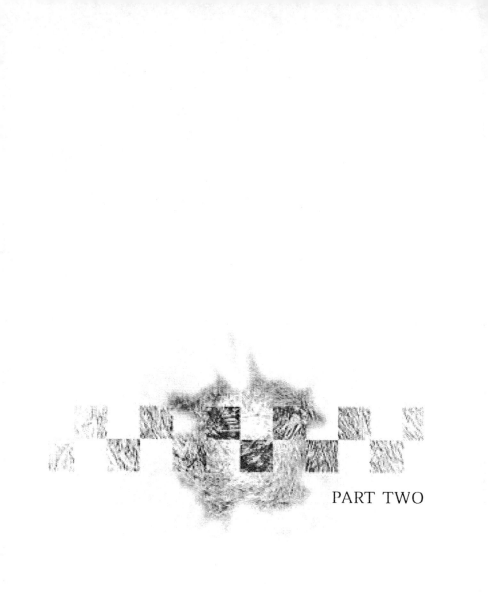

PART TWO

11

Every member and his dog was seated around the large, highly polished oval table. The committee room was just off the mayor's robing room and the members of the Police Authority were in full attendance. It was quite an occasion. Assistant Chief Constable Frank Newhart had come to make his annual presentation on the state of crime in their city. A couple of months ago, they'd listened to the chief constable's annual report, and this was dessert. And the councillors were finding it fascinating. Zero tolerance was something they had read about in newspapers but didn't fully understand. They were none the wiser as Frank Newhart delivered his closing statements. "Therefore, we must accept that it won't happen overnight. To develop such a high level of public corporacy will take time. We must all act together." The last remark always impressed. It was we'll-fight-them-on-the-beaches time all over again. Strength in unity and all that.

"How much time, Chief Constable?" This was the fifth question from Councillor Knebbs. He'd been on the council for eons. Practically since they built the town hall at the beginning of the century. He always had plenty to say but nowadays not much that made any sense.

"Assistant," corrected Newhart.

"What?" Old Councillor Knebbs turned towards the lady mayor.

"He's the assistant chief constable," she said, carefully enunciating every word. Knebbs was still nodding when Frank Newhart replied to his question.

"Well, who knows? It could be a year. Might be longer. Whatever. I believe …" Newhart checked himself. "That is, we, the chief constable and I, believe that this is the right direction to take. Involving the community and working together towards a common goal." He stopped, head slightly bowed, waiting. Much to his relief, the applause began, drowning out Councillor Knebbs' next question. He'd cracked it. He'd whipped up sufficient enthusiasm to label support. He could go back to the chief constable and tell him about the tremendously positive meeting he'd had.

As the room emptied, Newhart gathered up his bits and pieces and prepared to make his way down the hall towards the buffet. The presentation had gone well, and that was a relief. You never knew how this bunch of clueless do-gooders was going to react. Particularly Paul Meade, the arrogant leader of the council. So far as Newhart was concerned the man was a right plonker. And a lying toad to boot. But thankfully he'd sat in uncharacteristic silence all the way through his presentation. Leaving the idiot Knebbs to ask his idiot questions. But now here he was, silent no more, jabbering away at his elbow.

"So, Frank," Meade gushed. "Sorry about the golf last week." He was back to his usual flamboyant self. There was gold wrapped around both wrists and most of his fingers. Aftershave by the gallon. Little black cigarette in its little gold holder. Before he'd met Meade, Newhart had only ever seen these in Agatha Christie films. It was an affectation that really pissed him off. But he was on duty tonight. So he nodded and smiled and wondered vaguely what the prat was on about. "I take it you got my message."

"What message?" Newhart did his best to pay attention. But his mind and stomach were on the buffet downstairs.

"From that young inspector. Can't think of his name. Presley? No, Priestley. That's it, Jack Priestley. I asked him to pass on the message."

"What message?" Newhart repeated. His stomach rumbled a little complaint.

"I asked him to pass on my apologies for missing you at the club."

"Well he didn't." Newhart decided he might as well head downstairs. If Meade wanted to talk to him, he'd walk with him. He did. Only now he was clutching at his arm. What's wrong with the silly sod, thought Newhart.

"We had quite a conversation the other day, did Jack Priestley and I," continued Meade. "In fact I'm not really surprised you didn't get the message." Newhart didn't like the sound of this. After a short pause, Meade pushed on. "Frank. Do you think you could have a word with him?"

"What?" Frank Newhart didn't have time for this. His eyes took in the splendid sight before him. A line of tables covered in the city's best linen tablecloths, groaning beneath a feast fit for an assistant chief constable.

"Priestley, Frank. Jack Priestley. He's been on to me about some bloody land deal or other. I don't know. I think he's got his wires all mashed up. Have a word could you, Frank?"

"Mixed up."

"What?" asked the leader of the council.

"He's got his wires mixed up."

"That's it, Frank. Mixed up. Have a word with him will you?"

Newhart looked at Meade, realising at last that a favour was being called in. Meade was satisfied Newhart understood and let go of his arm. But just to make sure the message really had hit home, Meade added some insurance. "By the way," he whispered, his mouth barely an inch away from the assistant chief constable's ear. "Keep this close to your chest. We're putting you up for the next honours list, Frank. Shouldn't tell you really. I'll get my balls chewed for it. But I'm sure you'll keep it to yourself."

He walked away, leaving Newhart standing at the banquet table, his face beaming. A little confused, but nonetheless delighted. Recognition at last. He'd have a word with Nolan in the morning. Put the kibosh on whatever Jack Priestley was up to. As he found himself a plate and started loading it with food, he wondered what it would be. OBE? CBE? Something more?

*　*　*　*　*

Priestley was certain he had done his job well. He hadn't left a single stone unturned, so far as he was aware. The vast amount of energy he'd dedicated towards putting Paul Meade out of circulation was reflected in the neatly stacked pile of papers which sat on top of his desk. In a nutshell, Cheapside Surveyors had purchased the land in Rowntree Lane from the council for three quarters of a million pounds. The council had acquired the land two years before for one and a half million. The previous owners sold the land to the council having repeatedly failed to obtain planning consent. Over the last ten years, twelve planning applications had been made to the council, and they'd all been turned down. Until Cheapside came along that was. Priestley was happy with the way his investigation had gone. And now he was ready to submit the papers. The only problem, niggling away at the back of his mind, was his brief conversation with Jim Nolan earlier in the week. At the time he hadn't treated it very seriously, but now it was worrying him.

Priestley had only called into police headquarters to pick up some files and to visit the gents, but he could have sworn that the head of CID had been waiting to ambush him. He had the impression that Nolan's sudden appearance had very little to do with splashing the porcelain.

"Meade is a big ally, Jack. We really mustn't antagonise him," he'd said.

"You know about my inquiry?" Priestley had replied, thinking, of course he does.

"Be careful, Jack." Nolan had been standing beside him at the basins, washing his hands as well. "He's a very powerful man."

"What exactly are you suggesting? That I drop the investigation?" Priestley had asked.

Nolan had sighed and shaken his head. Like he was trying to explain rights and wrongs to a particularly stupid child. "Jack, all I'm saying is be careful." Then, abruptly, he turned and walked away. Without even drying his hands.

Priestley considered the stack of papers on his desk in front of him. Paul Meade was a big cheese and his report strongly recommended prosecution. The fruits of one month's labours. Finally he decided, to Hell with them all.

* * * * *

Three weeks later, Priestley found himself pacing up and down outside Frank Newhart's office. He glanced at his watch. He had no idea why the assistant chief constable had asked to see him, unless it was to congratulate him on a pending promotion. Wishful thinking. But he was confident he wasn't in any trouble and it was only for that reason, or promotion, that officers at his level were summoned to the dizzy heights. He felt a little apprehensive as he studied the pictures of the old fogies who'd proceeded the current ACC. Each one, the first dating back to 1879, stared sternly down at him from the dimly lit corridor walls. He glanced at his watch again. If he had to wait much longer, he'd piss himself.

"Mr Priestley?" The secretary was a middle-aged woman and she dressed the part. But she greeted the detective inspector with a warm smile. "Mr Newhart will see you now."

Newhart sat behind a large oak desk, examining a huge bundle of papers. He eventually stood and shook Priestley's hand. "Sit down Jack. I won't keep you long."

Priestley obeyed but wished he could have remained standing. "You wanted to see me, Sir?"

"I'll get straight to the point, young man. Paul Meade. I've read your papers," he said, pointing at the pile on the desk. "And I must admit I'm a little concerned about your recommendations."

"The evidence supports a prosecution surely?"

Newhart pushed his chair away from his desk, but remained seated. He linked his hands together across his belly. Newhart was a big man. In his youth, he'd been muscular and athletic. But by now the muscle had run to fat. All his clothes were just that little bit too tight. "Maybe so. Your inquiry is extremely detailed and well put together. But I'll come straight to the point," he repeated. "The chief has a vested interest in this particular investigation and doesn't favour any further action."

What! What kind of bollocks is this? Jack felt his collar tighten and his face light up like a firework against a black sky. Newhart continued calmly. "You see what we have to look at is not just whether a prosecution should follow an inquiry such as this, but also the consequences for the force and other associated departments."

More bollocks. "But, Sir, Meade has used his position to obtain financial benefits and the Theft Act distinctly ..."

"Jack, Jack, I know," Newhart interrupted, waving his hands in a gesture intended to calm. "And I know that you'll have misgivings about this. I have them too. But, Jack, think of the press if this thing goes public. And you know it will, Jack."

No. Jack shook his head. Unbelieving. This was a cover-up. There was no other way to describe this. But what Newhart didn't know was that the press had initiated the inquiry and Priestley certainly wasn't going to enlighten him.

Newhart stood and walked around to the front of his desk, placing his plump arse on the edge of it. "You see," he said, "in this game, politics is important and at the moment Paul Meade is very supportive of this force. Now if this gets out, Jack, he'll be destroyed. If that happens, Jack, the way will be open for the left wingers to jump in and that could spell dire trouble for everybody. Do you follow? Of course you do. Now, let's agree to file these papers and say no more about the matter, eh?"

Priestley was astounded. Flabbergasted. Everything he believed the police service represented had just gone down the drain. Integrity. Honesty. His whole investigation slung out the window. And whatever the reasoned arguments, this was manipulation. Abuse of authority. What he could never have believed would happen, just had. And there was nothing he could do. He stood and nodded his compliance, an urgent need to get out into the fresh air pushing him towards the door.

"You know it makes sense, Jack, and I'll tell you this, the chief won't forget it in a hurry."

* * * * *

Priestley didn't go back to his office. He needed to make a telephone call. But not from his desk telephone which would be monitored. He used his cell phone in the park across the street from HQ.

"Hi babe," chirped Carol Guardia. "How's the inquiry going?"

"It's been spiked."

"Don't piss me about, Jack."

"Believe it, Carol."

"Who's killed it, Jack?"

Priestley's loyalty only went so far, but he wasn't going to breach it. Not even for Carol. "You know I can't tell you that. Anyway, it's not important. Run the story, Carol."

On the other end of the line, Carol Guardia's clever brain swung through 180 degrees. "No. At least not yet. The council elections are in a few months. I'll have a word with Eddie. I think we'll run this then. And that'll be the end of Mr Meade. File your papers, pending prosecution in the summer, Mr Detective. Revenge will never be sweeter."

On his end of the line, Priestley shrugged his shoulders. It was her story. She could do what she liked with it. He didn't have the energy for games. He'd heard about this happening before, but never believed there was any truth in the rumours.

12

Colin Causer was twenty-three years old. He was in Gartree to serve eight years after having been convicted for a series of armed robberies on building societies along the south coast. For two years he and his girlfriend had taken out various branches with a sawn-off shotgun. No one knew how much this modern day Bonnie and Clyde team had made from their exploits, least of all the culprits themselves, but it must have run into thousands – money which they had spent like water running through rapids. That was as much as Blade was able to discover in the two days between receiving his instructions from Frankie and young Colin's arrival.

"Do anything? Apart from pull a face?" he said the first time he saw him. To Blade the boy looked like a rabbit in headlights. He had blond curly hair, a slim figure, and fast-looking feet. All the attributes, in fact, of an athletic armed robber. But his wispy beard made him look more like a college student, innocent of the ways of the world. And in many ways he was. He didn't bother to reply to Blade's quip and from the look on his face, Blade wasn't optimistic that their relationship was going to flourish. Nevertheless, he had Frankie's instructions and tried again. "Steve Blade," he said and offered the hand of friendship. It was taken. Good sign. Might be able to do something with this kid after all. "How do you fancy a tour?" he suggested. "To take in the sights and all that?" There was a timid nod in response. Maybe the kid just lacked confidence.

Slowly, over the next couple of weeks, Blade developed a close relationship with Colin Causer. He felt sorry for the boy. Recognised parts of his own younger self in him. As his affection for the kid grew, it became harder and harder to stand witness to his obvious pain. Something was clearly bothering the young man, but so far Blade had failed to make the breakthrough. He knew he had to, and soon. Because if ever there were a candidate for topping himself, this was it. In fact Blade was faintly surprised Colin hadn't done it already. The lad was keenly vulnerable and prone to frightening fits of introspective depression. Something deeply rooted inside his mind was causing him a great deal of heartache and Blade knew he had to get him to open up. It took a lot of time, patience and effort, but one afternoon it happened. And then the whole sorry tale came flooding out.

"Son, you're carrying the problems of the world on your shoulders and you know what happened to the last geezer who did that – they crucified him. Why the black clouds all the time?" They were in Blade's cell. Blade was sitting comfortably in the only easy chair. Causer was parked on the table top, swinging his legs to and fro in the void underneath. He had a mug of coffee in one hand and a biscuit in the other. Blade had managed to smuggle a load of them from the kitchen two days earlier.

Causer sighed, as if suddenly reaching a decision long held at bay. "It's a long story, Steve." The kid stared at the floor.

This was the closest Blade had got, and he knew he had to get the next question right. Or Causer would run away again. "Try me, son." Blade wouldn't have a better chance to get into the lad's mind. "You know what they say. Two heads are better than one. Perhaps it might help to get whatever's giving you so much grief off your chest?"

"There's nothing anybody can do for me." He looked up. "Even you." Had he fallen back into his black hole already?

"That bad, eh?" Blade felt he had to persevere with this, but didn't have a clue what to say next. So there was a long period of silence, except for the occasional sound of something being dropped in another cell and the normal daily rumpus that goes on in one of Her Majesty's prisons.

Then suddenly the floodgates opened. "We'd just done a job. Like always, I did the business and she waited in the motor a few streets away." Blade didn't dare to speak. Only to listen. "We were going to run back to her mother's place, you know, where we knew the law wouldn't be waiting. That was our safe house, as it were." He stopped and Blade could see that his eyes had begun to fill with tears. He knew that if he spoke now, he might destroy the kid's only chance to unload the grief that had so obviously been clawing away at him since he first landed. "I reached the motor and Joanna had the engine running. She always sat in the passenger seat. You know? I always did the driving." He was choking but getting there. "Anyway, it looked good and I started moving off. All nice and slow like. Then this police car came from nowhere and rammed us in the back." The trembling increased and his voice cracked and became louder as he struggled to get the words out. "I took off like a bat out of hell but couldn't shake him, Steve. He just stayed with us, his sirens blasting. We got out into the country, into some little lanes, but he was still there, like a fly on gum paper. I even thought about stopping the motor and giving it him." Blade knew he was referring to the sawn-off he'd have been carrying at the time and thought what a stupid thing to do that would have been. Seeing off a copper. Jesus, he'd have been spending the rest of his life emptying boilers in the kitchen.

"But then that would have implicated Jo even more, so I carried on. It was pissing down with rain and the car started to go its own way." The trembling intensified. It was getting hard for Blade to understand what he was saying. "We must have been doing 80 or more and I just ran out of road. The car hit a tree and she just sat there not moving. She died while I held onto her. They told me later she'd broken her neck, Steve. And I'd really shit out."

"How long had you known her, son?"

"Long enough. Since school." The tears in his eyes hadn't yet fallen. They needed to. He needed to scream. But they balanced there on the edges of his lids. Not quite ready to run. "I was roped in and charged with death by dangerous driving."

"The bastards. They did that knowing what she meant to you?"

He nodded. "It was dropped eventually and they just went ahead with the blaggings." The mug fell from his hand and smashed onto the floor, but neither man paid any attention. "But I should have died with her and there's not a moment in the day or night when I'm not thinking of her. It's like a living death. Everywhere I look, I can see her face. At night, when everything's quiet, my mind fills up with the memories. The laughs we had and the way we led the law a merry dance. But it keeps coming back to the accident."

"But that's it, son." Blade was trying hard to think of something to say which would help the kid. "You've just hit the nail on the head. It was an accident and life has to go on." He held onto Causer's shoulder. "I can understand you grieving, but you can't keep drilling yourself. It wasn't your fault. Listen to me. You're serving your time in here for what you've done and nothing you do now will bring your bird back. You've got to make the best of it and try and get that madness out of your head. You owe that to Joanna, surely?"

Causer nodded and wiped his eyes. At last he'd opened up his heart to somebody else. The tears finally started falling and Blade held the boy as he wept to mend a broken heart. Eventually the sobs receded and Blade loosened his hold as Colin regained his composure. "Listen," said Blade. He'd had an idea. Something that might help the kid get his mind off things. "I want you to give us a hand with something. We're going to throw a party. You and I. A right booze up, savvy? What do you think?"

"How?" It was working. Despite himself, Causer was intrigued.

"Hooch, my son." The broad grin on Blade's face confused him even more. "We are going to make some hooch. Okay?" He slapped the kid across the back. "Get your head on sunshine. I need a mate for this one." Causer grinned. It was the first time Blade had seen him look genuinely happy. He breathed a quiet sigh of relief. Colin Causer was going to be okay after all.

13

The pub was overflowing with people, congratulations and cigarette smoke. Priestley looked around the room and was suddenly overwhelmed by a sense of foreboding. He remembered the day, just four weeks ago, when he'd been summoned once more to see Frank Newhart. He remembered waiting outside Newhart's office thinking, you are here either because you are in the shit again or because you really are going to be promoted this time. And now here he was, holding a party to celebrate his elevation to detective chief inspector. The promotion had been unexpected to say the least, although he'd been qualified to go up a rank for some time. But if he was honest there was no way he believed it would come so soon. And to be given a post on the Regional Crime Squad? Well, that too was unexpected. It meant secondment away from his force, but the work would involve supporting his own as well as other forces. However, as with all good news, there was a downside. Instinctively he knew his promotion was a direct result of dropping the Paul Meade investigation. It had come so suddenly and the vacancy at the RCS must have been too good an opportunity for his senior officers to distance him for a while. He wasn't sure, but he had a bloody good idea that was the case. Just to cool his heels a little. The thought left a sour taste in his mouth. He felt himself to be tainted with a vague whiff of corruption. He sighed and reminded himself that now was not the time to worry. Now was the time to go through the motions. And celebrate.

"Jack, over here," called a voice through the crowd. It was Ernie Machin, editor of the local rag. Ernie was barely an inch over five foot and was dwarfed by the six-foot police officers standing around him, his chin supported by a large, brightly coloured dickie bow. "Jack, sort this one out for us. This lot reckon you need us more than we need you. What about it, Jack? True, or false?"

Priestley opened his mouth to answer but young Vince Bragg interjected before he had a chance to utter the first syllable. Vince was an earnestly enthusiastic member of his team. Or, rather, his ex-team now he was moving on. Vince was always willing and eager to please, but a little impulsive. He didn't always take enough time to think things through. Hopefully these were just symptoms of his youth and, if so, Priestley was certain his future would be bright. "Gaffer, Ernie and his mates phone us up every morning, right? Now all we're saying is that without the information we give them, they'd be struggling."

"Not so. Not so," shouted Ernie. "We already have half the story when we ring. All you lot do is cut corners for us." Bragg shook his head, enjoying the attention and support of his mates, who humorously jeered the suggestion that they were merely a support facility for the local press.

Priestley became the mediator. "Okay. So let's agree to differ. In fairness to both of you, we need each other." This was greeted by howls of derision from the young officers, but Priestley pushed on. "Come on. Think about it. Whenever we want to make public appeals for help, the press support us. And then when things are a little quiet for them, we give them a pointer or two. It works both ways."

Ernie liked that. "Well said, Jack. I'll settle for that." He took Priestley's hand in his own and shook it enthusiastically. You couldn't help liking Ernie. He exuded bonhomie from every pore. "By the way, Jack. I don't think I've congratulated you properly. Congratulations! I'd like to talk to you sometime about doing a piece on you. Hot-shot police officer and his meteoric career. I gather you're one of the youngest detective chief inspectors in the country. I thought Carol could do the interview." His words fell thick and fast, he barely took time to draw breath, his eyes all the time scanning the room. "And here she is," he said, spotting the girl in question. "The delightful Carol. Come to add her congratulations to mine."

Carol didn't have time for congratulations. "Did you see it, Mr Policeman?" she said impatiently.

"See what?"

"The article on Meade. In tonight's paper. Congratulations by the way. Suppose we won't be seeing so much of you now?"

"You ran it?"

"Sure we did. It's in the public's interests that they know all about that bastard."

"I thought you said you were going to wait until the elections."

"We did. But, you know. Things are a bit slack at the moment. Ernie wanted it, didn't you Boss?"

" 'Fraid so, Jack. Needs must. Besides, it was Carol's story anyway. And the elections are next month in any case."

"For fuck's sake, Ernie. You've really dumped me in it."

"Oh come on, Priestley. You've got your promotion. What's to worry about?"

Jack sighed. What's to worry about? They'd think it was him. Promotion or no promotion they'd have his balls in a vice if they thought he'd leaked the story to the press. Meade had had it. His political career was over and, even if he wanted to, there was nothing Priestley could do about it. Except that Jim Nolan suddenly grabbed him by the elbow. "A word if you please, Jack," he murmured and steered him to an out-of-the-way corner of the room. In his hand he held the evening paper. "Are you responsible for this?" he hissed, holding up the paper for Jack to see the headline. It read 'Local Politician in Land Deal Fraud'.

"No, Boss."

"Then where the hell did it come from?" There was no need for him to lower his voice. The hubbub in the bar was so loud nobody had a chance of overhearing.

"Not from me."

"You sure about that Priestley?"

"Yes, Boss. I do know that Carol Guardia's got it in for Meade. Ever since he got caught with his pants down. She probably investigates every move he makes. There was nothing in my report that wasn't already in the public domain."

"Did she tip you off in the first place?" This was an uncharacteristic and unexpected flash of insight. For an instant, Priestley felt guilty about betraying Carol. But only for an instant. After all, she'd just dumped him in it. Still, he had to protect his sources.

"No, Boss," he lied.

Nolan backed off. "You did the right thing, Jack. Dropping your inquiry. Meade has been a good supporter in the past. He's been there for us when we've needed a favour or two from the council. And in return, we've given leeway back. Understand?"

Oh yes, Priestley understood very well. "You mean you scratch my back and I'll scratch yours?" He couldn't hide the sarcasm in his voice and Nolan screwed his face up in response.

"Not exactly."

"Then what are you saying?"

"I'm saying ... I'm saying, Jack, you've got a bright future. But you need to learn the difference between ..." Priestley stopped listening. This conversation was going nowhere. In his book, whatever label you put on it, coercion, for whatever reason, was corruption. And he had problems with that. Nolan's voice faded away as Priestley's gaze skimmed across his shoulder and focused on a soldier, sitting alone in the far corner of the room. His head nodded from time to time in acknowledgement, but he could no longer hear what Nolan was saying. He gazed at the oddness of the soldier. He was obviously an officer but he appeared to be very frail. He had an astonishing lack of physical bearing. A mop of unkempt black hair exaggerated his unhealthy white face. He sat hunched on his seat, alone in a room full of people. Except that the table in front of him was lined with pints of beer, queuing up for his attention.

"… so use your loaf, Jack." Nolan's voice penetrated his mind once more. "Take advantage of every opportunity. Learn now about the ins and outs of politics. You've got a good future in front of you. Don't spoil it." Nolan stopped, awaiting some acknowledgement.

Priestley woke up. "I understand," he lied. "Thanks for the advice, Boss."

Nolan slapped him on the shoulder. "I knew you would understand Jack. You'll enjoy it on the RCS. The change will be good for you." He lowered his voice. "And you can make yourself useful while you're there. Keep this to yourself, Jack, but we've been having problems with some of our informants." Priestley stiffened and held his breath. The word 'informant' was very sensitive. Not one to be mentioned in public. Especially not at a gathering such as this, inside a public house, full of flapping ears and loose tongues. "There's a leak somewhere. Someone's giving out their details. We've had two or three done over lately. So keep your ears open and your eyes peeled." Nolan nodded his head and placed a forefinger to his mouth. "Keep it to yourself, Jack. Let me know if you hear anything."

Nolan patted Priestley's arm and wandered off, clearly satisfied with his lecture. But his conversation with Jim Nolan, the bits he'd heard anyway, had unsettled Priestley. He looked around the smoke-filled room again. The party was going well. It was in full swing all around him. And he was the host. He looked at his watch. God, he hated this kind of thing. Right now all he wanted to do was go home and go to bed. Or preferably to Sonia's home. And to bed with her. But he had his hostly duties to fulfil. And now was the time. He asked the barman to ring the bell behind the bar, and when he had everyone's attention he invited them all to have a drink on him. Naturally there were no dissenters and it cost him dear.

A voice behind him said, "Drink, Mr Priestley?" He turned. It was the regimental sergeant-major from the barracks, resplendent in full uniform. Part of Priestley's job at CID had been to maintain a close and friendly relationship with the local army camp. So naturally they'd accepted his invitation to join him for a drink or two now that he was moving on. Typical soldiers. They'd take any opportunity for a piss up!

"I've just bought you one," he replied. "By the way it's Jack."

The RSM stood as all RSMs do. Straight as a rod, as though he were still on the parade ground. Priestley recognised him from a social gathering he'd attended at the barracks months ago, before Christmas sometime. "It was very good of you to invite us tonight," the sergeant-major said. "I'm all for social as well as working liaison. Congratulations, by the way."

"Thank you, Sergeant-Major. Glad you could all come." He paused briefly. "I was wondering. That chap over there. On his own in the corner. Who is he?"

The RSM didn't have to look. He knew exactly who Priestley was referring to. "That, Mr Priestley," he said, ignoring Priestley's request to use his Christian name, "is Captain Carpe from the Bomb Disposal Unit."

"He doesn't look much like a captain. He ..."

The RSM interrupted. "Captain Carpe is the bravest man I have known in fifteen years of military service. And I think that goes for the rest of the men. We're all proud to know him. He and his men are with us for a few weeks. Up from Herefordshire on exercises. Would you like me to introduce you?"

"No, it's all right." Priestley found himself staring at the strange, solitary figure. "If you'll excuse me, I'll introduce myself."

* * * * *

"Jack Priestley," he said, holding out his hand. "Detective Inspector Jack Priestley." He'd already forgotten about his promotion. He sat down opposite Captain Carpe. He was even more mystified by the man's appearance now he was up close. It was obvious the man was in a lot of pain. It was written all over his face. But his eyes showed no emotion. You could be forgiven for believing that the captain was as pissed as a rat. But that wasn't so. It was simply that there was something different about his eyes. A strange kind of alertness about them. "You must be a very popular man, Captain," Priestley said, indicating the line of full glasses on the table, now totalling five, and another in his hand.

"Help yourself, Inspector." Carpe smiled, but only slightly, as though his head would fall off if the crack in his face broadened any further.

Priestley held up the pint in his hand. "No. Thanks anyway. The RSM tells me you're up from Hereford on exercises?"

"Yes."

"He tells me you're the bravest man he's ever met. That's quite an accolade."

"He exaggerates."

"But diffusing bombs ..." Priestley couldn't think how to continue.

"There are others who do the same job." Carpe stared at him without any expression at all.

Confused, Priestley stood up to leave. He hadn't even begun to satisfy his curiosity but he felt he was already on the verge of outstaying his welcome. "It's been good to have met you," he said weakly and held out his hand a second time. The captain's grip was dry and firm. Steady. As Priestley turned away, he suddenly said, "Inspector?"

Priestley turned back, eyebrows raised in enquiry. "One of my lads was sentenced to twelve months' jankers last week."

There was still no expression or movement, except by the hand which was nursing the pint on the table. "He's been using drugs. Coke."

"Must be a fair bit of that going on in the army, I suppose."

Ignoring the comment, Carpe continued. "He told us he got the gear off an officer in your force." Priestley's eyes widened in amazement. He waited for more, but more didn't come.

"Any name? Or rank? For the person who supplied your man." The answer was just a shake of the head. "Any other information which might help us?" Another expressionless shake of the head. "Was he telling the truth?"

"Yes, I believe he was."

Priestley fished in the inside pocket of his jacket and pulled out a card. On it was printed his name and his mobile telephone number. He handed it to Carpe, saying, "Call me if you find out more. And I'll look into it."

* * * * *

The RSM was still guarding the spot where he was standing when Priestley had left him earlier. "What about that drink now, Jack?"

Still absorbed in his conversation with Carpe, Priestley appeared not to hear the question. "Doesn't say much, your captain, does he?"

"Doesn't have to. Did he tell you what he does for a living?"

"Diffuses bombs."

"That's true. But he does a bit more than just that."

"How can you describe diffusing bombs as being just that?"

"Well, imagine a three-week-old body decomposing in the middle of a field on the Northern Ireland Border." The RSM lowered his voice. "The body is probably booby trapped. In addition, you've got reason to believe the field is mined. Right? Well, Captain Nicholas Carpe is the poor bastard who's dropped into the field and tasked with clearing the area. And that's before he even starts on the body."

Priestley's intake of breath was sharp. No wonder. "You're right, Sergeant-Major. The man is a hero. He's a living bloody legend."

* * * * *

Why is it, thought Priestley, that every time you have to visit a senior officer they always seem to be busy reading something when you first walk into their office? Jim Nolan was no different. Except that he was reading a newspaper. He eventually finished the article he was reading and looked up. "Right, Jack," he said curtly. "You've got three minutes. I've got a meeting with the chief in a minute. What can I do for you?" No, "Good to see you, Jack. Always a pleasure. Do take a seat. How's the new job going." No. Just, "You've got three minutes." So, better get straight to the point.

"Do you remember the army captain at the pub the other night?" Nolan lit a fag and shook his head, as he began to gather up papers from his desk and stuff them in a buff coloured folder. "He mentioned something to me which I thought you should know about."

"Oh?" Nolan didn't even bother to look up.

"He told me that one of his men had been banged up by the army for taking cocaine and the bloke who'd supplied him was on our force." He watched eagerly for Nolan's reaction. Instead of the response Priestley anticipated, howls of horror and the assertion that such an allegation should be investigated immediately, Nolan smiled nervously and without any real sincerity.

"Rubbish, Jack. Bloody rubbish. How's the Regional going?" This was a deflection which Priestley didn't appreciate. He hadn't come all this way to discuss the bloody RCS. Apart from that, he'd only been on it a couple of days. He looked closely at Nolan and thought he recognised a man dismissing something he knew to be true. Priestley's experience in the interview room warned him that Nolan might be lying.

So he persisted. "Captain Carpe believes what his soldier has told him."

"Any name, Jack? That's the important thing." Priestley had to admit that there wasn't. "Well there you are. Load of crap." Nolan stood up, ending the meeting. "Have to go now, mate. Catch up with you another time. Oh, and by the way, that stuff I was telling you about informants. It was a load of balls, Jack. I was pissed. Forget it."

*   *   *   *   *

As Priestley walked slowly back to his car, he wondered whether he was reading too much into what had just happened. Firstly, an allegation that an officer on the force was selling drugs had to be investigated. Everybody knew that. Brushing it under the carpet was out of the question. Secondly, he had the impression that Nolan was lying in some way. He didn't know how exactly. But he sensed a lie. And thirdly, why would Nolan tell him about informants being done over at the party and then change his story today. It didn't add up. Nothing that had just happened in Jim Nolan's office made any sense. And for sure Nolan wasn't drunk at the party. Not then anyway. Later on he was roaring drunk. But when he'd given Priestley his little lecture, he'd been sober as a judge. None of it made any sense.

Just as he reached his car, his mobile phone started up. It was about bloody time he changed the bloody tune. Beethoven's finest. It gave him the pip every time it went off. Irritated, he answered it as quickly as he could. "Jack? It's Nick Carpe."

14

"Jack, surely you're not going already?" Sonia's voice was blurred with her newly departed dreams. He turned and looked back at her as he walked towards the bathroom. Christ, she was gorgeous. Even rubbing the sleep from her eyes, with her hair all over the place.

"I have to. I'm sorry. I didn't mean to wake you." His watch was telling him that it was already seven o'clock and he had a long day to get through. First, he had to get down to Hereford for his meeting with Nick Carpe, and that was one appointment he didn't want to miss. Then he had to go on down to Gartree to see Steve Blade.

"Jack, I want to talk to you." She raised her voice so that it would carry through to the bathroom. When there was no response, she tried again. "Jack, I need to bloody well talk to you." For a learned counsel, she certainly had a way with words, but they were drowned out by the sound of the shower coming on. She waited impatiently for him to finish, twisting the beautiful satin sheet in her hands. The moment she heard the shower stopping, she shouted out again. "You've been here all night. Surely, another ten minutes won't hurt?"

Smearing shaving foam on his chin, Priestley called from the bathroom, "Sonia, I'm late. I really have to get going." He didn't need this. He really didn't need this.

"But Jack," she persisted. "It's important." Silence came from the bathroom. He was shaving. "It's a matter of life and death, Jack," she solemnly continued. "You're the only person I can talk to." Now that did sound serious. Perhaps this wasn't a female ploy to get him back into bed after all. Shaving foam still covering half his face, Priestley walked back into the bedroom, prepared at last to listen. "Can you come back later, Jack. I really have to talk to you. It's very important that I talk to you."

He didn't like the sound of this. "Should I be worried?" he asked.

She sat up and turned on her side, one shapely breast falling out from beneath the sheet. He pretended not to notice. This wasn't fair. He had to leave. "Not about you and me," she reassured him. "But there's something that's been preying on my mind for a couple of days now and I need to run it past you. I think it's something you should know about."

He sighed. Obviously this was important to her. He sat down on the edge of the bed and took her hand. "Okay. Okay, I'll come back here this evening. About eight. You can give me dinner and tell me what's on your mind. Okay?" Soothed, she nodded. "Right," he said, business-like again. "I really do have to get going. Better get this crap off my face first though."

* * * * *

The market in the town square was crowded with people chasing each other from one stall to another, searching out bargains or anything else to attract the money burning a hole in their pockets and purses. But gathering clouds glowered overhead. They hadn't yet blocked out the sun, but Priestley wondered how long the activity could continue before the inevitable burst of rain. June was such a changeable month, but, he supposed, no more unpredictable than the others.

He could see Nick Carpe sitting in the window of the café as he crossed the busy square. He looked just as he had at their first meeting in the pub. Pasty-faced and completely shot through. The only difference was that this time his smile was sincere as he stood to welcome Priestley, and to offer him a coffee. "Thanks for coming down, Jack," he said, with surprising warmth in this voice.

"No problem. It's good to see you again. Have you seen Private Gardiner."

"Yes. Went up to Colchester yesterday. We had a long talk about whether or not he would still have a career in the army when he comes out."

"Will he?" asked Priestley.

"Oh yes," said the captain, nodding his head. "He will now. I told him it was conditional on his providing the name of the man who supplied him."

Priestley smiled. He liked the way this man operated. "And will he make a statement."

"I told him he had to. That was the second condition. The officer's name is Boyle. Detective Sergeant Colin Boyle." He paused. "Does that ring a bell?"

It did more than ring a bell. Boyle was one of the best known detectives in the force. And Priestley had had dealings with him before. He remembered the man's smirk the day he arrested Steve Blade and Boyle and his bunch of cronies had tortured him half to death in the interview room. Boyle had been on the Force Crime Squad at the time but had transferred, if Priestley remembered rightly, to the Drugs Squad a couple of years back.

"Yes, sadly it does. The man's an animal, Nick." His coffee arrived and he paused until the waitress had left. "Did he describe Boyle to you?"

"Sorry, I never asked him." The rare smile reappeared on Carpe's face. "I'm not a policeman, unfortunately."

"Did he tell you anything else?"

"No. Just that he'd only been supplied by Boyle three or four times. They were only small amounts and infrequent.

Seems as though he only used Boyle when he couldn't get hold of his regular supplier."

"Did he say where he met him?"

"Yes. Somewhere called the Tiger Bar. In Birmingham city centre." The name obviously meant nothing to Carpe, but Priestley knew the place well. It was a seedy little pub frequented by students and drop-outs. They went there to get pissed up on the cheap. It had been busted several times in the past but not, so far as he knew, recently.

"Could I see your man?" The copper hoped he wasn't asking too much, but he needed that statement.

"I can probably arrange something. When would you like to go?"

"No particular hurry. It sounds as though your man's told you all he can. Can I give you a ring in a week or so? Give me a chance to ask some questions my end."

* * * * *

The rain was falling heavily now, pouring from the sky in torrents. The narrow lane was pitted with rain-filled craters and Priestley had to keep all his wits about him just to keep the car on the road. He supposed, by necessity, high-security prisons had to be built miles from civilisation, but why did the only road accessing this one have to be a virtually impassable country track? Eventually he arrived and parked his car in the not surprisingly almost empty car park. He was hustled quickly and efficiently into an interview room by a terse, monosyllabic guard. Steve Blade was waiting for him, sitting on one of the two chairs that were either side of the inevitable table.

"Thanks for coming, Jack. Any smokes?"

Straight down to business then, thought Priestley. No holds barred. He looks well though. Prison life must be suiting him. Or maybe it's all the country air he's getting out here in the middle of nowhere. Priestley knew all about the sign at the prison entrance, pointing out that it was illegal for visitors to provide prisoners with tobacco (amongst other things) so he dropped the two packets on the floor and slid them over to Blade with his foot. "It's been a while," he said.

"Yeah. I wasn't sure you'd come."

"I'd do anything for an old mate. You know that."

Blade's laugh was more like a bark. "Yeah, right!"

"So why am I here, Steve?"

"I want your help, Jack." Priestley's eyebrows shot up. Of course you do, he thought. Blade ignored him and pressed on with what he wanted to say. "When I get out of here, I'm going to change my ways, Jack. I want this to be the last stretch I do. I never want to be banged up again."

Of course you don't, thought Priestley, understandably cautious. Who would? He was unsure how to take this declaration. Somewhere there would undoubtedly be an agenda. Blade was coming up to the time when he could apply for parole. Priestley waited – all would be revealed in a moment.

"And I thought I might be able to help you Jack," Blade finished.

"Why would you want to do that?"

"I don't know. For old times?" He grinned. "Maybe because I want a fresh start?"

"Okay. And how do you think you could help me?"

"There are a lot of things I hear inside these walls. Things that might be of interest to you."

"Such as?"

"Well, Frankie Richardson's in here ..."

"I know that, Steve. What about it?"

"Frankie Richardson's in here," Blade repeated. "He's practically running the whole fucking prison from his cell. I don't know why they bother paying for the governor. It's Frankie who's in charge. Frankie who calls the shots. Plus he's running his business from in here. Being in prison hasn't made the slightest difference to his operation. He's been running it very smoothly from his cell for the last twenty years. You know he's always been into drugs, extortion. He's up to his neck in other people's blood. He'll be out of here in a few months and he's been getting some interesting visitors lately." He paused. Here it comes, thought Priestley. "And I thought if I managed to help out in some way, you might be able to put a word in later with the parole board." Bingo. "Besides, you owe me a big favour, Jack. What I did to that filthy copper, I did for you. And the couple of months' bail was nice, but I've served my time. I want to get out of here. You owe me this much, Jack."

The policeman stood up. He'd heard enough. He hadn't even bothered to take his coat off. "Okay Bladey, suits me. Anything to help the fight against crime," he remarked, knowing how corny he must sound. "I'll leave it to you, Batman."

"No Jack, I'm Robin. You are the overgrown pillock in the black cape."

Priestley turned to leave, but Blade stopped him. "One more thing, Jack. How's Sammy? Have you seen her lately?"

Priestley shook his head. "No, Steve, I haven't. Hasn't she been visiting?"

"Yeah, couple of weeks ago. I just wondered," he said forlornly. Priestley laid a sympathetic hand on his shoulder as he passed Blade's chair on the way out. There was no way he wanted to be the one to tell the man that it was open house with his missus. Nor that she'd been having it away with Harry Nesbitt ever since he'd been inside. So, guiltily, he left.

Driving away from Gartree, Priestley couldn't decide whether Blade had been serious. He was offering himself up as an informant. Priestley was amazed. This was the last thing he would have expected of Blade. He wondered if anything had happened. Still. Time would tell. He'd just sit back and wait for the phone call. In the meantime, he had a call of his own to make. He picked up his mobile and dialled the number for HQ. Within a couple of rings the call was answered and he asked to be put through to Jim Nolan.

* * * * *

Usually Priestley only saw Jim Nolan four times a year in an official capacity. But now here he was again, keeping another appointment with the head of CID for the second time in as many days. He wondered whether or not he could trust Nolan. Yesterday's meeting had left him uncertain. Instinct had told him that something was wrong. But Nolan had also been in a hurry. And what Priestley had told him no senior officer ever wanted to hear. Without hard facts wouldn't he too have brushed the allegation aside? He'd decided, after his meeting with Carpe, that he had nothing to lose in telling Nolan the name of the officer who had supplied Private Gardiner. If his suspicions were wrong, all would be well and an investigation would be initiated. Conversely, if his instinct was right, Nolan would probably reveal his hand. He didn't know what he'd do if that happened. Best not to think about it. After all it might never happen.

He related everything that Nick Carpe had told him. Nolan listened carefully to every word. There wasn't a flicker of reaction on his face. "You did the right thing, Jack. Coming to me with this, I mean." He stood up and walked over to the window with his back to Priestley. "Who else knows about this, inside the job I mean?"

"Nobody, as far as I'm aware."

"And this captain? Is he likely to talk to anybody?"

"I doubt it."

Nolan returned to his seat, clearly perturbed. But then who wouldn't be? This was a serious issue. "Boyle's a good man, Jack," he said. "I can't believe he'd be involved in anything like this."

Priestley knew that whatever Boyle was, he wasn't a good man. But to be fair, Nolan may mean that Boyle was a good policeman. How could he possibly know? He only had the incident with Steve Blade to go on for that. And that was years ago. And anyway, he put the blame for that one fair and square on Oberon's plate, as the senior office involved. Still, there had to be a thorough investigation of this allegation, so he said, "It has to be looked at, Boss."

"Of course, Jack." Thank Christ, thought Priestley. "I don't want anything on paper, just yet," Nolan went on. "I'll have the secret squirrels put on Boyle and we'll take it from there." Relieved, Priestley nodded. "Keep this to yourself, Jack, until you hear from me. Then you can go and get that statement off Gardiner. Okay?" Nolan looked hard at him, clearly requiring some kind of commitment.

"Don't worry, it won't go anywhere else."

A look of satisfaction swept across Nolan's face. "Let me know if you hear anything else."

Priestley left, convinced he'd done the right thing. Reassured, he felt as if a heavy burden had been lifted from his shoulders. As soon as Priestley closed his office door, Jim Nolan snatched the receiver from its cradle and started dialling. He didn't have to look up the number because he knew it by heart.

15

After his brief session with Priestley, Blade made his way quickly back to his cell. He'd done it. It hadn't been easy but he'd done it. Well, needs must. He had to get out of this place. There were days now when he wasn't sure he could stand it any longer. It was like claustrophobia. The fear would build up inside him until he could hardly breathe. Ever since he'd helped young Colin Causer through his crisis it had been like this. Not all the time. Just some days. It was like he'd taken the kid's burden onto his own shoulders. And now it had become a simple matter of survival. And he, Steve Blade, was a survivor. He had to do whatever it took. So now, in exchange for getting out of Gartree, he had turned grass. He would have to live with the consequences for the rest of his life. But at least he would be free. At least he would be with Sammy. The pain of missing her, and wanting her, was worse each day. At least Jack Priestley was a safe pair of hands. He'd look after him. It'd be okay. Jack Priestley had always looked after him.

*   *   *   *   *

"Bang, bang; you're dead, Jack Priestley." The nine-year-old Priestley turned and fired his wooden machine-gun in retaliation. But he was too late. Steve Blade had already claimed the victory. "I said you're dead, Jack Priestley."

"No, I ain't. You missed. I shot you first." So they sorted out their difference with the inevitable fight. Neither ever won. And the spoils were always shared out equally: a fair distribution of sore chins, grazed knees and black eyes.

Running home after one such incident, Blade remembered seeing his mother standing on the doorstep, arms folded, careworn pinafore wrapped around her skinny waist. He could still hear her voice. "Steven, what have I told you about playing with that Jack Priestley? He always gets you into trouble. Look at your knees." She turned towards the uniformed copper standing beside her. "It's true, you know. That Jack Priestley's the one you want to go and see. He's always getting him into trouble." And yet he knew even then, all those years ago, that Jack Priestley was the one who got him out of trouble, not the other way around.

* * * * *

Colin Causer was waiting for him when he got back to his cell. The hooch party was planned for this weekend and Colin was practically beside himself with excitement. He'd really come out of his shell since he'd opened up. Blade was proud of his handiwork, even though it seemed to be causing him his own particular crisis. But that was sorted now that he'd seen Priestley. So he smiled and winked at Causer. "Okay mate?" he said. "Shall we go and check the brew?"

He'd chosen a bank holiday weekend for the party because it was usual for security to relax during holiday periods. In the majority of cases, a home-brew party was the answer to all a prison's evils. Although undoubtedly there was always a heavy penalty to be paid – in the form of the world's worst hangover – all the participants believed that getting pissed out of their brains was the best cure for the release of pent-up pressure within the nick. No one knew whether or not the screws were ever aware of what was going on. If they were, they never seemed to be too bothered about it. Staffing levels were always reduced dramatically during a holiday period. Perhaps they understood the benefits too.

Whatever the story, for Blade, the risk of possibly getting caught making illicit liquor was well worth the excitement and adventure involved in the brewing and concealment. The main ingredient for hooch is yeast and that wasn't easy to obtain in the sort of quantities required. The only place was the bakery and the cons working there had to be careful not to steal too much at any one time. If an allocation of yeast sufficient for making 50 loaves of bread only made 25, questions would be asked, and the scam discovered. So it had taken three weeks to gather a sufficient quantity. They also needed sugar, potatoes and fruit. All much easier to acquire. And, easiest of all, a five-gallon drum. The drums that cooking oil came in were perfect. They stashed the brew in the boiler room. Warmth was needed to help the fermentation along, and, besides, there were lots of good hiding places for a five-gallon drum in the boiler room. The only problem was getting in there to check the brew from time to time without being seen. Another three weeks had passed since they had set up the brew and by now it should be ready. They slipped quietly into the boiler room. The brew was perfect. "Right, then!" whispered Blade. "Tomorrow. We'll get the stuff up tomorrow."

16

Priestley went straight from his meeting with Nolan to Sonia's flat. By the time he got there it was well past eight o'clock and he was tired. He'd had a long day and it wasn't over yet. The moment he arrived, Sonia thrust a glass of wine into his hand and launched straight into whatever it was that was bothering her. Without so much as a welcoming kiss. He wondered how much of the bottle she'd already drunk by herself. The answer was soon apparent. Her glass was almost empty and as she spoke she busied herself opening another bottle. He'd never seen her so agitated. He had to relieve her of the bottle before she snapped the cork.

"I interviewed a new client earlier this week. Saw him again this morning. He was up for a lorry hijacking on the M6 last month." She paused and looked at him, to make sure he was listening.

He was. "Was?" he said.

"Was. He was found dead in his cell this afternoon. He hanged himself." She paused to take a gulp from her glass, then continued. "The lorry he is alleged to have hijacked came from France. It was carrying a mixed cargo of goods for delivery all over the country. Hidden in the cargo was a consignment of drugs. Obviously, this was what my client was allegedly after." She looked at him. Priestley smiled a wry smile to himself. Even in the state she was in, she couldn't help barrister-speak.

He nodded. "Obviously."

"His police record states that he was suspected of involvement with one of the big criminal organisations in London. But this is all background. He and I had two quite lengthy meetings and he told me some things I don't think he intended to. At our first meeting, he told me there were a number of unsolved murders in this area. Apparently they all involve police informants."

Involuntarily, Priestley stood up from the sofa, spilling his wine as he did so. "What?!" he shouted spontaneously.

"This morning he told me they'd all happened recently and that the police were covering them up."

Priestley was aghast. This was unbelievable. He couldn't even begin to comprehend what she was saying. He couldn't stop himself from asking. "Who is he, Sonia?"

She didn't reply at first and he repeated his question. Still she didn't answer. She was rattled. His response to her revelation frightened her. "Jack, the man was petrified." Priestley knew that Sonia wasn't the type to be over dramatic and he credited her with a great deal of common sense. "I shouldn't disclose a client's name, Jack. I really shouldn't. But we both know you'll find out anyway." Priestley forced himself to be patient. "His name was Peter Murray."

"Did he say anything else, Sonia?"

She sighed. "No. No, I think that's everything."

"Was it suicide?"

"There's no reason to think it was anything else."

Numbly, Priestley slumped back onto the sofa.

* * * * *

He sat like that for a long time. Sonia had the sense to leave him to it and soon the little flat rang to the song of water running through pipes as she ran herself a long hot bath. In which to wash away the horrors of the day. The need for

116

wine obviously passed, the newly opened bottle sat untouched on the sideboard. He couldn't believe it. The police covering up the murder – murder – of their own informants. What the hell was going on? It couldn't be true. It could not be true. But this was what Nolan was one minute telling him. And the next not. And this man Peter Murray clearly believed something serious was going down. Serious enough for him to be frightened out of his wits. Serious enough to kill himself. And he must have known more. He must have told Sonia more about what he knew. Or thought he knew. He'd have to talk some more to Sonia about it.

But now was not the time. He stood up. He had to go home. He needed a few hours' peace and solitude. His cottage was in a small village on the outskirts of the city. It was very rural. Very quiet. His escape. He'd only had it a few months. Was glad to move out of that pokey flat at last. He was finding solace from the frequent brutality of his working week in slowly doing it up and working in the tiny garden. Digging, he'd discovered, was an incredible cure for quieting a troubled mind. Perhaps he'd go home and dig all night.

Sonia knew better than to ask him to stay. She, who had lived alone for years, understood the need for solitude better than anyone. She held him. Kissed him. Told him she loved him. Which was music to his ears and salve to his heart. And let him go.

* * * * *

It was a foggy night. The mist crept in and out of his headlights. Today's torrential rains had cleared the air and through the fog he could occasionally catch glimpses of a clear, starry sky. He was almost there. The narrow lane twisted and turned, but soon one of these bends would bring him home.

He didn't see anything. Just felt the bump as the front wheels, then the back wheels, of his car pitched upwards, landing heavily on the road surface. His heart skipped a beat. Fuck! He must have gone over a dead animal. Road kill from some previous passer-by. People came down this road like maniacs. There was a campaign going on in the village to get something done about it. Petitions and meetings of the parish council and such like. Probably it was a badger. Or a fox. One that the local hunt wasn't going to get a chance at.

He could hear the car's tyres hissing as soon as he opened the door to get out and look. All four of them. Fuck! And fuck again! This was ridiculous. He slammed the car door and went to the boot for a torch, cursing under his breath. He shone the beam back in the direction he'd just come. There was something in the road, but it wasn't an animal. He walked towards it. A plank of wood full of nails. "Bastard kids," he muttered.

A twig snapped. Somewhere behind him. He half turned to look and it was then that he felt the blow. Hard across his right temple. "Jesus," he gasped, legs folding beneath him. He collapsed onto the tarmac. His ribs took two forceful blows from a couple of boots and he struck out with his own. He managed to connect with one of the three pairs of legs dancing around him and was gratified to hear a yelp of pained surprise. Then he was lifted off the ground and propped up against his car, one assailant on either side, whilst the other pounded his stomach with what felt like rocks. Finally, the assault stopped, and the three hoods stood back and allowed him to slip back down to the ground. A muffled voice reached his ears through the darkness closing in on him. "Keep out of business that don't concern you, Chief Inspector. Or the next time, you'll need an ambo." The sickly smell of one of the men's aftershave invaded Priestley's air space. As the footsteps hurried away, he was violently and painfully sick. Wine and bile. There was nothing else.

Priestley lay there for some time beside his car. Praying that another car didn't come along. And flatten him. Or, alternately, praying that another car did come along, and rescue him. There was no way he was moving just yet. He couldn't.

* * * * *

Eventually he limped his crippled car the short distance home. He fumbled for the right key, let himself in and stumbled upstairs to his bedroom. He collapsed in a heap on the bed. He'd worry about the shoe-less car in the morning. He'd worry about his injuries in the morning too. Right now, all he wanted was the relief of sleep. He passed out almost immediately, only to be awoken a few hours later by morning sunlight pouring through the open curtains at the window. He peered at the clock on the table beside the bed. Six o'clock. He hauled himself off the bed and staggered into the bathroom to assess the damage. Cuts and bruises. Nothing too serious. There was a nasty cut above his right eye. Ordinarily, he should have had it stitched. But it seemed to have closed up okay. He turned on the shower, peeled off his clothes and submitted to the healing power of clean, running water.

As the water poured its torrent over his head, he wondered what had happened. At least he knew what had happened in actual terms. The evidence was there to see in the bruises on his face and body. The cuts and scratches. The aching agony of his every limb. But what had happened? He was going home late at night and he was attacked by three goons in balaclavas. Several things struck him as important. Firstly, they knew where he was going, which meant they knew where he lived, and they knew roughly what time he'd be going there, even though it was practically the middle of the night. They knew it was his car coming down that lane. And not somebody else. So someone had been watching him. Secondly, the one that had spoken had known his rank. He had called him chief inspector. He'd only officially been chief inspector for a week. Thirdly, the man had said 'ambo'. 'Ambo' was a word used almost exclusively by coppers when referring to ambulances. So that man at least was likely to be a copper. Fourthly, the stink of the aftershave. He knew it. He'd smelt it before.

He climbed out of the shower. Gingerly, dried himself off. And collapsed into bed again. Once more sleep took him immediately.

* * * * *

Later that morning, he lay perfectly still in his bed. His mind raced. He thought over all that he knew. Or thought he knew. Police informers were being murdered, but the police themselves were covering it up. Jim Nolan, his force's head of CID had told him that there was a problem. And then said there wasn't. Meanwhile, a man arrested for hijacking a lorry carrying drugs, and a suspected member of a gangland organisation, had told his barrister that police informers were being murdered, but that the police themselves were covering it up. He was so frightened about what might happen to him that he committed suicide. Further, Nicholas Carpe, a captain in the army and, as every instinct told him, an honest and sincere man, had told him that one Colin Boyle, an officer in his force, had supplied drugs on at least three occasions to one of his men. Apart from Nick Carpe and Private Gardiner, so far as Priestley was aware, only Jim Nolan knew about this.

The aftershave, thought Priestley. That aftershave. Boyle. Colin Boyle was one of the men who had attacked him last night. That aftershave was the same as the one he'd smelt in the corridor after Steve Blade was attacked. He'd recognise that sickly-sweet smell anywhere.

So, what do you think, he asked himself. I think serious shit is manifesting itself. I think scumbags on my own job are ripping off the system. I think I was being warned off. Who sent the gorillas into my cage if it wasn't Jim Bloody Nolan?

17

This was the best weather possible for surveillance; tipping it down in torrents. Your average British summertime. He was still a little worried that his decision to use Carol Guardia was misguided. When he'd telephoned her that afternoon and suggested that she came along, she'd thought he was having her on. But, apart from the major scoop she'd been promised, this particular adventure wasn't something she wanted to miss. When she'd picked him up half an hour ago, she'd told him she felt like the girl in a Bond movie. But for all her thrilled enjoyment, what he was asking her to do was dangerous. She could very easily get hurt. In fact, as they sat waiting in her car, he was on the verge of calling the whole thing off. It was futile. It was endangering them both. It was foolish. What did he hope to achieve?

Priestley sat deep in thought. From now on, he couldn't afford to make any mistakes. After last night and what Sonia had told him that afternoon, he knew this was way heavier than anything he'd ever dealt with before. Eventually he would have to go to the chief with the bad news. But his real problem for now was that most of it was based on suspicion, and logical reasoning told him he could finish up making a prize prat of himself. He needed more, concrete proof to support his suppositions, before he stood on the thick red carpet and spouted off to one of the highest ranking officers in the land. He still felt a little groggy after the attack.

Gently, he touched the scab above his right eyebrow. No, he'd learned his lesson. Next time, he would be the one dishing out the punishment. Fair and square. Carol had told him he looked like he'd been in the wars. In a way he had been, he'd told her, but refused to tell her more. Apart from anything else, what did he have to tell her? For now, all he'd told her was that he had reason to believe that one of the coppers on his force was dealing in drugs. And she was coming along to give him a hand with the stake out. And that had been a sufficient lure.

"What about them, Jack?" Carol's voice interrupted his reverie. He came to with a jolt and followed her pointing finger towards the two figures walking down the station steps. They headed towards a car parked opposite the entrance. Immediately, he recognised Colin Boyle. The other was also vaguely familiar. He was dark and considerably taller than his ginger-haired compatriot.

"That's the little shit. The one on the left. You sure he doesn't know you, Carol?"

"Jack," she said, exasperated. "How many times do I have to tell you?" He looked at her, reminded yet again just how determined this little lady was. "Anyway," she continued. "What if he does? I'm nothing to do with you, am I? I work for the *Mail* for God's sake."

Which, he reminded himself, was exactly the reason he'd asked her to help him. She had the perfect cover. Plus she was practical. Resourceful. Loyal. In Carol Guardia he had a strong ally. She was the right person to have on side. If anything bad came out of this, it wouldn't be because of her. Satisfied, his confidence in what they were doing restored, he watched Boyle and partner climb into their car and drive off into the Friday evening traffic.

They followed the vehicle through the rain-washed streets and into the city centre. Priestley slowly realised where they were going. The car stopped. Right outside the Tiger Bar. Perfect. Priestley pulled over and they watched

Boyle and his mate enter the seedy little public house, which was already humming with early evening activity.

"That's it, Carol. Go and do your stuff, lady."

She looked straight ahead, her hand resting on the door release, and took a deep breath. "Don't you dare move from here, Jack Priestley," she said, and an instant later she was out of the car and halfway across the street. He was filled with admiration as he watched her trim figure disappear beneath the neon lights at the bar entrance. What she was doing took a lot of courage.

* * * * *

It had taken him until lunchtime to decide what to do. Lying on his bed, he had run through his options. There weren't many and they all came down to one single fact. What he needed was proof. The question was, what of? He knew something was going down. But what exactly it was, was still a mystery. Drugs and informants. He had no reason to think they were in any way connected. So he'd start at the beginning. Drugs. Colin Boyle. He knew Colin Boyle was involved, and he would soon have Gardiner's statement for that. But he needed corroboration. And getting Boyle on his own was not enough. He knew that this very probably went wider and further than he'd yet imagined. What about Nolan, for example? But for the moment, he'd decided to keep it simple. He'd just watch Boyle. He picked up his mobile phone and dialled the number for the *Mail*. He'd ask Carol Guardia to be his foil. Plus, he needed her car. Boyle knew this, and it was going to have to go to the garage for a new set of shoes anyway.

* * * * *

The minutes ticked by. He had no problem staying on full alert. Not when his new partner was alone inside that bar, rubbing shoulders with the two slime balls they'd followed there. He looked at his watch. Nine o'clock. She'd already been half an hour. The rain pelted the car's roof with a rhythmic beat. Ten past. Twenty past. Half past. The daylight was beginning to fade now. The Tiger Bar was still heaving with activity. People going in and out the whole time. He shot forward in his seat to get a better view of the three people walking towards the bar. It couldn't be? But there could be no doubt. The woman was Sammy Blade. And she was clinging to the arm of Harry Nesbitt. Priestley guessed that the third individual was Leroy Henderson, Nesbitt's bodyguard. They were laughing, little Harry in his platform shoes. Christ! What on earth was such an attractive woman doing with the biggest little shit in town?

* * * * *

In the end Sonia didn't have much to add about Peter Murray. But what she did have to say was astounding. She'd insisted on coming over and giving him some of her very special tender loving care. In truth he was delighted. So, sitting on the little terrace he'd only recently finished laying at the back of his cottage, they waited for the truck to come and collect his injured car, and ate the picnic lunch she'd brought. Wine, quiche, salad. Very chic. Just what you'd expect from Sonia. And in the meantime, she told him what she knew.

Peter Murray had confirmed that he did indeed work for one of the big organisations. He took his orders directly from a guy called Bernie Hemp. All he had to do was hijack lorries as directed and drive them to wherever he was told. He didn't have much past form. Petty theft, nicking cars and joyriding when he was younger. He'd been a professional lorry driver for a while, but got laid off, and it was then that he'd hooked up with Bernie. He said he was also used as an occasional driver. He knew about informants being murdered because he'd been the driver on one of the killings. The murderer had told him he didn't have to worry about being involved because the police would cover it up.

Sonia had even had the wit to ask him if he knew the name of the assassin. But apparently the organisation he worked for was very hierarchical (not his word; Sonia's) and organised on a need-to-know basis. Bernie's was the only name he needed to know. It had only dawned on him slowly that Bernie himself had a boss.

* * * * *

It was well past ten when Priestley saw Boyle and his companion leave the Tiger Bar. He slumped down in his seat, certain they hadn't noticed him, as their car drove away. Shortly afterwards, the passenger door opened and Carol slipped into the seat beside him. "Well, that was a waste of time, Jack Priestley." She was disappointed. "All they did was sit on their own and drink."

"They didn't meet anybody then?" He was also disappointed. He was secretly hoping she would have seen three or four yobbos approach them and hand over bundles of crumpled cash in exchange for little packets of white powder. But at least he'd confirmed that Boyle used the place, which corroborated part of what Carpe had told him.

"Yeah. But only some poncy little guy and his bimbo girlfriend. Little prat even had a minder."

"What?!" Priestley was aghast.

"Yeah. That's it. Zilch. Nada. Nothing." It may have been nothing to Carol. But not to Priestley. What the heck was Boyle doing meeting Harry Nesbitt? Well-known crook. Extortionist. Bent as they come. Harry Nesbitt was reputed to have a finger in every crooked deal around. "I tell you this though, Jack. You could get them done on a breathalyser easy enough."

* * * * *

"I want my roll-up now, Harry. Understand? I want it now." Even when she was half pissed, Sammy still looked like a page three model out of the *Sun* newspaper, despite the

125

sulky expression on her face. There was going to be a tantrum. He knew it. And it was all costing Nesbitt a small fortune. And for a man who was renowned for tight-fisted meanness, that was really something. But he was besotted by her. Always had been. All he wanted was to be seen with her. So far as he was concerned she could have anything she wanted, whenever she wanted. But not her roll-up. Not now. Not here. Not just yet.

"Not in here, my love. Wait 'til we get outside. We'll be leaving shortly, just hang on."

"Bollocks, Harry. I want it now." There was fury in her eyes.

Nesbitt sighed. He hated scenes and he wasn't going to win this one. "Come on, buttercup, let's go." Nesbitt stood and offered her his arm.

"Buttercup? Buttercup? Don't you dare call me that. I'm not your buttercup."

Nesbitt winced. This wasn't how it was meant to be, but he nodded towards his minder, summoning him over. Leroy Henderson came from Jamaica. What little spare time he had he spent in the gym. All those hours lifting weights had turned his body into a rippling mass of muscle. He walked across from his stool by the door and helped, or rather lifted, Mrs Blade out of her chair and escorted her from the bar.

Nesbitt followed quickly. Once outside and in the car, he lit the tapered end of the joint and pushed it into her mouth.

* * * * *

Carol dropped him outside Sonia's apartment building. They both enjoyed her half-hearted attempts to persuade him to come home with her. Once upon a time he'd have been more than a little tempted, but not now. So he declined as gracefully as he could. "Probably just as well," she said, and winked. "I don't think my boyfriend would appreciate it if I turned up with you. He's a bit possessive." She grinned.

18

The following Tuesday morning, Priestley still hadn't worked out what the Nesbitt/Boyle connection was about. He'd spent the whole of the bank holiday weekend puzzling over it, while at the same time lapping up Sonia's loving care and attention. So far as he was aware, Nesbitt wasn't into drugs. Protection rackets were his game nowadays. Once upon a time he'd been into blagging in a big way, but never drugs. He'd have his detective inspector look into him. Chris Barton was one of the good guys. Efficient, capable, honest. Utterly trustworthy and loyal. Priestley had had him transferred with him to the Regional. He was going to have to put him in the picture soon. He was also going to have to help with Peter Murray and Bernie Hemp too. His research skills would be invaluable in investigating the story behind the murdered informants. But in line with his decision to concentrate on Boyle first, he'd get him started on Nesbitt the moment he got into the office. If he ever got there. Christ, the traffic was terrible. The weekend's rain didn't help much either. They were saying on the news that there'd been widespread flooding to the south and more rain was forecast for today. Fucking weather. It'd arrive sooner rather than later judging by the look of those clouds. He swore again as his mobile rang. When was he going to get around to changing that bloody tune?

Well! What a surprise! Steve Blade. Wanting to see him. That was quick. It was urgent, apparently. So Harry Nesbitt would have to wait. At the next roundabout, Priestley turned his car around and retraced his journey, before heading out of the city towards Leicestershire, and Her Majesty's Prison Gartree.

* * * * *

"You sent for me," he said, the moment the door banged shut behind him.

"Yeah. Good to see you, Jack. Thanks for coming so quickly. I've got some big news for you, I think."

"Okay," said Priestley slowly. He'd had so much big news recently, he wasn't sure he wanted more.

"Frankie Richardson's the top con in here, right?" Priestley nodded. "Well, I'm well in with Frankie. I'm his blue-eyed boy. Owes me his life and all that, follow? Some cons tried to knife him in the exercise yard a few months back. I was his heroic rescuer." He pushed himself back into his seat. "Now, he's got a large organisation, with satellite companies in most major cities. Follow?" He was sounding more like Tony Lambesi every day. "The one in your locality is run by a geezer called Hemp. Bernie Hemp. You won't know of him, Jack. They deal in drugs."

Priestley shifted in his seat as his mind registered the name. "Go on, Steve. I'm all ears."

"Well, they've got some filth-sorry Jack-coppers working for them and pretty high up as well." He stopped to light a cigarette before carrying on and Priestley had to be patient. "This bunch of wankers helps them with distribution and stuff. It's pretty well organised, Jack."

Priestley grabbed the edge of the table, forcing himself to remain calm. "Any names, Bladey?"

"Yeah, but only for parole, Jack. I need your word." Blade's *coup de grace*.

"You've got it," declared Priestley, without hesitation, and that was enough for the con. Jack's word was as good as they come. Blade was amazed at the effect his words were having on his friend. He knew he had good information but he hadn't expected it to strike such a sensitive nerve. Priestley's face had completely drained of colour. His knuckles were bright white as his hands gripped the table. His body had become utterly rigid. His usual elegant flexibility had vanished.

"I've only got one name, Jack. He visited Richardson about a fortnight ago."

"What, in here?" Priestley was surprised. Frankie must be very sure of himself.

"Briskett, Jack. I think he might be a biggy in your outfit."

"John Briskett?"

"I just know it's Briskett, because I saw it written on Frankie's visitor's pass. He left it on his table." Priestley sprang out of his chair. John Briskett was the detective chief inspector in charge of the Intelligence Department. A man with security clearance at the highest level and all that shite. Blade ignored Priestley's pacing and continued. He had a lot he wanted to say. "Listen Jack, there's more. A young kid called Colin Causer. He's in here for blagging. Been here a few months. I've been looking after him for Frankie. Nice kid, but a bit screwed up. In fact, very screwed up. Killed his bird in a car smash somewhere down near the Smoke. They were being chased by the cops and he lost control. Can't forgive himself. Anyway, I arranged a little party the other night. To help him take his mind off things. So Colin got pissed out of his head and started gabbling on and on about Joanna, the dead girlfriend, and her uncle. Apparently they used to visit him sometimes. He runs a place called Dale End Books. It's on your turf. The geezer's name is Chrissie Dean. Looks like an ordinary bookshop from the front. But sells video nasties out of the back. You know the sort of thing. Now, Causer tells me that one of Dean's regulars is a copper called Briskett. According to Causer, he supplies details of police informants in exchange for a bit of gratis, follow? I didn't put two and two together until this morning. Took me ages to remember where I'd come across the name before. Anyway, I thought you should know. Thought it might be useful. Thought it might help you write that letter to the parole board."

Priestley had a thousand questions flowing off him like melted treacle off a stick, but all of them stuck in this throat. He had enough here to crease his thinking cap in all kinds of directions for days. He sat back down and gazed numbly at Blade. Unconsciously, his finger rubbed the scar above his right eyebrow, now nearly five days old.

* * * * *

After his meeting with Priestley, Blade headed off back to work in the laundry. "How's things, Stevie boy?" Tony Lambesi intercepted him. "Frankie wants to see you." As usual it wasn't a request, it was an order.

"Okay, I'll pop in after work."

"Sorry mate. He wants to see you now." Blade shrugged. When Richardson wanted to see you, you grew wings. Lambesi walked with him. Making sure the order was obeyed, like the good lieutenant he was. When they reached Frankie's cell, the big man was sitting in his armchair dressed in the habitual silk dressing gown. The one with that huge fucking big dragon on the back.

"Come in, Croaker. Come in and close the door." A big fat hand summoned him in.

"You look well, Frankie," he said, as the cell door slammed shut behind him. That was unnerving.

"I am, Croaker. I am. But how have you been, Croaker? What's been happening? You okay in the laundry?"

Something was up, thought Blade. It wasn't like Richardson to ask about your health unless he was planning to change it for you. "Fine, Frankie. Thanks for asking."

"Good. That's good." Frankie nodded. "I, meanwhile, have had some good news. Some very good news. They're letting me out of here. In two days' time." The fat man grinned, delighted with his good news.

"That's wonderful, Frankie. Congratulations." It was very important he sounded sincere and Blade did his best.

"You'll be out of here soon too, Croaker. Won't be long."

"Yeah. Just a few more years unless I get parole."

"Everything comes to he who waits," quoted Frankie, his mood growing ever more expansive. "So I've asked you in to say goodbye. And to tell you to get in touch with me when you get out. I might be able to do something for you. Savvy?"

* * * * *

Priestley was cruising down the M6 when his phone peeled out. There was so much water on the road that it really was just like cruising. You had to keep all your wits about you just to keep the car from aquaplaning. He fumbled awkwardly in his pocket for the phone. Why couldn't he remember to change its tune? And why couldn't he remember to take it out of his pocket before he got in the car and started driving? Eventually, he retrieved the phone. It was Blade.

"Jacky-boy, I've got something more for you. Thought you might like to know that Frankie's coming out the day after tomorrow."

A passing car cut in front of him and dumped a sheet of water on the windscreen. Momentarily blinded, Priestley could only manage a weak "Oh," as he fought the steering wheel one-handed.

"I thought you'd be a bit more interested than that."

"I am. Sorry. The weather's shit. I am interested. Thank you for letting me know, Steve."

"No problem. I'll let you go." He was about to hang up, when he remembered something else. "Oh, and by the way, you might like to know he's offered me a job." Priestley's car swerved dangerously on the motorway.

* * * * *

By now, Steve Blade was very late for work in the laundry. It was almost lunchtime and hardly worth going in. Still, it was something to do, and he wanted the brownie points. Immediately he walked through the laundry doors, he looked around for a screw so he could offer his sincere apologies for being so late. He couldn't find one. But Mickey the Cricket stood facing him, holding a pile of linen towels in his arms.

"You all right, Bladey?"

"Yeah, sure." Blade walked past him towards the top end of the room, where he and Causer worked. Causer wasn't there. Must have gone for a piss or something.

The Cricket called after him. "You sure you're all right, Bladey?"

"Shit, Cricket, you do go on. Why shouldn't I be?"

"Colin?" The Cricket shrugged his shoulders. "You don't know about Colin?"

"What about Colin?" Then he saw the look in the Cricket's eyes. It said trouble. A surge of alarm swept through his body. He ran from the room. Up the iron staircase. Towards young Causer's cell. A group of screws was gathered outside it and as he reached the landing he feared the worst.

"Take it steady, Steve." A screw placed an arm across Blade's chest in a futile attempt to prevent him from barging into the cell. Horses couldn't have stopped him, although later he wished they had. There was a strong smell of burning coming from the mess lying on the bunk. That was Colin Causer.

* * * * *

Every year two or three prisoners in maximum security prisons commit suicide. The favoured methods are hanging or suffocation – by placing a plastic bag over the head. A few cut their wrists and bleed to death. Causer hadn't chosen any of these more orthodox methods. He had wrapped a plastic mat around his face and head, securing it with pieces of torn sheeting. The youngster had then poured oil over his body. He got it from the engineering shop. Then he lit a match. It was the most painful imaginable way to die. What his friend saw on the bunk that day was unrecognisable. The mat had melted and stuck to the disturbed man's face. The only consolation was that inhaling the mixture of toxic fumes would have hastened his death. Blade left the room and vomited violently.

19

By the time he finally drove through the gates at the rear of the RCS building later that afternoon, Priestley had a rough idea what he was going to do. First, he was going to have a little chat with Ron Birch. Then he was going to have a brief word with Chris Barton. So once he'd slotted his car into the only available parking space, he picked up his mobile phone, dialled the number and asked to be put through.

*　*　*　*　*

"Jack, do you know what you're asking?"

Priestley was well aware that the last thing he should be doing was asking Ron Birch to disclose confidential information. "Ron, have I ever bothered you before?" The DCI wasn't going to give up. Even if Birch refused to help now, Priestley would hound him until he provided him with what he was after, or stuck him in to the chief constable. But he knew he was on safe ground. Ron Birch wasn't that sort of bloke. "This is important, Ron. I only want to know if you're doing a number on DS Boyle."

"Jack, you know perfectly well that I can't tell you anything about any of the operations we're doing. You should know better than to ask," said the superintendent. "However, what I will say to you, Jack, is this," he said slowly. "If there is an operation in the future on the man you've mentioned, you'll be the first to know. Obviously, you have some information that you feel might be constructive." Ron Birch hung up. But that was enough. Thank you, Birchy. And thank you, God.

The message from the head of the Internal Investigations Department was clear. He hadn't been asked to investigate the life and times of Detective Sergeant Colin Boyle. And Priestley wasn't remotely surprised. The last thing he had expected was for Nolan to keep his word. He had had plenty of time but he hadn't done it. And that was because he was up to his neck in this shit. Whatever this shit was. And Boyle had been left to continue with his hobbies without the secret squirrels up his arse. Priestley pressed the end button on his mobile and got out of the car.

The ever-diligent Chris Barton was ready and waiting for him outside his office when Priestley got upstairs. Barton was the type of man who rarely smiled. He was also the height of discretion. Priestley knew that if he wanted to, he could discuss his own mother with Barton and it would go no further. He was a tall, thin young man with an already receding hairline. His face had an appealing intelligence about it and Priestley very much appreciated the man's straightforwardness and honesty. Such qualities were refreshing in a world Priestley was finding increasingly difficult to cope with.

"Right, Chris," he said, immediately business-like. "Come in and take a seat." He closed his office door firmly behind them and sat down on the other side of the desk before continuing.

"I'm not sure how to begin. But I'll try and be brief. No point in beating about the bush with this one."

"Yes, Boss," responded Chris, examining him closely. "I'm sorry, Boss," he went on. "But what happened to your face? That's a nasty cut you've got there."

Priestley's hand involuntarily reached up to touch the cut. It was becoming like a nervous habit. He had to make a conscious effort to take his hand away. "That's all part of what I have to tell you, Chris," he answered. "So here goes.

135

First things first. Remember my promotion party?" Chris nodded. "Well, two things happened that night. Firstly, Jim Nolan asked me to keep my eyes and ears open because several informants have been murdered recently and to report back if I discovered anything I thought might be relevant. Secondly, a member of the army fraternity, a captain, mentioned that one of his men had been convicted by an army court of cocaine abuse. Captain Carpe told me the soldier acquired the cocaine from an officer in our force." He paused. "Okay? You with me?" Chris nodded again and Priestley went on. "I met with Captain Carpe on Thursday morning. The officer in question is DS Colin Boyle. He's on the drug squad."

"I've heard of him. Not a pleasant character."

"You jest not, Chris. So, on Thursday night, I reported this little lot to Nolan, who said he would look into it. In fact he said he would get the secret squirrels onto it. Well I've just spoken to Birch, who tells me that they've not been instructed to conduct an investigation. Additionally, after my meeting with Nolan, I was attacked on my way home. Three men ambushed my car and threatened me. I'm certain one of them was Boyle. That's how I acquired the cut." Priestley paused to take a deep breath before continuing. "So on Friday evening I decided to conduct a little impromptu surveillance. I followed Boyle and friend to the Tiger Bar in the city centre ... know it?"

"Yes, Boss."

"And while he was there he met up with Harry Nesbitt."

"Nesbitt? Harry Nesbitt's not into drugs."

"That's what I thought. See what you can find out. Okay?"

"Yes, Boss." Barton blinked. "And what about the informants?"

"Ah," said Priestley. "Nolan made a mistake when he told me about that. The next time I saw him he told me he was talking bollocks and to forget it. And I'd have willingly believed him except that since then I've heard a very similar story from Sonia. One of her clients, a Peter Murray, has told her that he was used as the driver for some of the murders. Apparently the assassin told him he needn't worry about being a witness because the police were covering up the murders."

"He what?!"

"You heard correctly. Now Murray was arrested when he was caught hijacking a lorry containing drugs. He told Sonia that he was acting under orders from a man called Bernie Hemp. Both are suspected of being part of one of the big crime organisations."

"We should try to get an interview with Murray."

Priestley nodded. Ordinarily, Barton was quite right. That's exactly what they should do. "We can't. He's dead."

Barton deflated into his chair. "Oh. Suicide?"

"Apparently. You with me so far?"

"Yes, Boss." This time he nodded as well.

"Well, this is where it gets complicated. I think the Boyle/Nesbitt/drugs thing is connected to the Murray/Hemp/informants thing. Today I went to see an old friend of mine who just happens to be in Gartree. Steve Blade."

"I know of him. You've mentioned him before."

Priestley raised his eyebrows. "I have?" He shrugged. "Possibly. Anyway. One of Steve's fellow inmates is none other than Frankie Richardson."

"Whose release, I gather, is imminent."

"You gather correctly. Frankie Richardson is Bernie Hemp's boss. Hemp runs his racket for him in this area. Now I'm not sure how this all fits together but I'm certain there is a link somewhere. But if informants are being murdered, then it's John Briskett who's supplying the details."

It was Barton's turn to raise his eyebrows. "What makes you think that?"

"Blade tells me he's been to see Frankie in Gartree."

"What!" Barton exclaimed. "That's ridiculous."

Priestley smiled, "Isn't it. Very careless. Nevertheless, I think he's supplying the details in exchange for cheap thrills from some porn shop in town. Dale End Books. Heard of it?"

"No."

"Nor'd I."

"And who's covering up the murders?"

"I don't know. That's where you come in. As well as looking into Nesbitt, look into these murders will you. See if you can find any unsolved murders that might involve informants. Okay?"

"Yes, Boss."

"Good. Now get off home and get a good night's sleep. See you in the morning. I'll be late in by the way. I'm planning to pay the Intelligence Department a little visit."

20

John Briskett was a man Jack Priestley hadn't really had much to do with. Most of their previous encounters had been across a table at pre-arranged meetings they'd both had to attend. They'd never actually worked together and, even at those shared meetings, Briskett had always appeared to be a solitary figure. One who kept his own counsel; which was probably the reason why he was the DCI chosen to be in charge of the Intelligence Department.

Briskett's office was adjacent to the main indexing room and Priestley found the door open. He was a large man with three chins supporting an over-sized head. His dark brown hair was greasy and cut very short. He looked uptight in his suit and tie. He certainly didn't look like the type who would indulge in dirty flicks. But then, who did? He welcomed Priestley quietly. "Good to see you, Jack. How can I help you?"

"Frankie Richardson, John. He's a London villain. We're doing a number on him and I wondered what you had?" Briskett wasn't quick enough to hide the surprise that swept across his face. Instead, he had to stand up and turn to face the window to conceal his horrified expression. Ignorant bastard, thought Priestley. Obviously the guy knew nothing about body language. Briskett quickly regained his composure, however, and said to the window, "Well, if he's known to us, we'll have something on him." Briskett's performance was rock-solid from then on. He turned and faced his visitor, an ingratiating smile on his fat face. Obviously well rehearsed. "Whilst you're here, let me introduce you to Charlie."

Charlie, the secure computer, was one of the reasons Priestley had come, so he accepted the invitation with alacrity. "Why not?" To find out more was exactly why he was here. "Ready when you are."

Briskett led the way. "Jackie," he said to one of his assistants. "Get me the file on a Frankie Richardson if we've got one, will you please." Jackie's pair of firm young buttocks slipped across the room towards her computer terminal, ready to do her boss's bidding.

The long, thin room was full of computers, all of them identical. But appearances are deceptive, because Charlie's insides were very different from all the others. Briskett patted the top of the monitor. "This is Charlie. Our secure system," he said proudly. "All the information contained in Charlie is secure. That is, restricted to people who work here. Charlie's information is highly sensitive."

"And where do you keep the registered informants' details, John?" asked Priestley, fully alert and waiting for any unusual reaction Briskett might make. There wasn't one.

"In here," he said. "In Charlie, along with the porn material." The answer was delivered in the coolest manner imaginable.

"So, in a nutshell, John, if I had needed to find out whether an individual was involved in electronic porn or was a police informant ..." Briskett couldn't be bothered to help out, he stood his ground and waited for Priestley to find his own answer. "... then I have to come directly through you?"

"Yes," he smirked. "Or the chief constable," he added as an afterthought. It was obvious that Charlie was Briskett's pride and joy. But whatever Charlie was it didn't matter. Priestley had got the answer to the question he'd come with. In reality, the only person in the entire force who had complete access to informants' details was Briskett. He was the only person who was in a position to be selling it to Frankie Richardson.

The girl, Jackie, returned and explained that Richardson was on record, but that the details were housed at New Scotland Yard. That was exactly what Priestley expected she'd say, but he smiled his most charming smile and said, "Well, we can't win them all, now can we?"

"Want me to try the Yard for you, Jack?" asked Briskett.

"No. Thanks anyway. I'll pay them a visit myself."

And maybe he would. There wasn't much he could do now except sit back and wait while Barton made his quiet, discrete investigations. Then he'd find out the whys and the wherefores. And find out what the hell was really going on. And at that point, he'd take his story to the chief. And ruin his day.

PART THREE

21

So far as Priestley was concerned, the summons to the early morning briefing in London had been nothing more than an irritation. He was finding it increasingly hard to concentrate on the daily round of RCS work, so absorbed was he becoming in his conspiracy theories. He reckoned he had more important fish to fry than helping the customs boys out with some heist. But the briefing had been a revelation to Priestley and Barton. Afterwards they'd felt as though they'd completed the outside edge of a jigsaw puzzle. The inside was still in pieces, but the corners and all the edge pieces had been found and slotted together. It wasn't proof exactly, but it crystallised part of the bigger picture.

Richard Parker was a dedicated customs officer who didn't really trust anybody outside his own department. So, naturally, that included Jack Priestley and Chris Barton. But Parker had been given no choice. He'd had to summon the help of the Regional Crime Squad to support the kind of operation he was dealing with. He was a short man, medium build, in his early thirties. He was smartly dressed in a hacking jacket and grey flannel trousers. His neat brown hair matched the thickish moustache which embraced his upper lip. He looked more like a 1950s school teacher than a modern day customs investigator with an excellent track record. Priestley was impressed by the way the assembled company immediately settled when Parker walked across the room to the lectern and wished them all a very good morning. "Can I also welcome Detective Chief Inspector Jack Priestley and Detective Inspector Barton who are going to help us on this case." The customs officer smiled and launched into his briefing.

"As you are all aware, Team A is now in Turkey with the targets. The latest we've got is that the targets have made contact with the suppliers over there and should be returning to the UK in the next couple of days, once they've purchased the goods. Now, we know that the targets are trying to purchase heroin and that they're trailing a caravan. It'll take them a few days to drive across Europe and Team A intend to follow them back. We're expecting them to cross the Channel on the Calais-Dover ferry." He paused. "That, of course, assumes that they come back the same way they went across. Once they're back on home soil, bump; we'll stop and search them. I expect it to go down within the next seven days. If we find the goods on them, you'll get your call and then it's your turn for your team to take out your individual target. Jack, in your case that will be a man by the name of Nesbitt. Harry Nesbitt. The details are in this file," he said, handing Priestley a buff-coloured folder. Priestley did his best to hide his surprise as he took the folder from Parker. He quickly flicked through the papers and little pieces of information flashed out from the pages of numerous intelligence reports. There were also photographs of Nesbitt in the folder; one of which, he noticed, also featured Sammy Blade.

"Why aren't you using our Drug Squad officers for this Richard?" Priestley believed he was making a valid point; the RCS had little experience of investigations involving drugs. "They've got the expertise for searching in situations like this."

Parker looked slightly embarrassed. "There's a small problem there, Jack. I'll update you after the briefing." Priestley glanced at Barton and found him looking at him already. He was thinking the same thing. Boyle. Colin Boyle.

This might be the Nesbitt/Boyle connection they were looking for.

"So what are we looking for?" asked Priestley. "Heroin? And on what grounds do you want us to take Nesbitt out, Richard?"

"We think Nesbitt has been one of this organisation's main contacts for heroin distribution in the Midlands for some time. So obviously we're looking for heroin inside his house. That means you'll have to be quick on his doorstep. Or, he'll have time to get rid of it. If he's got some, nick him. If not, still nick him on suspicion of conspiracy to import."

* * * * *

When Parker had finished his briefing, Priestley asked Barton to wait outside while he hung back, waiting for the room to empty so that he could have a word alone with Parker. "Tell me, Richard, what's that you said about the Drug Squad up our way?"

"You've got a problem up there, Jack. We're not sure, but we think some of your blokes are involved in this organisation." Obviously this didn't come as a complete shock, but Priestley decided to play dumb.

"I don't believe it. Our Drug Squad?" A picture of Colin Boyle's face came to the forefront of his mind. "You mean backhanders?" Parker nodded. "Anything being done about it?"

"I don't know, Jack. I've just been told to steer clear of them." He shrugged his shoulders and continued. "There might not be anything in it. But you know what it's like. The slightest rumour and we can't afford to take the risk."

* * * * *

Five days later the DCI felt that the time had come to brief those of his people he'd selected for Richard Parker's operation.

* * * * *

Two days later, at four o'clock in the morning, Priestley's phone rang. "Jack? It's Richard Parker. We've pulled the main targets down at Dover and found a few kilos of heroin hidden inside their caravan. The stuff was inside some baked bean cans, believe it or not. You need to move now. Quickly," he said urgently. "Before word gets out."

Priestley's arse was already in gear. Using a pyramid communications system it took only seconds for the eight-man team to be warned. They assembled at the nick nearest to where Harry Nesbitt lived, where Priestley briefly reminded his people what was expected of them. Three officers would go with Priestley to the front door, whilst the other three covered the back of the house with Barton. Although Priestley had obtained an entry warrant, he knew they wouldn't have time to go through the usual procedures. It was vital they crashed the door, before Harry had chance to flush any dope down the toilet.

Within minutes of finishing his briefing, Priestley and his men were in the street outside Harry's house. "Right, Chris, take your three round the back. We'll give you three minutes before we hit the door." Barton didn't waste any time in leading his men off, while Priestley and the remaining members of the team huddled out of sight behind a hedge.

Three minutes ticked slowly by. "Okay people. That's enough. Let's go and do it." Priestley and his team approached the front of the house, down a long gravel drive. The house was large, the fruit, Priestley supposed, of Harry's ill-gotten gains. When he got to the front door, Priestley banged on it loudly. Almost immediately a light came on in an upstairs window. Shortly afterwards the window was flung open and voice shouted, "What the fucking hell's going on?"

"Morning, Harry," Priestley shouted back cheerfully. "Get down here and open the door. I want to look around. I'll give you two seconds. Then I'll break the door down." Harry didn't need to bother with the door, though. There was a loud, rending, crashing sound from the back of the house and a moment or two later, Barton appeared in the newly opened front door.

Priestley immediately sent his team to work and decided to start on the upstairs himself. He was particularly interested in Nesbitt's bedroom. He firmly believed that Harry would have whatever there was to be found close to where he slept. Always assuming the little shithole hadn't had time to get rid of everything.

He was right. Or so he thought. As he stepped onto the landing, he came across a small set of scales on a table top, presumably for the purpose of measuring out the dope. Priestley was confident forensic tests would find traces on the scales and called to Chris Barton to seize and bag them as exhibits while he went in search of the bedroom. When he found it, he was amazed to be confronted by a four poster bed with what appeared to be a body hidden beneath the bedclothes.

"Mrs Nesbitt?" he said. Stupid question really. He knew Harry wasn't married. There was no answer and the body remained still, completely covered by the blankets. So, without hesitation, Priestley flicked back the sheets. To reveal the naked figure of Sammy Blade. She stared at him furiously, folding her arms over her breasts. "Hello Jack," she said. He stood there speechless. "Cat got your tongue has it? What did you expect, Jack Priestley?"

"Not this." There was a slight tremble in his voice, but his words were truthful.

"Obviously not." Her lips seemed to move out of sync with her words. "Well, Mister High-and-Mighty, I suppose you can't wait to go and see your old mate and tell him all about it, eh? Well, go and do your dirty tricks, Jack. He's been away a long time." Still he said nothing. "Well piss off then. Or do you want to search me as well? Or, perhaps you'd like a freebie. Eh, Jack?"

Suddenly he found his voice. "I only want to search the bed, lady. Get off."

22

It was amazing. Unbelievable. Impossible; but true. Harry's scales came back clean from the lab. There wasn't the slightest trace of any illicit drug on them. He was clean. They couldn't make the charges stick and Harry walked. But under the bed, Priestley had found a slip of paper. On it was written a telephone number. No name, just a number. Furious that the raid was not going well, (well, actually, the raid was going fine, it was Sammy Blade that had upset Priestley's calm – knowing about her relationship with Harry Nesbitt was one thing, but having it shoved down his throat was quite another) Priestley angrily pushed the piece of paper into his pocket.

Two days after the raid, Chris Barton followed him into his office and closed the door. He had a bundle of papers under one arm. "That research you asked me to do, Boss? On the informants?"

Priestley shifted upright in his chair. "Go on, Chris."

"I've found five unresolved murders, all committed in this region and going back two years. But I think you'll find that three of them in particular are interesting." He placed three separate piles of papers on top of Priestley's desk. "The first involves a young bloke named Kenny Mulch." Barton picked up one of the files and started to read from it. "Kind of a loner. Lived on his own. Had form for supplying drugs.

He was found in his flat. With his throat cut. They never found his killer."

"Who dealt with that one, Chris?" asked Priestley.

The answer was unexpected. "Superintendent Nolan, Boss." Barton put Mulch's file down and picked up the next. "This was a strange one. The victim came from London. He was up here visiting some business associates. Name of Wesley Richards. Again he had form for drugs. According to the records, at the time the investigating officer thought it was a contract killing. He was found slumped over the steering wheel of his car with his brains blown out."

"Shotgun?"

"Yes, left at the scene. Apparently there was talk of Richards owing money to some London organisation."

"Sounds like a contract to me." Every copper knew that most professional killers left their hardware behind. Always completely clean, without even the slightest print or traceable mark. Once the weapon left their possession, so did the evidence to tie them to the murder. "Who investigated that one, Chris?"

"Nolan." Priestley raised his eyebrows. Two out of three. What a busy boy.

"The third murder involved a woman by the name of Annette Colby. Prostitute, but also known to deal in drugs." Barton stopped and looked a little blank.

"Go on, Chris," directed his DCI.

"I wish I could, but most of the papers on this one are missing."

"When did it happen?"

"Twelve months ago."

"Probably they're still with the investigating officer. If the murder is only a year old it's too soon to file it."

"But once again, Boss, the investigating officer is Superintendent Nolan."

"Cause of death?"

"Strangled."

Priestley stood up. "Okay. Who were their handlers?"

"Mulch and Colby had the same handler. A Detective Constable Andrew Jones. Drug Squad."

"And the other?"

"Richards was registered in London. So his handler was a Met. Officer. A DS Simon Cranby, from West End Central." Priestley flopped back down into his chair. This didn't look good. He shook his head. None of this looked good.

Barton turned to leave, but as he reached the door he remembered something and turned back to look at his boss. "Oh, one more thing. That number you found when we busted Nesbitt the other day?"

Priestley looked up. "Yes, Chris. Whose is it?"

"It's down to a John Briskett of 23 Colonial Road, Redditch."

"You mean Detective Chief Inspector John Briskett of 23 Colonial Road, Redditch?"

"The very same. Why would Harry Nesbitt have his mobile phone number?"

"My question exactly." But no wonder the bastard had been clean.

23

"So what's it about, Jacky?" Priestley had never felt comfortable meeting Jacky Benson in this pub, which was used by so many market traders. But it was Jacky's local. Or, rather, it was two minutes from the stand from which he sold newspapers and magazines. Jacky Benson eyed the second pint sitting on the bar, as he downed the first Priestley had bought him. He'd known the DCI since he was a young copper who'd turned his back on the old man after finding him with a set of nicked cutlery. Gear which Jacky had tried to convince him had come off a bloke in a pub. Over the years he'd repaid that debt many times by providing the policeman with information concerning a number of jobs, including the one Steve Blade was eventually caught on. He hadn't been involved in what he described as 'real crime' for a few years now, but he still wouldn't look a gift horse in the mouth if it presented itself to him. There wasn't much going on that Jacky Benson didn't know about, and today he clearly had something he wanted to get off his chest.

"I don't believe this," muttered Priestley. Some old geezer had decided the saloon bar was too quiet and had sat down to earn a free drink or two, hammering out the black and white keys. Either he was too pissed to play properly or the old Joanna was well out of tune.

"Don't worry, mate. A little singsong never hurt anybody. Besides, nobody will be able to hear what we're saying over the racket he's making." Jacky's eyes were bloodshot. He didn't look at all well. He never looked well.

"So why am I here?"

"Nesbitt. Harry Nesbitt." Priestley pricked up his ears. The prospect of possibly having another go at Harry ten days after dropping the last lot of charges was delicious. " 'Those old red flannel drawers that Maggie wore,' " quavered across the room from a few who'd decided to join the old pianist.

"What about him?" " 'They were tattered. They were torn. From the crutchpiece, they were worn.' " The rendition continued in the background.

"He's been shafting Steve Blade's missus."

"So I hear. Been at it for years. Ever since he went back inside."

"And feeding her drugs too. Bastard. She was off her head last time I saw her. His latest scam is to sell cardboard to the Indians."

"Cardboard?" Priestley didn't have the faintest idea what Jacky was on about.

"Inside cigarette packets," he explained. "He sells thousands of them by the van load and then pisses off with the money. He's been doing it for ages."

Oh, I get it, thought Priestley. Fake cigarette packets. "Where?"

"Coventry. Leicester. Not here. He wouldn't dare shit on his own doorstep."

"When?" Priestley needed more.

"I don't know. He's always at it." Jacky paused while he made inroads into the second pint and Priestley had to wait for him to pick up the conversation again.

"Keep talking, Jacky," he had to say eventually, when the pause became a full stop.

Jacky shook his shoulders. Like he was making a decision. "Tonight. You'll be able to get him tonight. He's also been running a racket. That's where the real dough is coming from. And he'll be at it tonight. He's going to call on a bloke called Malik. He keeps a shop on Lozells Road. Apparently, he's well behind with his payments. Harry was mouthing off last night about him owing five grand and tonight he's gonna have his come-uppance."

"How?"

"Jack. Use your imagination. Do you want me to dress you as well?" Jacky sniggered. "Harry's going round there to torch the shop."

"That sounds better than busting him for selling bent fags."

"Yeah, thought you'd be pleased."

* * * * *

The red Jaguar crept slowly down the cobbled street towards the brightly lit corner store and stopped outside. A small man, smartly dressed in a camel-coloured overcoat, opened a rear door and climbed out onto the pavement. In his hand he held a newspaper parcel containing the remains of his fish and chip dinner. The car's driver joined him on the pavement. He also had a parcel wrapped in newspaper, but his was tucked under his arm.

The coppers watched and waited in silence while the little man finished eating. When he was done, he slung the empty wrapper on the ground. Jack Priestley grunted. "Well, at the very least I can do him for littering," he muttered under his breath. He watched Harry Nesbitt rub his hands together and say something to Leroy Henderson before heading towards the shop. His head spun every which way as he went, looking for signs of trouble. Satisfied all was well, Harry and his muscle entered the shop. Immediately, Priestley gave the word and he and Chris Barton were out of the car and across the street in an instant.

Inside the shop, Harry was shouting at the shopkeeper. He poked the man in his chest and yelled out in fury, "You've got this coming to you, you Paki bastard. I've given you enough time. Let's see what you make of this." Harry signalled to Henderson who responded by unwrapping his parcel. He placed a milk bottle on the counter beside the cash register. A strip of rag hung limply out of the top. Your average petrol bomb. From the display on the counter, Harry selected an orange Bic lighter and handed it to Henderson.

Right, thought Priestley. Enough. Time to break up the party. Making as much noise as possible, he wrenched open the shop door and charged in, Chris Barton following close behind. "Hello, Harry," he said. Harry's face hit the floor. Henderson dropped the lighter and, turning to face the intruders, searched under his jacket with his right hand. Presumably for his defence. "Don't even think about it," Priestley warned.

Outside in the street, all hell had broken loose as the back-up arrived, setting up a cordon surrounding the shop, preventing escape. Harry's shoulders slumped. And his muscle had sufficient intelligence to realise that resistance was useless. His hand dropped to his side and Barton immediately grabbed him, turning him roughly around so that he could cuff his wrists.

"Very nice, Harry," said Priestley. "Barbecue laid on for tonight was it?"

Harry glared at him. "I'm not saying a word."

"You don't have to. I've got all the evidence I need to put you away for years right here."

"I'm not going anywhere, Mr Untouchable."

"Don't be silly, Harry. 'Course you are. You seem to have been caught with your trousers down, again."

24

His elbows locked together and he paused, just for a second. Seventy completed; thirty to go. He watched the beads of sweat drip from his brow onto the floor. His shirt was saturated. It always was when he did a hundred. That was the idea of the exercise. He slowly lowered his chest, then pushed up hard, keeping his legs taut. Seventy one. Come on, he told himself. Not far to go now. Determination drove him. Ignoring his aching biceps, Blade pressed on. His cell wasn't the best place to exercise, but he felt such a tosspot working out in the gym with all the heavies looking on. Show the slightest sign of weakness and they all took the piss. Seventy two. Seventy three. Seventy four. Still, he thought, the prison had been a different place since Frankie had left. Not that he'd paid much attention at the time. Causer's death had knocked him sideways. The screws had been really good about it and let him spend as much time in the exercise yard as he wanted to. Walking round and round. Around and around. And while he walked away his pain, things changed in the prison. It became a dangerous place after Frankie left. Different factions developed and fought for control. Fought to fill the void that Frankie's departure had left. Blade was well out of it. And he'd stayed out of it since. Now he was just biding his time. Waiting for the result of his parole application. Any day now he'd know. And the agony of waiting would be over.

Ninety eight. Ninety nine. One hundred. Thank Christ for that. Blade collapsed onto the cell floor and lay gasping for air. The chilly linoleum cooled the heat seeping out of his flesh. But not for long. Keys jangled in the lock and his cell door opened. "The governor wants to see you, Steve. Now. So look sharp."

Blade pulled himself off the floor and stood before the screw, his arms raised to indicate that he wasn't really dressed to see the governor. "Any chance of a shower first, Frank?" He was still breathless.

"Sorry son," the screw shook his head. "No time. You'll be all right as you are. The governor will understand, don't worry."

The two men walked along the landing and down the metal staircase. Taxi driving, he thought suddenly. When he got out of here he'd get himself an old taxi and see where it led him. He smiled to himself. Why hadn't he thought of that before? It was obvious. He followed his escort across the yard towards the administration block where the governor's office was situated on the top floor. He'd only been there once before. He remembered that the room had a big window, which looked out over miles and miles of flat, unchanging Leicestershire countryside.

Blade was instructed to sit on the wooden bench in the corridor outside the office door. Blade did as he was told and stared down at the floor while he waited to see the governor. He was in a reflective mood. He often was these days. Prison had changed him. Colin Causer had changed him. It had been a shock. Colin Causer's death. And the way the young man had chosen to do it. It had ripped Steve Blade apart. He'd put a lot of time and effort into that kid. Trying to help him. Trying to straighten him out. He had really believed that he had influenced the boy. Made a difference. So what really hurt, apart from the loss of friendship, was the fact that he hadn't.

God. He hoped he'd get parole. He hoped that was why he was sitting here now. Possibly, just possibly, the governor had the result of the application. He knew he'd become institutionalised. He'd played the game and not caused any hassle during his time inside, especially in the couple of months since Frankie'd left. He remembered the big man offering him work and, although he was reluctant, knew he would probably take up the offer. Taxi driving, my arse, he thought. What a crap idea. But sitting there waiting, he remembered the promise he'd made to Jack Priestley before Colin died. He had an idea. The only question was, did he have the balls to do it? Could he work on the inside of Frankie's organisation and pass information to the outside? It would be a reversal of everything he knew and understood. And if he did, what was in it for him? And what about Sammy? He'd need to rebuild his relationship with her when he got out. Settle back down. See if they could make it work. Prison destroys marriages. He missed Sammy desperately. Recently, she'd not been visiting. And he knew she must have somebody else.

"Blade!" The screw's voice woke him up. He'd been waiting ages. "You can go in now." The con stood up and entered the governor's office. Nothing much appeared to have changed since the last time he'd visited. It was even the same governor looking up at him from behind the same shabby desk.

"I have the result of your parole application, Steve. The Secretary of State has approved it." He stopped to give the prisoner a chance to digest the news, and then stood up to offer his hand in congratulations. Blade grasped the proffered hand, his face splitting in two in his delight. He couldn't believe it. Free! Freedom at last. He had no words to say. He was aware his head was nodding up and down. Inanely. No way could he could stop it. Freedom! "Congratulations, Steve. A lot of influential people have supported you in your application. Detective Chief Inspector Priestley for one." Good old Jack! "Even Assistant Chief Constable Frank Newhart." Blade didn't recognise the name and it barely made any impression in his ecstatic mind.

He still found it impossible to speak. So he stood before the governor, nodding and grinning, until the screw took him by the arm and steered him out of the room.

He was still dazed when he got back to his landing. Outside his cell, he shook himself, as if re-gathering his wits. He had a telephone call to make. Two telephone calls.

* * * * *

It was three o'clock in the afternoon when the telephone in Sammy Blade's flat rang out. Sammy was stoned. She lay on her bed grinning almost as foolishly as her husband had been a few moments ago. The phone rang and rang. Eventually the answer phone picked up. So far as Sammy was concerned, that was the best thing about her answer phone. As long as the caller was patient and held on long enough, the answer phone would eventually click in. Saved her from having to remember to turn it on. The recorded message announced to the empty living room that Sammy was unable to take your call, so please leave your name and number and she'll get back to you. After the bleep, her husband's voice filled the room and floated into the bedroom. Sammy struggled up onto her elbows. "Sammy! Sammy, it's me. They're letting me out. On Thursday. I'm free! Can you come and get me? Can't wait to see you. I'll give you a call later. Christ! I can't wait to see you." Sammy slumped back onto the bed. The excitement in his voice had been palpable. It was too much for her to bear. Sammy burst into tears.

* * * * *

In Gartree, Steve Blade replaced the handset on its cradle and leant against the wall. Home! Going home. Two more days. He could hardly contain his excitement. He rubbed his face with his hands. Right. Priestley.

* * * * *

Priestley couldn't believe it. It wasn't just the fact that Andrew Jones was the same face he'd seen going into the Tiger Bar with Colin Boyle that day he'd followed them with Carol Guardia. It was also the sickly smell of his aftershave. A smell which had haunted him since the night he'd met the three jokers in the country lane. And now it was in his own office. His first reaction was to blast the bastard from here to Kingdom Come, but he decided it would be more prudent to open the window instead. His mind was racing. Why hadn't it occurred to him that this might happen? The window looked out over the car park and he watched someone struggling to park their car in a space that was much too small as he tried to marshal his thoughts. He was going to have to tread very, very carefully. It occurred to him, not for the first time, that he was getting in way out of his depth. He straightened his shoulders and turned to face one of the enemy.

"Thank you for coming to see me, Jones," he said, gesturing towards one of the two chairs on the other side of his desk. But the detective constable had already made himself comfortable. Why wait to be asked?

"That's okay, Boss," he drawled. "What's it all about then?"

Priestley looked hard at the young man and wondered how much he knew. More than he did, that was for sure. Bombastic git. "Coffee, tea?" Priestley offered, buying time. He hadn't been expecting this.

"No thanks, Boss. Just had one."

Still playing for time, Priestley asked, "Still on the Drug Squad, Andrew?"

"No, I came off a few months ago. I'm in Intelligence now. Working for Mr Briskett."

Priestley feigned interest. "Really? I've never worked in Intelligence. Is it as good as they say?"

"Not really, Gaffer." The young detective was certainly giving off a laid back attitude. His eyes were all over the place. "It's all right," he continued, "but you don't get out much. Most of the work's done sitting at a desk." So you're just running with Boyle for the exercise and excitement, are you, thought Priestley, as his cell phone started singing its tune. He rummaged about on his desk until he found it.

"Jack Priestley," he shouted.

"Jack? It's Steve. I wanted to let you know. They're letting me out."

"That's wonderful. Congratulations."

"I wanted to thank you for supporting my application and …"

"Look, I've got someone with me, can you call me back later?"

"Sure, Jack. No problem. This evening okay?"

"Fine. Speak to you later." He turned the phone off and switched his attention back to Jones. "I've asked to see you Andrew, because we've got a problem with a couple of informants that are registered to you." Priestley watched Jones's face carefully as he said this, but his expression remained unchanged, like a plastic mould, a mask of barely concealed insolence and boredom.

"Which two are they, Gaffer?"

"Well, you see the thing is we've had two registered recently and when we checked them out we found that their names are very similar to two you used to handle. We wondered if there was any connection. The names in question are Mulch and Colby." He was still searching for some sort of change in the man's demeanour, but there was nothing. He hoped the smoke screen was sufficient.

"You mean Kenny Mulch and Annette Colby. They were both topped."

"What? Murdered? Were they connected, or what?" The surprised and bewildered Jack Priestley act wasn't that convincing. But hopefully this tosspot wasn't bright enough to see through it. The man's expression was still one of vacuous boredom.

"No. Well I say that, but they were both into heavy drugs. But they didn't know each other from Adam, as far as I was aware, Gaffer. I didn't get a tripe supper from either of them."

That was enough. The bent bastard's first lie. From the files Barton had dug up, Priestley knew that this wanker had paid a total of three grand to Mulch alone, over a period of two years. To justify that would have meant a lot of information. But Priestley pretended to accept Jones's point of view. "Why were they murdered, Andrew?" Priestley turned his back on him again.

"Don't know really, Boss. I put Mulch's murder down to a rip off. You know, he'd probably done a deal and then legged it with the money."

"And Colby?"

"No idea. She was just a brass who used to pop a name in now and again. But only small stuff. Now I was surprised when she got topped, but I thought it was probably a dissatisfied customer. From memory, I think she was throttled."

This time it was the phone on his desk that rang. It was Jim Nolan. "Jack, can you pop in and see me as soon as you can?"

"Half an hour?"

"Fine, see you then." That was a surprise. What the hell did Nolan want? He looked at Jones and tried to drag his mind back to what the bastard had been saying. He'd got all he wanted. Jones was as bent as they come. He wasn't going to get any more.

"Well thanks for the help, Andrew. You've cleared up one or two things for me. Anything else you think you should tell me?" he said, as Jones appeared to hesitate before getting up to leave. As if he'd mislaid his shopping list.

* * * * *

Priestley was losing his touch. He should have guessed this would happen. Should have known he'd find Colin Boyle sitting comfortably in Jim Nolan's office, self-satisfied smirk plastered all over his face.

"I'll get straight to the point, Jack," Nolan said. "Harry Nesbitt. I understand you've just done him for ..." He checked a piece of paper on the desk in front of him. "... conspiracy to commit arson?"

Here we go, thought Priestley. He wondered what the reason would be this time. Supports the force to the hilt? Or perhaps, if Harry went to prison, all the lefties would come marching in and take over the drugs scene? Still he said, "Yes. He tried to burn out a shopkeeper and his family."

"You know DS Boyle from the Drug Squad?"

"Yes, vaguely," he replied, meaning, yeah sure, this is the guy that puts plastic bags over prisoners' heads and tortures them half to death.

"Well, Nesbitt's one of his informants." Knew it, thought Jack. Another stitch up. He waited for Nolan to finish. "In fact, Jack, he's one of the best the Drug Squad's got at the moment and he's in the middle of a major operation." Priestley was motionless. There wasn't even a nod or shake of his head as he let the bullshit roll. "The bottom line is, Jack ..."

Priestley came to the end of his tether. "That you want me to drop the charges?"

Nolan stood up and stuck his hands in his pockets. Aggressively. Priestley wondered if it was a deliberate act of intimidation. "I was just saying to Colin here," said Nolan, "that you'd understand. Thanks a lot, Jack." The superintendent turned to Boyle. "Make sure he delivers, Colin. This is a big favour, but a one off. He only gets this one chance."

Priestley couldn't tell if he meant him or Nesbitt. But it didn't matter. Now the cat was truly amongst the pigeons, thought Priestley, as he raced out to get some fresh air.

* * * * *

A couple of hours later, Sammy sat silently on the edge of her bed, trying to use the corner of the sheet to cover the upper part of her naked body. Harry Nesbitt lay beside her. He tried to stroke her arm but she snatched it away furiously. The room was full of the smell of his newly acquired Parisian aftershave.

"It's over Harry," she said. "Steve's coming out the day after tomorrow."

"So?" he replied. "Why does it have to be over? We can up and sling our hook right now if you want."

She turned sharply to look at him, opened her mouth to speak. Harry held up a hand to stall her, "Okay, okay," he soothed. "I know. You don't need to tell me. That wasn't part of the deal."

"That's right. The deal, if you remember, was that we'd do this while he was inside. The moment he comes out, it's over. That's what we agreed. That's the way I want it."

"One in and one out, eh?" he said aggressively. "What about me?"

"What about you, Harry?"

25

"For he's a jolly good fellow," was usually the refrain to which long lost souls were greeted back into the fold, and Steve Blade was no exception. The public bar was heaving with people and the ex-con almost lost his footing as the blast of the noise hit him as he stood in the doorway. He surveyed the scene. Everything and everybody looked exactly the same as four years before. But he was different. He felt nervous now, with so many people around him.

The hand-shaking started immediately, as his old friends joyfully greeted him. They'd all turned out to celebrate his release. As the beer flowed, pint after pint, it slowly began to feel as though he'd never been away at all. As if the latest episode in his life hadn't really happened. He surveyed the room, looking round for Sammy. It had been so good to see her, to hold her. And now he didn't want to let her go. Didn't want her out of his sight. Eventually he spotted her in a distant corner talking to Harry Nesbitt. Good old Harry, thought Blade, wondering what he'd been up to these last few years. The sight of the little man reminded him of the time they'd worked together in the parcels business. He watched them for a while, closing his ears to the hubbub around him. It was odd, the way Harry and his missus seemed to be so engrossed in their conversation. Strange because, although he and Harry had been close all those years back, Sammy had never really taken to him. He wondered if maybe she owed the little git money. He'd sort it out later, he decided, as his thoughts were interrupted by another Harry: Harry Ventnor; his one-time partner-in-crime.

"Good to see you, Steve. Long time, no see." They greeted one another with an affectionate hug.

"Have a drink, Harry." Blade noticed his voice was beginning to slur. And no wonder, he must have been on his seventh pint by now.

"Had one off you already. Sammy put some dough behind the bar. You're looking good, Steve. Any plans yet?"

"Not yet, mate. Bit early. I need a bit of time to get sorted. How's life been treating you? Anything happening?"

"No. Quiet as the grave since I got out. Been keeping my head down. Nothing round here's changed much, except of course for that over there." His eyes went across to where Sammy and Nesbitt were gassing.

"I don't follow."

"Harry Nesbitt. He's been going up in the world since you've been inside. Every bent which way you can think of. Just walked away from one Jack Priestley tried to do him for. Rumour is he parted with some cash to get himself off the hook."

"You telling me Priestley's bent?"

"Not telling you anything. But I do suggest you keep an eye on that one," he said, jerking his head in Nesbitt's direction.

"What?"

"Well, I guess you'll find out sooner or later. It may as well be me that does the telling. Harry's been having it off with your missus all the time you've been away. Never came up for air."

A bombshell exploded in Blade's head. World War Three. Hiroshima and Nagasaki all over again. He took a deep breath. Trying to get his brain to take in what Ventnor had said. "Harry, can you say that again?"

"Nesbitt and your missus," he said. That was enough. Ventnor didn't have to say any more. The news was devastating. Blade could feel his lower lip start to tremble. His senses froze. He sobered up very, very fast. The chattering voices all around him faded into the distance and his legs felt paralysed. He couldn't move. His wife. Who he loved more than life itself. In bed with Harry Nesbitt. The bastard. The thought of Sammy sitting astride that scumbag was too much to bear.

Sensation slowly started to return. The voices and bright lights that surrounded him gradually seeped back into his consciousness. Ventnor was gripping his arm. Restraining him. Blade glared at his wife and her midget lover. "Not now," warned Ventnor. "Not now." Blade shook his head. "Don't worry, Steve. The bastard's not the most popular around here. There's a few of us that owe him some grief. You'll have plenty of support when the time comes. Don't worry. We'll hand him to you on a rope."

Blade pulled away from Ventnor's grip and buried his face in a pint of lager. "I'll sort my own business out, Harry. Just as I've always done," he said. He appeared to relax. "Don't worry," he continued. "I've learnt a few things inside. I'm a bit more streetwise."

Relieved, Ventnor patted his shoulder, while Blade finished his pint. The glass still in his hand, Blade sauntered over to Harry Nesbitt and his wife. "Hello, Harry," he said. "How's things?" Very deliberately Blade shook the other man's proffered hand.

"Welcome home, Steve," he said. "Got any plans?"

"Well that's what I wanted to talk to you about H.. There's something I've had on my mind for some time now. A little tit-bit from inside, you know?"

"I'm always interested, Steve. You know that." Nesbitt looked steadily into Blade's eyes.

"Well this isn't the place or the time, Harry." Blade's quickly prepared plan was going well. It looked like Nesbitt was falling for it. "Perhaps we could meet somewhere less public?" He paused. "Say, tomorrow night?"

"Fine by me, mate. Whatever you say. Where were you thinking of?" Harry's smile was sickly. It was beginning to get on Blade's nerves. He concentrated hard on keeping himself under control.

"Small Heath Bridge." That would be dark enough, thought Blade. Unless they'd built floodlights on it while he'd been inside breaking rocks.

"Okay. What time?" Nesbitt's downfall was his cocky self-confidence.

"Nine o'clock? Perhaps we could talk over old times. After I've put you in the picture with this little venture I've got going?"

"Sounds good to me. I'll be there." He raised his glass and took a gulp – toasting the arrangement. The corner of Blade's lip curled as he turned away. His legs felt like putty. Then the voices around him dimmed again as he heard Sammy's voice calling after him. Questioning. He fingered the empty glass in his hand. Turned and retraced the few steps he'd taken. Overtaken by fury he shoved the glass into Harry Nesbitt's ugly, laughing face. The little man received a reverse face-lift. New fashion. Blade then kicked him in the stomach and in the head as good old Harry fell to the beer-sodden floor – a spread-eagled bloody mess. He could hear his own voice yelling, "You bastard. You slimy, filthy bastard," as two strong arms grabbed him and dragged him from the scene as the room collapsed into uproar. Welcome home, Steve Blade.

26

Priestley was in his office the following morning, catching up on his paperwork, when his phone rang. It was his bloody bank manager! For Chrissakes! This was a man he'd never met, let alone spoken to. "Mr Priestley, our services are here to help you invest your money in the best way possible," he offered, his voice smarmily submissive. The man was obviously trying to help. The bank must be promoting a better quality service, thought Priestley. Just exactly what customers needed. And about time too.

"And what would that involve, Mr Knott?" Five grand was all he had, but if Mr Knott's investment schemes could turn it into six grand, then obviously he would be very interested. Who wouldn't be?

"All I need to do is arrange an appointment for you with one of our financial advisers. I know you are a busy man, so if you would prefer, Mr Priestley, we could always arrange a home visit for you, perhaps one evening next week?"

This was service at its best, thought Jack. "I'd prefer that Mr Knott, if that's possible."

"We do it for all our customers who deposit such large sums with our bank."

Priestley's heart skipped a beat. What large deposit? Had he missed something here? "Mr Knott, what's the large deposit you're referring to?"

"Why, the twenty-five thousand pounds you deposited into your current account yesterday."

Priestley felt his legs begin to tremble. He replaced the receiver and sat down sharply. His face turned a whiter shade of pale. Nesbitt. Nolan. Boyle. The bastards. A twenty-five grand backhander for letting Nesbitt off the hook. What a complete prat he'd been. He hadn't read it. Hadn't seen it coming. And now he was into the same game as they were. Into it up to his neck. He picked up the phone again and dialled Sonia's number. He needed her legal expertise to help him out of this one.

* * * * *

Blade, meanwhile, had taken refuge in Harry Ventnor's flat after the fracas the night before. He was going to have to lie low for a few days. The rumour on the street was that Nesbitt was on the war path. His looks were ruined and he'd sent out his minder to deal with Blade. No way was he feeling forgiving. Ventnor had come home at lunchtime full of it all. Delighted to be in the middle of so much drama.

But Blade knew that it was too dangerous to stay. So he made a snap decision. He was going to London. He was going to take up Frankie's offer. He didn't think he had an option. His marriage was over. And that bastard, Priestley, was as bent as everyone else. He wondered how much he'd taken. Wondered what his price was. The pain and sense of betrayal was indescribable. He'd throw himself into whatever life Frankie could offer him and hope it numbed the hurt.

27

This was one beautiful car. It was red. It was sleek. It was shapely. Sex on wheels. And when you put your foot on the gas it gave out a satisfying roar. Raw power. Great torque. Harry Nesbitt loved driving it. He felt ten foot tall when he drove it. But he didn't often get the chance. He'd decided long ago that a man of his stature needed to be driven. So usually, Leroy drove and he sat in the back. But tonight he'd given Leroy the night off and he'd taken the car for a spin. Out and down the motorway to put it through its paces on empty open road.

The car was a great place to think. And Harry Nesbitt had a lot to think about. First, he had twice escaped the clutches of the law by the skin of his teeth and that was two occasions too many for Harry. Frankie was furious with him. He was going to have to be much more careful. Vigilance. That would be his key word as long as Jack Priestley was sniffing around. Hopefully the cash in his current account would be sufficient to keep him off his back. Frankie had insisted. And what Frankie said always went.

He checked his face in the driving mirror. The cut was hideously livid. That was the second thing. That bastard Blade. He'd opened up the whole left side of his face. All he'd done was show his wife a good time while he was inside. The cut ran in a jagged curve from the edge of his eye to his mouth. He'd get his come-uppance soon enough. Nesbitt hadn't decided what that would be but Blade had it coming. He'd just let him cool down first. He must be shitting himself wondering when the attack would come. Nesbitt sniggered. Probably couldn't even pluck up the courage to leave Ventnor's poxy flat. Vengeance would be his. Vigilance and vengeance. His watch words for the month.

Approaching his exit off the motorway, he checked the mirror again. "Sod it," he whispered. A red and white was approaching his rear, lights flashing. Where did that come from? Apart from them and him the motorway was deserted. He thought about pushing the peddle to the floor but the cop car was approaching too fast. He'd seen it too late. So much for vigilance. He'd try pragmatism instead. He reached for his wallet to pull out a few notes to stuff inside his driving licence. Then he remembered he hadn't had a drink. Stuff them instead. He was clean. The blue lights lit up the inside of his car and, disgusted with himself, he pulled over to the side of the road. This was ridiculous. The filth, hell-bent on wrecking his night. He was only out for a quiet drive. Bastards.

Two officers walked towards his car. Nesbitt pressed the button in the arm rest and the window slipped smoothly down. "Good evening, Sir." The greeting was cordial but, in the light of the headlamps of the police car behind him, it was clear that this one was a hard bastard. A man who enjoyed his job. Slashed peak. Sideburns. Definitely a hard bastard. Harry was glad he hadn't had a drink. "Can I see your documents please?"

Nesbitt reached across for the glove compartment. "Don't piss me about tonight will you, son" he said, his arm outstretched. "I'm trying to make a very important meeting."

"Like fuck you are in the middle of the night." The driver's door was wrenched open and Nesbitt was dragged onto the roadside. He felt a thump on his head but before he could even cry out he found himself being lifted and frog-marched to the police car. Another smack and he was lying on the back seat of the vehicle, sprawled across the lap of a third traffic cop, who placed his arm firmly around Nesbitt's neck. He tried to kick out with his feet but they were already bound together and the door slammed shut. The car sped off with a shriek of rubber on tarmac.

Minutes later, the police car stopped. Nesbitt didn't dare to speak. Already, he'd been clubbed across the mouth for trying to converse with these animals. It was pitch black outside. He hadn't a clue where he was. Woodland somewhere. He could just make out the shadowy shapes of trees. They were going to top him. Of that he had little doubt. These coppers were actually going to see him off. He tried to tell them … what? He was gabbling. Incoherent. Senseless with fear. He was shitting himself. He was hauled roughly out of the car, lifted under his arms, propped upright, pushed forwards.

Nesbitt was knocked unconscious the moment his head hit the newly felled tree trunk. But his assailants had been instructed to make doubly sure their job was properly done. They put the boot in one after another, in perfect rhythm. One. Two. Three. Over and over again. Pounded his body to a pulp.

28

At least the black stripper moved with more finesse than her predecessors. They had reminded Hemp of two old bags lifted off the streets to perform for a couple of quid each. This one was better. Nice body too. Still, he was getting impatient. Usually he didn't mind being kept waiting but today he was a busy man. He looked at Furnace, whose eyes followed the rhythmical movements of the figure moving about on the stage. Hemp said petulantly, "It's been thirty minutes so far, Dave."

"What?" It was unusual for Hemp to show irritation, especially here of all places. Furnace was a lot calmer than his boss. But then it wasn't his head in a vice.

"We've been waiting for thirty minutes," Hemp said again. He looked away. His mind was on the load which was due in later that night. A load which represented just over a million in readies on the streets. But the buyers had postponed their collection until tomorrow. And he needed to get back and organise storage for twenty-four hours. Frankie would nail his head to the floor if it went wrong.

He walked up and down the bar, throwing disgusted glances at the heavy behind it, who was polishing glasses just like they did in the films. Waiting for Frankie went with the territory. Hemp knew that, but today, when he had matters to attend to, he didn't have the time to hang around for a briefing just because Frankie felt like giving one.

"Gents?" It was Lambesi. Neither of them had seen or heard him approaching. Hemp practically jumped out of his skin.

"Where'd you come from? Through the fucking floorboards?"

"Sorry, Bernie." Hemp's remark was exactly the type of thing that made Lambesi come unhinged. Especially since he'd come out of the nick. Lambesi had always been an unpredictable bastard. But nowadays he'd go off into orbit at the slightest provocation. Hemp and Furnace froze for a moment, waiting for Lambesi's response. It could easily be broken bones for both of them. But the white teeth flashed behind the sudden grin on Lambesi's face and they could breathe normally again. All was well. "Come on through, my friends. Frankie's ready for you." He beckoned for the visitors to follow him.

Frankie Richardson's office, as he liked to call it, was palatial. Paintings covered the walls. The heavy drapes were closed, as they always were. It was as though, thought Hemp, the infiltration of daylight would turn Frankie to dust. Frankie the vampire. It occurred to Hemp, not for the first time, that that wasn't a bad analogy. The only lights came from concealed strips on three of the four walls and from a few carefully positioned spots in the ceiling. The two suites of furniture were clearly made from the very finest rich brown leather. And the carpet? Well, neither of them could feel the carpet beneath their feet. It was like walking on air. They didn't step towards the massive teak desk, they glided towards it.

The big man was on the phone. "Frank, we can't have any more problems," he was saying. There was a pause. "Then you make sure you do. I've had Nesbitt seen to. The next time, he'll get a wooden box, Frank." Another pause. "Blade's a good man." And yet another. "If twenty-five grand doesn't do the trick with your man, he'll get the same as Nesbitt. Earn your money." And he hung up. Why bother to say goodbye? Frankie simply slammed the receiver down, before warmly welcoming his visitors.

"Bernie. Dave. Good to see you. Come and sit yourselves down. Sorry about the wait. Business, you see," explained Frankie. "There is always some little matter requiring attention." Hemp and Furnace felt like a pair of bookie's runners, brought in to be given their instructions about tomorrow's race card. "Tony, drinks for our friends."

As Lambesi went off towards the bar in the corner of the room, Frankie got straight down to business. "Now, Bernie. Tonight's delivery?"

"Sure, Frankie, we're ready." Hemp needed to look confident. He always made bloody sure he looked confident whenever he was in Frankie's presence. It didn't pay to look nervous or uncertain. "I'm going to meet it myself, as soon as we leave here." That was intentional. A hint to Frankie that he should pull his finger out and cut out the delaying tactics.

"And the buyers? Are they bringing their own sampler, Bernie?" Christ. Obviously Frankie knew there were problems. Hemp cleared his throat before answering.

"They always have their own, Frankie. The problem is ..."

"Problems don't exist in my business, Bernie," interrupted Richardson. "Will they be there tonight?" Christ. He knew they wouldn't be.

"No, Frankie. They can't come until tomorrow night."

"Why not?" Christ. The big man knew all the answers before he asked the questions. That was the problem with working for Frankie.

"We've got to store the dope for twenty-four hours." Hemp shrugged his shoulders and then accepted a large scotch off Lambesi. He was going to need it. "They've got problems their end, Frankie."

"So we store it." The big man was far from pleased. "But once only. As a sign of goodwill, Bernie. It won't be repeated. You tell them that. This is the only time. Make sure they understand." He pointed a fat finger at Hemp.

"The next time this happens, I'll deal with them direct. And then I'll deal with you, Bernie." Hemp nodded, relieved that Frankie hadn't thrown him out of the window there and then. "By the way, Bernie, Harry will be tied up for a little while. Had a run in with the law apparently."

"So I heard."

Richardson roared with laughter and the usual coughing fit followed. Everyone waited. "I'm sending you a replacement. Steve Blade. He's a good bloke. Look after him, Bernie. He's a strong man to have on our side." In other words, Bernie, fail me once more and I'm going to give you a new and permanent resting place on the bottom of the Thames.

PART FOUR

29

They walked down to the river and then strolled along the bank, away from the cathedral and the hundreds of tourists with their flashing cameras and out-of-control offspring. There was a bite in the air – summer had been short-lived and autumn was moving in fast – and the gravel made a satisfying crunch beneath each step. Priestley had known David Greswolde for years. Ever since he first joined the force and had been assigned to his department. Greswolde was a tall man, well over six foot, and he was still as slim as he had been when Priestley had first known him. In fact, there wasn't much about him that had changed, which made David Greswolde a rarity. Usually, when someone like him reached the dizzy heights, they suddenly developed a falsely cultured set of manners and a new accent. Came up with all sorts of airs and graces. Not Greswolde. He was unscathed by his elevation to the top echelons of the police service. The country yokel's twang remained intact and his feet were planted firmly on the ground.

"Worcester is a beautiful city, Jack," he said. "Being able to live in this place is probably one of the main reasons I've stayed here for so long."

"So the promotions didn't influence you in any way at all?" quipped Priestley. "They certainly couldn't have done you any harm." David Greswolde had recently been appointed the deputy chief constable for the force that neighboured Priestley's own, beating off tough competition to become one of the highest ranking officers in the land.

"Oh, I don't know," Greswolde responded wryly, and then glanced at Priestley, a broad smile splitting his face in two. "It's been a long time, Jack."

"Sure has. It's got to be ten or eleven years."

"That long?" Greswolde shrugged. How fast time flies. "I suppose so." He grabbed Jack's arm. "Hey, remember the time you saved my neck, Jack? In the Piccadilly Club? The geezer with the chair? He'd have turned my head into a ravine if you hadn't been there, Jack." Priestley looked away. He didn't enjoy dealing with other people's gratitude or raking over past exploits. And he was anxious to get on. Fortunately, David Greswolde had sufficient subtlety to understand this and asked, "So, how can I help you, Jack? What's on your mind?"

"I'm after some advice really, David." And Priestley related everything he knew and everything that had happened. Greswolde listened intently as the sorry tale unfolded. Priestley concluded with the cash payment sitting in his bank account.

"Where's the money now, Jack?"

"Still there. I haven't touched it. I have a barrister friend and she's prepared an affidavit for me, stating that I have no knowledge whatsoever about the money."

Greswolde frowned. "Don't you think you should inform your chief about all this?"

"Yes. No. Probably," Priestley blustered. He stopped and took a deep breath. "David, I'm confused. I don't mind admitting, I'm frightened as well. This is heavy shit. But it's all supposition. I've no real evidence and Private Gardiner is my only witness. Everything could be coincidental. I don't think for a moment it is but I'd look a complete prat if I blurted my mouth off to the chief, and it all turned out to be nonsense."

"And you think you look less of a prat talking to me?" Greswolde smiled.

"Okay. Okay. But what have I got to go on really?"

"What about this man Blade? Might he be a good witness?"

"I thought he might be but he's disappeared. He was released from Gartree a few days ago and the first thing he did was push a glass into Harry Nesbitt's face. And now he's vanished. I think he may have bolted and gone to London."

"Why do you think that?"

"Frankie Richardson. He offered him a job while they were inside."

"Ah." Greswolde paused while he thought about this, and then said, "So you think he may have changed his mind about becoming an informant?"

"Probably." Priestley stopped walking and turned his back to some children who were feeding bread to a group of ducks. "I'm at my wit's end. That's the only reason I'm here with you now, David, I just don't know what to do. I've even thought about getting out. The alternative is to investigate this lot myself. After all, I'm not accountable to my own force any more since the RCS is Home Office governed."

Greswolde took his arm and they continued their stroll. "I know that." It was obvious he was giving the matter some serious thought. "But why don't you? Investigate it yourself, I mean. But look, I want you to think about making a statement to someone in my complaints department. Just to cover your own back." Greswolde stopped. He picked up a stone and examined it briefly before slinging it across the water. You don't see many chiefs of police doing that, thought Priestley. "At least it will give you some insurance, Jack. My main concern, and I'm sure it's yours, is that these bastards might be setting you up, Jack. A statement now will protect you."

"And what happens to the statement?" asked Priestley.

"There will be a time, when we shall have to disclose it to your own chief constable, Jack. But for the time being, I'll keep it in my safe. Let's take it one step at a time and do what's necessary to protect your back, Jack. First things first."

* * * * *

When they parted, Priestley felt calmer than he had in months. At least he'd been able to share his concerns with somebody and he felt that that would give him the strength to carry on with his own discrete enquiries. He thought back to the good old days when he first joined up. Complications like these didn't exist then. Coppering was a respectable profession. It hadn't been tainted with all the shit he'd been learning about recently. Briefly he wondered about putting a team of specially selected covert blokes together and giving them the job of following these goons until there was enough evidence to get rid of them, but his mobile interrupted his thoughts before they had a chance to crystallise.

"Jack?" Why did everybody who rang him always ask if it was him on the other end?

"Yes, Carol? How's my favourite reporter."

"Cut the crap, Jack. You're not funny." Obviously this was strictly a business call. "We've heard a rumour that the Drug Squad office has been burgled. Any truth in it?"

"What?" Priestley was incredulous. What Carol had just told him was impossible.

"We haven't had it confirmed yet, because they're 'no commenting' us, but apparently it was broken into last night."

* * * * *

His foot was almost though the floorboards all the way back to the office. The Drug Squad office screwed? That couldn't be. The place was constructed like Fort Knox. He remembered the alarm system on the drugs vault and, for Chrissake, it was right in the middle of the nick. Impossible. Or was it?

"Apparently so," said Barton. "Somebody tied the security bloke up and cut the alarm system's wires."

"How?" asked Priestley.

"According to the lad who spoke to us this morning, they just walked in, did the business on the guard and then emptied the vault. Brazen as anything."

"Emptied it?" Priestley couldn't believe what he was hearing. "How much?"

"Well, I don't think it was actually emptied," Barton corrected himself. "But there was a load of coke and heroin that went apparently. Jim Nolan's doing the inquiry."

"I bet he is."

Barton was just turning to leave, when he stopped and said, "Oh, and Boss? Did you hear what happened to your pal Harry Nesbitt last night?"

Priestley looked up from the briefing document he'd just selected from his overflowing in-tray. "No. What?"

"He was found out at Greenacre Wood this morning. Beaten to a pulp."

"You're kidding! Is he dead?"

"Not quite. He's in a bad way though, but apparently they expect him to pull through. I should think he'll be out of action for a while. I mean, he's only just had his face glued back together after that glassing."

"Do we know who did it?"

"Not yet. He's in no shape to do any talking at the moment."

"Fall out amongst villains do think?" he said. "Keep an eye on him, Chris."

* * * * *

Meanwhile, back at his desk in Worcester, David Greswolde had summoned one of his most trusted aids on the telephone. "Simon, I want to you check out a man called Steven Blade. He's just been released from Gartree. Only a few days ago. He's probably now in London. Find out as much as you can. I want to know everything. And then I want to meet him. See what you can do. Make this a priority. Do it as quickly as you can. Report to me in two days."

30

"You wanker. You're not paid to think." Nolan was outraged, like a bull shown a red flag. "Do you realise the shit you and your little group of bandoleers have landed us in? If the press get hold of this we'll all be ducking and diving 'til the cows come home."

Boyle's face was white. Not from fear, but because he was furious. He thought he'd done the right thing. "Priestley isn't going to take that twenty-five grand off of Frankie."

Nolan stood up, towering over the junior rank. "Don't change the subject." He paused to give himself a chance to regain control over his voice. It wouldn't do to be overheard. In a quieter voice, he continued. "Well anyway, you jerk, he hasn't put it into me yet. So what does that tell you?"

But Boyle didn't believe that Priestley could be bought so easily. He and his boss could argue it out until they were both blue in the face and never agree. So he switched back to the original topic. "Listen, Boss, if we'd had an audit on that vault they'd have found out there was about ten kilos missing. It was noted in the books but we wouldn't be able to account for it. That's a lot of smack."

"So now we've got an internal investigation on top of us instead." Nolan understood the detective sergeant's reasoning, but he was still angry that Boyle hadn't bothered to consult him before going ahead with the dummy burglary.

"But you're doing the investigation so that doesn't signify. Anyway, there's another problem we need to consider."

Nolan had been just about to sit back down but decided to remain standing while the next pearler was delivered. "Go on."

"Steve Blade."

"What about him?"

"He's tied up with Jack Priestley."

"Bollocks. Priestley locked him up."

"He might have done." Boyle was cocky now. "But he's still close to him. Priestley used to visit him regularly when he was inside. And now Frankie's recruited him onto our team."

Nolan stared at him while he considered the situation. "I'm not sure. An armed robber isn't Jack Priestley's cup of tea. For heaven's sake, he's been locking them up for most of his life." Boyle gave up. There was nothing he could do about it anyway. Once the big man had decided Blade would come on side, that was it. Nobody argued with Frankie. Still, he was more than a little reassured when Nolan finished, "Keep an eye on him, Colin. If we see him hand in hand with Priestley, I'll ring London."

* * * * *

Priestley drove onto the pub car park and swore quietly under his breath. It was full. He'd have to park somewhere else. In the past this had always been a nice quiet country pub. But it was some time since his last visit. Obviously things had changed. The world had moved on at the White Elephant. In fact, the last time he came here, he'd met the same man as he was meeting today. Jamie Bunting. The best undercover cop in the country. He was a Met. officer who not only did live operations but who also organised the training of other agents from other forces. Priestley had known him for a number of years. There had always been a great deal of mutual respect between them. They'd both drunk themselves silly in this very pub after Bunting was awarded the British Empire Medal for selling a container full of armaments to the IRA. The result was a major coup for the British Army and the IRA's control and command were out of action for months.

Priestley scanned the bar cautiously when he eventually entered. The boozer was packed to the brim. Still, he spotted Bunting waving at him from the other side of the room where he'd managed to find a corner table.

"So, how's life, Jack?" Bunting took the first gulp from his pint of best bitter.

"Not good, Jamie. Not at the moment anyway."

"No doubt that's why you belled me after all this time."

"I've got a small problem, Jamie. I need a covert to go into a drugs team up my way, but there's bent law in there as well."

Bunting sighed and nodded. He wasn't surprised. "Most of the jobs I'm involved in these days have an element of corruption attached to them. Sign of the times I'm afraid, mate. So. You want one of my boys to help you out?"

"I was thinking more in terms of yourself, Jamie?"

"Couldn't do it mate. I've too much on as it is. But I can give you a good lad. Or lassie. Which is it to be?"

The suggestion took Priestley by surprise. He hadn't considered using a female covert for this job, although he'd used them in the past and they had always been very good. He pondered for a moment and then decided. "No, I think it has to be a bloke. A bloke would have more credibility with this lot. He'd have to be well up on the drugs scene."

"Obviously. Okay. When do you want him?"

"Soon as possible. Oh. And one other thing. Frankie Richardson."

Bunting raised his eyebrows. "Mad Frankie Richardson? Involved is he?"

"Yeah. He's running the sham from a distance."

"And so you need somebody who hasn't been connected with him?" said Bunting, anticipating Priestley's next request.

"Fine. So when do you really want this superstar of mine?"

Priestley lifted the his pint mug to his mouth and peered at Bunting through the chunky glass. "Tomorrow?"

Bunting choked into his own glass as he burst out laughing. "Haven't changed at all have you, Jack?"

* * * * *

Steve Blade left the meeting a happier man. One or two things that had been bothering him since he came out of Gartree had been explained. And all he had to do was follow his instructions and he'd be looked after. He knew that he couldn't take another stretch inside and the arrangement he'd just made guaranteed he'd never be locked up again.

His first task was to regain Jack Priestley's trust.

31

The Carpenters Arms was a quiet, businessmen's pub near to the city centre and, as far as they were both concerned, a safe one. They hadn't seen one another since the last time at Gartree. A lot had happened since then and Blade knew that Priestley believed he had reneged on the deal they'd made. He knew it was going to be hard work convincing Priestley he hadn't and that he still wanted to be his informant.

"So come on, Steve, let's have it," said Priestley. "How many more acts of madness are you going to drop on me before I have to lock you up again? Or was that just a one off?" he said, referring to the glassing of Nesbitt's face. "To make sure everybody in the bloody police force knew you'd come home?"

"You're still an expert at taking the piss, Jack." Blade's grin cracked his face in two as he tried to make light of the situation.

"And what about the three so-called coppers who put Nesbitt back in the hospital?"

"Alive, isn't he?"

"No thanks to you," Priestley retorted bitterly.

The comment stung Blade and he sucked in a sharp breath as he bit down on his tongue. He mustn't allow Priestley to bait him. He had a job to do. "It wasn't me that did that, Jack. You have my word."

"What good's that to me, Steve. Your words aren't worth the breath you use to make them."

Blade studied the half-empty pint glass on the table in front of him. "Look," he said. "I know you think I've let you down, Jack. But I've got some plans, Jack. And I need your help." Blade wanted to enter the ballpark with Priestley backing him. He made a quick decision to take Priestley into his confidence; maybe that would help his cause. "But first I've got a few domestics to sort out."

"Nesbitt?"

"No, I've told you." He paused. "Well, yes and no. Not Nesbitt directly."

"Sammy?"

Blade nodded. "She's pregnant, Jack."

"Well there's a thing." Priestley folded his arms and sat back from the table. "No chance of it being yours then." It was a statement, not a question.

"Not unless one of the Lord's Angels spirited me out of the nick, no."

"So it's Nesbitt's then?" Blade shrugged his shoulders and Priestley continued. "So, what's on your mind?"

"What's on my mind?" Blade raised his voice. "What do you think is on my frigging mind, Jack? You certainly aren't backward when it comes to behaving like a prize prat are you. How would you feel if your missus told you she'd been babbied by some other jerk?"

"I mean, what do you intend to do?" Good, thought Blade, it's working – Priestley sounded almost apologetic.

"Well. We've discussed it and I've made a decision." He paused and Priestley watched him with amazement written all over his face. "I've made a decision to stay with her and we'll bring the babbie up as our own."

"Well done." An embarrassed Priestley had to cough to clear his throat. "Yes, well done. You obviously know what you're doing."

"But that's not what I wanted to see you about, Jack."

"It isn't?" Priestley's face was still pink with embarrassment.

"No. I don't want to go back inside, Jack. And with the baby coming and everything, I've got commitments." Blade sounded almost proud.

"You don't have to. Nobody forced you to take out that post office van the last time, did they?" said Priestley sarcastically.

"Okay. That's true," Blade conceded. "But remember Frankie Richardson, Jack?" Priestley nodded. He wasn't saying anything. "Well, he's offered me a job."

"Taken it?"

"Yes. But I want to go in there working for you. Did you know he's got half your bloody force sewn up?"

"I've got my suspicions," Priestley responded guardedly.

"So. What's the starting price, Jack?"

"That's all according to what you give me, Steve. I'm sure we can work something out. Are you certain you're game for this?"

"I don't want to go back inside, Jack," Blade repeated.

"So you keep saying." Priestley looked hard at Blade. He wondered if he could trust him. He decided to take a punt. It was always risky, dealing with informants, in any case. Blade would be no different in that respect. You could never guarantee the truthfulness of what they told you. "Okay, Steve," he said. "Let's take it one step at a time."

Blade handed him a piece of paper with a list of names written on it. "How about this for starters? They're the local branch of the firm and deal with the hard stuff."

"Heroin?"

Blade nodded. "And amphetamines too."

"Okay," said Priestley and studied the list of names – bent coppers and criminals; they were all familiar to Priestley, so at least Blade's first piece of information appeared to be true and confirmed what he already suspected – while Blade continued.

"The main man is Bernie Hemp, but the team's well supported. In particular by bent coppers."

Priestley nodded, resisting the temptation to tell him everything he already knew. "So how do you want to play it?"

"Well, Frankie's put me on Hemp's team. I'd like to take one of yours in with me. Undercover. But he'll have to be a diamond, Jack. A real diamond. I don't want any over-excited wanker coming in there with me and spoiling it for all of us." That ought to convince him that I'm on his side, he thought.

32

Dave Curtis had a swarthy complexion with Latino features. He wore his dark hair at shoulder length and he always seemed to have a two day growth of stubble. He was casually dressed in a red-and-black checked shirt and a blue denim waistcoat which matched his jeans. Priestley had never worked with him before, but Bunting had assured him that Curtis was one of the best he had. His pseudonym was Sparky and he was going to be working with Blade to infiltrate Hemp's ring. They'd both been carefully briefed and now it was time for the trickiest, and certainly the most dangerous, part of the operation to begin.

There were only a few bodies inside the snooker hall and that suited Blade. So far as he was concerned, the fewer people that saw them together, the better. Introducing the new boy to the group was going to be difficult enough as it was without an army of spectators. Especially since Blade himself was a newcomer, even if he did have Frankie's full backing. As they pushed their way through the swing doors the irony of the situation was not lost on Blade. Only a few weeks ago he would have laughed at the thought of working with the filth and now here he was entering the very heartland of Bernie Hemp's organisation with one on his arm.

The man standing behind the bar must have weighed at least thirty stone. He had a long, black beard and a cigarette permanently stitched to his bottom lip. He greeted Blade with a deeply hoarse voice. "Nice to see you, Bladey."

"You too, Shovel. Bernie here?" The big man nodded towards the far corner of the room. And there he sat, Frankie's mimic, flanked by a pair of minders, at one of the little round tables that edged the hall. As they headed over, weaving between the dozens of snooker tables, Sparky asked how Shovel had got his name. Blade's answer was simple enough. "Because whenever he throws anybody out of here, they need a shovel to get them off the street afterwards."

As they crossed the room towards Hemp's table, Sparky scanned the faces and recognised some that were already familiar to him from the photographs Priestley had shown him during their briefing sessions: the man himself, Bernie Hemp, his assistant, Dave Furnace, and one Mickey Rambling.

Hemp greeted Blade with the flimsiest of handshakes. It always pissed him off when Frankie dumped one of his boys on him. Understandable really. Hemp liked to surround himself with his own people and didn't like having Frankie's spies around. "Sit down, Stevie boy. Good to see you," he lied. "Who's your friend?"

Blade introduced Sparky as a fellow ex-con who'd been a mate for years "Sparky! What kind of a name is that?" Hemp laughed.

"Used to be an electrician," responded Sparky, using a convincing cockney accent.

Hemp stopped laughing as abruptly as he'd begun and addressed Blade sharply. "Why's he here? Frankie told me you were coming into the firm. But he didn't mention two of you."

"Then he must be losing his memory in his old age, Bernie."

Unconvinced, Hemp turned his attention back to Sparky. "Sparky who?"

"You couldn't pronounce it if I told you."

"Try me."

"Ferenchino. It's Italian. Michael Roberto Ferenchino. Sparky."

"Where have I seen you before?" asked Hemp. Both Sparky and Blade knew that he would stand or fall depending on his answers to Hemp's questions. The whole scam depended upon the outcome of the next few minutes. Sparky would either get it right, and be accepted into the group, or get it wrong, and then things would get a little dangerous for both of them.

"You haven't." Sparky tried to sound cocky. "Unless you've worked on merchant ships, or done a stretch in Gartree."

"I've been in Gartree. When were you there?"

Sparky knew that was a lie. Priestley and Barton had checked Hemp out and Sparky knew from his briefing notes that Hemp had never served any of his three custodial sentences in Gartree. But he had to play along with the game. "Eighty eight to ninety two."

"What for?"

"That's my business." Still cocky.

"He isn't a paedophile, Bernie," Blade interrupted. He shrugged, "He gets a bit sensitive when the questions get too personal."

"Does he now?" replied Hemp, still staring at Sparky. "What wing were you on?"

"D for dogs."

"Near the old rehabilitation unit?"

Another lie. Nice try, Bernie, thought Sparky. Still, he continued playing. "There wasn't one when I was there."

"Who was the chief screw?"

"Foster." Any name would have done the trick because Hemp didn't have a clue. But Sparky had done his work well and Leslie Foster was the chief screw at Gartree during the time they were discussing. "Who was the chief screw when you were there, Bernie?" Sparky remained cocky. It was going well.

"Okay. That's enough," Hemp decided. He smiled and shook Sparky's hand. He'd successfully navigated his way through the first minefield. But that wouldn't be the end of the examination. Inevitably there would be more to come.

Hemp turned his attention back to Blade. "So how's things going with you, Steve?" he asked.

"I'm in the pink, Bernie, but I need work. So does he," he replied, indicating Sparky with a jerk of his head.

"Well it's lucky for you Harry Nesbitt's in hospital then, isn't it?" Hemp said sarcastically. Blade wondered if Hemp thought he was responsible for setting Harry up with Frankie. If so, that was bad news. It never went down well amongst the criminal fraternity for one criminal to set up another.

He tried to sound non-committal. "Life's a bitch," he said, shrugging his shoulders.

Mickey Rambling had wandered over to join the company. He'd been listening in on the conversation for a while and suddenly spoke up, directing his words at Sparky, "How's things with you, filth." The accusation took Blade completely by surprise. But not Sparky. Like the true professional he was, he'd been expecting it. He looked at Mickey but said nothing. Mickey picked up a glass from the table, emptied it, then replaced it amongst the muddle of ashtrays, bottles and half-full glasses. "You can smell them a mile off," he continued. "Trying it on with us are you, filth?"

"You talking to me?" Sparky said, his face expressionless, his eyes icy, and his voice calmly controlled.

"No, copper, I'm talking at you." Mickey was pushing it; quite deliberately. "You see, you don't need no warrant card for us. We can see right through you." Mickey sniggered. "What do you think we are? A bunch of green backs?"

"My name is Ferenchino. It's Italian. What's yours?"

"Fuck off, filth. You already know it. I bet you know what we all had for breakfast."

Sparky shook his head. "I couldn't give a fuck what you had for breakfast," he said. He knew that this was his opportunity to make it. He slowly picked up a glass from the table. The same one Mickey had just put down. Assuming that he was about to have the glass shoved in his face, Mickey stepped towards him, ready to grab his wrist. Nobody saw Sparky's leg move. Nobody saw him kick Mickey in the groin. The first they knew was that Mickey was folded double, groaning in agony on the floor. Then they saw the knife glinting in Sparky's hand. The blade pressed firmly on Mickey's throat. Hemp's eyes were out on stalks. "Next time you fancy your chances, dickless," Sparky hissed, leaning over his victim, marking his Adam's apple with a thin red line, "go and bully some other little shit. The next time, I'll break your skin and everything beneath it." Hemp was very impressed. He smiled at Sparky. He was exactly his type of man. Just the sort of person he wanted on his team. The knife disappeared as Sparky straightened up. There was fire in his eyes. He turned to Blade and said, "I don't like your friends." He turned to Hemp. "You can shove your job." Hemp's face fell as Sparky swung around and walked briskly towards the exit.

"For Christ's sake, Bernie," pleaded Blade, running after Sparky, past Shovel and out into the street. He caught up with him on the corner and tugged at his arm. "What the hell was all that about?"

"Part of the game plan," Sparky whispered and walked away again, leaving Blade speechless and confused in the street. But Sparky had only gone a few paces before Hemp called him back. Bernie stood in the shadows of the doorway to the snooker hall, as if afraid of the daylight. "Steve," he said. "He seems good to me." But then he had to because if any news of this crap got back to Frankie, there would be hell to pay.

"He's Italian, Bernie," Blade explained. "Always a short fuse with them High Ties, you know? He's always been a bit touchy, especially since the filth had him over with one of them undercover bastards."

"Sure, Steve." Hemp was well convinced. "There's no problem. He's welcome. Let's not let this get back to Frankie though, eh Steve?"

"No probs, Bernie," Blade smiled. That suited him just fine. There was no way he wanted Frankie hearing that he'd brought Sparky on board. Not for the moment anyway.

"If you're happy, Steve, I'll fix up a few meets and make sure both of you get involved. Okay?" Blade liked this. It was as though Hemp were pleading with him. He couldn't believe the way things had turned out.

He shrugged again. "Okay," he said coolly, in an I-can-take-it-or-leave-it kind of way. Then he and Sparky walked away. The first part of the job had been a triumph. But now the real work would start. They'd managed to get in. Now they had to make sure they stayed there.

33

It was a bright, sunny morning. An unseasonable early frost lay on the ground and there was an icy chill in the air. Priestley shivered. He'd forgotten his overcoat. Beside him George Cummings was better prepared for the northerly wind and well wrapped up in a jacket and scarf. They could already see Dave Curtis waiting for them on the other side of the lake. He had a bag in his hand and was throwing scraps of bread for the ducks to feed on.

It was too chilly to sit, so when they met up the three men paced slowly around the lake, their breath smoking into the air. Both Curtis and Cummings had worked for Jamie Bunting for a number of years, and both were highly skilled operatives. Curtis, being the older and more experienced and senior of the two, opened the briefing. He described the several meetings he'd had with Hemp and his cronies during the past couple of weeks. He said he was confident that he had been accepted into the fold. "It's early days yet, but I don't think I'll have much trouble bringing in Georgie here."

The words were reassuring to Priestley. He was anxious to press on and felt that they should move on to the next stage of his plan as fast as was safely possible. If it was feasible to bring in Cummings now, then he wanted to move ahead with all sensible haste. "Any scum showed up yet, Dave?" he asked. It was refreshing for Priestley to be able to talk to someone he felt he could trust.

"You mean bent law? No, no mention yet. Absolutely nothing."

"What about Richardson?"

He shook his head. "Nothing."

"And you're sure it's safe to bring in George now?"

"Yeah. I'm safe now to introduce another."

"Okay," Priestley nodded. He was pleased with the way things were going. It was a relief. More than anything, he wanted this over with. He turned to address Cummings. "I want you in there to back Dave. As a novice. Somebody who's just coming into the game, but who has money to burn. We need to move it on, now. If we can get a meet on with Hemp, through you Dave, and then make an offer – in time for the next delivery – that should put us in the pound seats. But I'm also after habits, places, meetings. You know the sort of stuff. And most importantly I need to be able to connect this team with bent coppers."

Both men nodded. They'd heard all this before and were well aware of the objectives. "I can get a first meeting on with George easily enough," said Curtis. "But he'll need to flash a lot of green stuff around to get the kind of credibility we're after."

Priestley showed no hesitation. "Ten grand? Real money. Is that enough?"

"It's enough," Curtis agreed.

"Okay. I'll leave it to you two to make the necessary arrangements."

* * * * *

Faces in oils stared down at them as they made their way up the stairs towards the top floor of the art museum. Former lord mayors and aldermen, hanging from the walls, watched over them as they passed underneath. The smell of beeswax lingered until they reached the restaurant, to be replaced by the stench of stale cooking oil. Hemp was waiting for them in his usual place – any corner table that gave him a facing view of the entrance. He had another man with him who wasn't known to either of the police officers.

"This is Arnie Stevens, Bernie." Curtis introduced Cummings. George Cummings was dressed for the occasion. Smart but casual. A man with money to spend. And no idea how to do it. "The geezer I told you about." Hemp smiled, while his associate, obviously an employee, looked like he had a broom handle stuck up his arse. Clearly he was there to protect his boss. And when he was instructed to fetch coffee, he obeyed without hesitation.

"So, you're interested in doing a deal?" said Hemp carefully. He had always been a cautious man. That's why he'd survived in this business so far. It was a game where a suspicious mind was far more useful than a clever one.

"That's all according to what's on offer," replied Cummings. Hemp watched his face closely. He looked cool enough. But it was obvious he wasn't carrying. Hemp had already scanned his experienced eyes over him.

"Well now." Hemp was still smiling. "As I understand it, you've come here to talk to me. So talk."

"I'm here to test the water, as it were." Cummings lifted his shoulders and spread the open palms of both his hands in a business-like gesture. "I want to know how much and how good it is."

Hemp stared at him. Curtis remained silent too. Past experience had taught him that it was usually best to leave the negotiations to the dealer and the 'novice'. Eventually the coffee arrived and then it was Hemp who took up the conversation again. "Okay." Hemp leaned forward. "What's your limit?" The question had come too soon, thought Sparky. Hemp's still suspicious.

"A hundred grand," replied Cummings without any hesitation, and his words certainly made their intended impact. The expression on Hemp's face seemed to be transfixed.

The dealer picked up the spoon from his saucer, dipped it in his cup, and then started to dribble coffee onto the table, as though dripping paint onto a canvas. "And how would you like the gear delivered?" he asked. His eyes didn't leave the apparition being created on the Formica tabletop. Careful, Georgie, thought Curtis.

"By canal barge." Again, there was no hesitation from Cummings, and this time Hemp's response was even more pronounced. He immediately switched his attention away from the tabletop and back to his visitor, eyebrows raised in surprise. But he didn't have to ask his next question because Cummings continued. "Tourist barges in Gas Street Basin. I own a few. There's no law down there. And in the middle of the night, no people."

Hemp burst out into laughing. "Mr Barge-man, I think you're taking the piss."

If this happened, they'd agreed that Cummings would stand up to leave. "Thanks for the coffee," he said sarcastically. Then, searching in his jacket pocket, he produced a thick roll of notes. Hemp calculated about ten or fifteen grand. Cummings threw them down on the table. "For your time," he said. "If you ever want to talk serious business, you can reach me through Sparky here." And abruptly he turned and left. Curtis followed him out. Hemp grinned broadly as he watched the two police officers leave. Then he reached for his mobile phone.

* * * * *

"Come on then partner, lighten my load." Curtis kept his voice low as they headed back down the staircase.

"He's hooked," said Cummings.

"Really? Now there's a surprise."

"No. Really. He's well and truly hooked." Cummings glanced at his colleague, a smirk on his face stretched from ear to ear. "Just you wait and see."

They soon reached the exit and walked down the short flight of stone steps onto the street. An elderly woman brushed past them, knocking into Cummings, and placing a bundle of newspaper into his hands. Then she disappeared as suddenly as she'd appeared, into the crowds of people milling around outside the museum. She could have been a ghost. Cummings unwrapped the parcel. It contained a small, clear-plastic sachet containing white power. He flashed it at Curtis. "Told you," he said. "He's hooked."

Just then, Curtis' mobile rang. A voice said, "Sparky, that was a gift from your Uncle Bernie. Your man has two days to come back."

34

Shovel didn't look his usual happy self. His face wore a stern expression as he glared at Curtis and Cummings, alias Sparky and Arnie, as they passed him, heading towards the little group in the corner. They were greeted by none other than Frankie Richardson, the chairman of the organisation. "Glad you could make it my friends," he said in a jovial voice. Bernie sat on his right. Behind him stood a couple of tough looking faces. Obviously minders. Various members of Bernie's team were occupying themselves on snooker tables in other parts of the room. The atmosphere was completely changed from the last time Curtis had been here. Then you couldn't exactly call it welcoming, but now it was downright threatening. From the bulges in the men's jackets it was clear that the big man had brought some heavy cover with him. There was no sign of Steve Blade.

"Am I supposed to know this man?" Cummings sounded as cool as ever as he addressed his question to Curtis.

"Of course Detective Curtis knows me," said Frankie. "But I'm not so sure who you are, my friend. Not yet." This was the moment all undercover officers feared. Being named. And Dave Curtis was no exception. He'd never been caught out before and had always worked in the hope that it wouldn't happen. But it had now. Unfortunately, Curtis had never decided what action he would take if he was compromised in this way. All he knew was that all his training and experience would now have to be unmercifully tapped into if he was to get out of the shit in one piece. "You mustn't even think about offering us a repeat performance of the first time you came here," continued Frankie. "But you are Detective Constable David Curtis of the Regional Crime Squad. And you do work for Detective Chief Inspector Jack Priestley." It was no consolation that he'd got at least some of that wrong. Obviously, whoever his informant was didn't know that he was a Metropolitan officer. "Don't you?" Frankie carried on when Curtis remained silent. "You've already had one of my men over." Obviously, Frankie was referring to Steve Blade, thought Curtis. The question was, was Blade working for Priestley, as Blade had led them to believe, or had he been working for Frankie all along? "Perhaps this gentleman too," Frankie finished, nodding in Cummings' direction.

A wave of optimism swept through Cummings. It certainly sounded as though he might still be running. He had to think up a feasible story quickly. Foolishly, perhaps, they hadn't planned for this eventuality. They'd figured if either of them was going to be exposed it would be him, rather than Curtis, who had appeared to be well in with the group. So he needed a believable explanation as fast as he could come up with one. Because, as sure as eggs are eggs, Big Frankie had topped more people than he could remember, and if he didn't think smartly he would be joining the forgotten many.

Curtis, too, had to remain calm whatever happened now. He also knew that his life was on the line. He spoke, and he knew as he did so, that his voice was giving him away, perhaps for the first time in his career as an undercover operative. "I don't know you and I don't know what you're talking about. Every time I come in here, I'm accused of being the filth." He knew he was finished. Excommunicated. Fucked from a great height. He could see there was no way out of this one. Clearly, Frankie had taken the time to do his homework. Curtis wondered what the penalty would be.

Bullet in the back? Swim in the canal in a pair of concrete overshoes? Or perhaps just a fractured skull to top up a few other broken bones? He glanced over his shoulder and saw the barricade across the exit in the form of Shovel and a man he recognised from the photographs as Tony Lambesi. Lambesi seemed to have appeared from nowhere.

Frankie waved his chubby hand dismissively. "I'm not interested in you or your damned lies, little man. You will leave now. Quietly. Alternatively, you can be carried out. You choose." Curtis knew he only had the one option. Offered what appeared to be a lifeline, he turned and walked away, taking care not to look at his partner. Lambesi opened the door for him and spat into his face as he passed. On any other occasion. At any other time. At any other place. And Curtis would have buried the gofer.

Once outside, Curtis realised his stars had come down from the heavens all at once and rescued him. That should have been very nasty. He exhaled violently and felt his body begin to shake. What the hell had just happened? Why? How? Who? When? And what about Cummings?

* * * * *

"I'm Frankie Richardson," the big man said. "I'm not from these parts, but I'm interested in knowing who you are, Mr Stevens?"

"Arnie. Arnie Stevens," Cummings said, pulling a chair from beneath the table, intending to sit down and join the company. He hoped he was getting through this okay. But he wasn't. He'd read it all wrong. At a signal from Frankie, two clowns grabbed his arms and frogmarched him across the room and up a flight of wooden stairs to a room on the upper level. He found himself sitting in what looked like a function room, although judging by the layers of dust everywhere it hadn't been used for that purpose for many years. Clearly it was time for heavy questions and answers, and Cummings knew he should expect the worst.

His two heavy escorts began their enquiries into his past. At least they were talking to him, he thought. At least they seemed to be undecided about him. Otherwise he'd probably be in a box ready to be packed away six foot under by now.

They asked him for his contacts in the drugs business. He provided them with the names of two known suppliers who he had genuinely dealt with in previous operations. They'd never got to know his true identity and he'd kept their identities to himself. Waiting for just such a crisis as this.

Finally, they appeared to be satisfied, and Cummings was reunited downstairs in the hall with Frankie and Hemp.

"So, how can we help you, Arnie?" asked the East Ender.

Now it was time for Arnie to act out the role of his life. It might actually be working. He might actually be able to rescue the situation and set up the bust despite everything that had just happened. Still, he must be very, very cautious and tread very, very carefully. His life might still be hanging by a thread. Blowing in the wind of Frankie's famous unpredictability. "Look Mr Richardson," he said. "I don't know nothing about that man, Sparky. I still can't believe he's the filth."

"What did you do with the sample you were given the other day?" asked Hemp, ignoring him.

"Tested it. It was okay. That's why I'm back for more." He realised he'd have to qualify that last statement. "I'm a businessman and can't afford any shit. There's been too many problems with tabs lately and the filth have been all over the place. That's why I'm interested in the other stuff."

"Have you dealt with Sparky before?" Again it was Hemp who was asking the question.

To negative the query would be too simple and possibly dangerous. So Cummings decided to complicate the issues a little. "Once before. But I didn't get anywhere. The bastard promised to deliver a load to me but then told me the law had intervened and blown him out. This deal was supposed to have made up for that balls-up."

"So you lost out?" Hemp asked. "By how much?"

"I parted with ten grand." He was doing all right. The answers were coming out of him like guided missiles.

"And you never saw that again?" Still Hemp.

"No. He was going to pay it back to me. After this job."

"I understand that you've got a hundred grand to invest?" Frankie now took over from Hemp.

Arnie's confidence was restored. He sat back, more relaxed, and said, "More, if it's good."

"You're not on your own in this, Mr Stevens, are you?" Frankie was testing him again.

"No, I'm not." It wouldn't be plausible to say that he was. Cummings knew that the next question might be the real bastard. The one which would decide his fate. He had to appear genuine. But if they asked for the identities of his supposed business partners, he'd have to refuse. And then pray.

There was a short period of silence, while Frankie studied Cummings and thought over all he'd heard and seen. Then, in a quiet voice, he surprised everyone. Most of all Cummings. "You know Spaghetti Junction, my friend?" A nod in reply was all Cummings needed to give him. Who didn't know it? "Be on the bench at the side of the canal at three o'clock tomorrow afternoon. The bench overlooks the reservoir next to the canal. I want the hundred grand wrapped in newspaper and placed in the rubbish bin next to the bench. You must put it in there at exactly three o'clock. Savvy?" Cummings nodded again. "Then you will wait for ten minutes. The deal will be delivered, my friend, once the money is in the bin. Savvy?"

Still playing his undercover role to the letter, Cummings overdid it. "There are one or two observations I'd like to make ..." He began, but was forced to stop as the East Ender grabbed his throat, squeezing tightly, and shouted, "There are no observations for you to make, my friend. It is for me to decide the arrangements. And you now have them. Is that understood? No money tomorrow, no life for you, my friend. Is that understood?"

"Perfectly," Cummings coughed and the vice-like grip was released.

"If no one has approached you during the ten minutes after you've put the money in the bin," Frankie continued, "then take your money with you and return on Friday. Same time. Is that understood?"

"It's a lot of money to carry," said Cummings, pushing it again. "I'll have two minders with me," he said, rubbing his throat.

Frankie had relaxed back into his chair and nodded his head in agreement. "I would do the same, Mr Stevens," he said. "It's good to do business with you. Let's hope this is the first of many occasions."

As Cummings was escorted from the building, he heard Frankie instruct Hemp, "Okay, tosspot. Make sure Bladey gets his two grand." And that was all he needed to know about who was responsible for blowing his partner's cover.

35

Later that evening the Regional Crime Squad offices were buzzing with Priestley's people – running to and fro preparing for the following day's operation. Priestley's anger was evident to everyone who rubbed shoulders with him. He was furious that Frankie had discovered Sparky's identity. He slammed his office door closed with all the force of a world heavyweight champion trying to floor his opponent, and turned to Chris Barton. "Right. We can't trust anybody. So this operation doesn't go up town. Understand?" His detective inspector reminded him of the need to inform other senior officers, but that only provoked a greater fury. "Are you deaf? Nobody gets to know about tomorrow until after it's over. Is that understood? Or do you want it repeated?"

"Jack." Curtis' voice was calm. "You've made your point."

Priestley parked his arse and stared at the ceiling. Taking a moment to reflect. A moment to cool off. An officer had been compromised and was lucky to have escaped without serious injury, let alone his life. And it was Steve Blade who was responsible. The dirty scab. The bastard. And it made him feel like a bag of shit. It was his fault. He should have trusted his instincts. On the up-side, he was lucky that Cummings had been able to hold it all together. The operation was on for tomorrow. And it was going to be a success. It had to be. And that would be an end to all this crap that had been washing about in his mind for months. He steeled himself. He was a professional. The operation was on for tomorrow, he reminded himself again. That didn't give them much time to complete the preparations. He apologised to Barton and instructed him to get Cummings wired up for his drop. "And I want a full surveillance team on Hemp, Rambling and Furnace from six tomorrow morning," he said.

"What about Richardson?" asked Barton.

"Forget him. He's not going to be there. He wouldn't want to get his hands dirty. No, he was only there today because Blade had told him about Dave. He wanted to make sure his little firm didn't make the same mistake with George. It's the hundred grand he's interested in. Greedy bastard. Too big a carrot to be ignored." He was beginning to look and sound more like his old self again. "No, we'll concentrate on Hemp and his main performers. I want Freddie and Grant to accompany George on the bench. Just to make it look good. Okay. That's it for today. Thanks, boys. Go home and see if you can get some sleep. See you in the morning. The briefing will start at four thirty prompt."

* * * * *

Forty eight yawning officers assembled for the briefing the following morning and Priestley quickly outlined the operation to them. Surveillance teams would stay with the three chosen targets until Priestley deployed them to make the arrests. The £100,000 would be made up in real money, wrapped in newspaper, as directed by Richardson, but with an electronic tracking device tucked inside the parcel. Priestley hadn't obtained the proper authority to draw the money because that needed to come from Jim Nolan. And if Priestley's suspicions about Nolan were correct, then this wasn't an operation he would support. Cummings was briefed to follow Richardson's instructions to the letter. He would be accompanied by Freddie Green and Grant Jacobs, two of Jack Priestley's most experienced undercover officers. Back-up teams, under Priestley's personal direction, would be positioned as close to the drop site as possible, and communication would be maintained from the DCI's car. It was anticipated that someone, some dogsbody, would approach George and hand over the drugs. As soon as George had confirmed to Priestley that he'd been given the dope, the courier would be arrested and Priestley would send out the order to deploy the back-up teams. He would also send in the surveillance teams to arrest Hemp, Furnace and Rambling for conspiracy to supply and illegal importation.

All in all, the briefing went down well and everybody seemed to know what was expected of them. Priestley was satisfied that nothing more could be done. All he could do now was wait. And hope that Blade hadn't also told Richardson about Cummings. It was possible, just possible, that Blade had shopped Curtis in order to buff up his star with Frankie. Blade believed he was in the ascendancy with Frankie, and he may have decided to risk revealing Curtis simply to remove any further doubt from Frankie's mind. If he had Frankie's total trust, then between them Priestley and Blade could blow his whole organisation sky high. If that was the case, Priestley wished Blade had had the courtesy to let him know. Especially since he didn't seem to be able to get hold of him. Blade appeared to have vanished. Because on the other hand, Blade could have lied to him. Reverted to type. Anything was possible with Steve Blade. Always had been. The uncertainty was crucifying him, and as the minutes of the morning ticked slowly by, Priestley became more and more agitated.

* * * * *

George Cummings and his colleagues slowly approached the canal-side bench and sat down. Cummings took the middle spot, listening to the calls coming in over his hidden receiver. "Two minutes to three. Confirm." He checked his watch and confirmed the message by scratching his head, the pre-arranged signal.

"Three o'clock. Place the parcel in the bin." Through his binoculars, Priestley watched as Jamie Bunting's undercover officer stood up and walked over to the bin, which was about three yards away from the bench. He placed the newspaper-wrapped parcel containing the money inside and returned to the bench.

For the next couple of minutes nothing happened. Multiple pairs of eyes scanned the area surrounding the bench, but there was nothing untoward. Suddenly a call came through from the communications car, which contained the tracking device for monitoring the whereabouts of the money. "There's movement on the parcel." Priestley's head spun back towards the bin. The three officers were still sitting on the bench, motionless. The bin was in the same position as it had been all along. No one else was anywhere near them.

"Repeat that last message," he demanded.

"There's movement on the money, Boss. It's heading away from the bench. Forty, fifty, now sixty metres. It appears to be travelling underneath the motorway link."

"That's impossible!" he exclaimed, before calling Cummings. "UC One, what's happening?"

"Nothing, Boss. The money's still in the bin. No sign of anyone."

"Victor One." It was the radio operator again, in the communications car. "The money has now passed beyond our signal. Its last position was two hundred metres north of UC One."

"UC One." Priestley was becoming uncharacteristically frustrated and flustered. "Check the bin." He looked at his watch. It was now five minutes past and there was still no sign of any other person near the bench.

Cumming's face was a picture as he gazed down into the black hole in total astonishment. The bin was empty. Underneath it was an open manhole. The bottom of the bin had been removed to allow the cash to fall through. One hundred grand was probably halfway to China by now. "You won't believe this, Boss." He spoke like a man in shock. "They've had it away from underneath the bin. There's a big manhole down there, with the cover removed."

There was a brief period of utter silence, before Priestley's voice came across the air again. "An open manhole you say?"

"A big, wide-open manhole, Boss."

"Then, what you're saying is, we've lost the money?"

"Yes, Boss."

"And we've got no drugs, either?"

" No, Boss. No drugs nor money."

There was another brief period of silence. "Get down there, George. Take those other two with you. See if you can catch up with them. We'll try and stay in touch with you from up here." At least Priestley was still thinking clearly. He even sounded reasonably assertive. Which was quite a surprise in the circumstances. His blood was running through his veins like ice. He shivered as a cold sweat broke out across his back. One hundred unauthorised grand had just disappeared down a hole in the ground. And it was his head on the chopping block.

He demanded an update from his surveillance crews. There had been no movement from any of the targets all day. So far as the surveillance boys were concerned, the villains were still tucked up in bed.

* * * * *

The next two hours saw the operation overtaken by confusion and frustration as police officers swarmed all over the area surrounding the bench next to the bin. Hemp, Furnace and Rambling were arrested and their homes searched. Cummings and his colleagues eventually returned to Priestley, soaked through and stinking of sewerage. Almost apologetically they explained that they had walked miles through the sewer but had found no trace of the villains. Priestley's eyes scanned the heavens as if searching for divine help. This was a nightmare of the first order. The money he'd just been parted from hadn't been sanctioned. He was going to be trussed up on a rack for this. His mobile rang. It was Blade.

"Don't hang up, Jack," he shouted. "It doesn't matter what you think of me, Priestley. These guys aren't wankers."

"Go piss on yourself, Judas." Furious, Priestley's finger was about to press the disconnect button when his brain registered what Blade's screaming voice was saying.

"Jack, don't hang up. Don't hang up. The money's with a geezer from London named Briggs. He's holed up at 43 Inkerman Street. It's a sting, Jack. They've got your dope stashed away in an empty petrol container in the car park of Smith's Garage in Yardley. It was brought down last night. They'll be moving it out in a few minutes."

Blade disconnected the call himself. Within seconds crime squad crews were flying towards both locations.

* * * * *

Ten minutes slowly went by. Priestley lit a cigar and lent against his car. Another five minutes. The tension inside him was at boiling point. After twenty minutes, the first call came through on the radio, "Victor One from DI Barton. We've one in custody and the money back." Priestley swore he would go to church at the first opportunity. He breathed out a deep, relieved sigh, one which came from the very depths of his soul. The radio burst into life once more. "Victor One from Sergeant Bakewell. Two in custody and a mountain of heroin recovered from Smith's Garage." Thank you God, whispered Priestley. His relief was absolute. One minute a failure, and the next a success.

36

The three of them leant against the bar in silence, watching the cabaret. One of the dancing girls sashayed across the room towards them. She swung her right breast into Hemp's face and was promptly told to vanish. Her buttocks slapped together as she made her way hurriedly back to the stage. The three musketeers continued to watch the remainder of the performance, each deeply engaged in their own thoughts.

Nesbitt was the first to be summoned into the big man's office. Now that they were alone, Hemp said, "So what went wrong?"

"You tell me," responded Blade. "It was your ball game, Bernie."

"You know that's what we're here for?" he said. "To get our balls chewed off."

"If it hadn't been for me, your little empire would have collapsed by now, Bernie. That man Sparky was going to rip you to shreds."

"But it was you who introduced him, you prat."

"Yep. And it was me who spotted he wasn't kosher. So you've a lot to thank me for."

"Then how can you explain the hits at Jimmy Briggs's and the garage?" Hemp was desperately trying to kick the blame into someone else's corner. He knew perfectly well he was responsible for this fuck-up. In Frankie's eyes, anyway.

"Bernie, how should I know, mate?"

Nesbitt reappeared, a broad smile plastered across his ugly, scarred face. He said nothing. Just nodded as he made his way towards the exit. Slimy bastard, thought Blade. Lambesi appeared a second or two later and signalled to the twosome to enter Frankie's lair. They followed him like sheep.

The welcome bestowed on Nesbitt was a great deal warmer than the one given to Blade and Hemp. But Blade felt confident. He knew the problem was Hemp's to deal with. After all, Blade was the one who'd severely damaged the police operation. But Hemp? Well, Hemp had screwed up big time, even if he didn't know how he'd done it.

The big man rose from behind his desk, like a huge hippopotamus leaving the muddy waters to reach dry land. "My boys,' he said. "Today is the first day of the rest of my life." He lit a Havana. "And that goes for you two, too." Hemp didn't have the brains to be anything other than relieved. Blade, on the other hand, sensed danger. Big danger for someone. "Tony," Frankie continued. "Drinks all round I think." He paused to study his employees. "The fighting stops now." What fighting? Hemp and Blade looked at each other in confusion. "We go forward together, my friends." Frankie certainly knew how to make an occasion. Blade and Hemp wondered what the occasion was. All was soon revealed. "On Thursday night we will be taking delivery of the biggest palette yet." To Frankie, a palette meant a consignment, whether it was a sack full or a lorry load. "Harry is going to take care of that, together with the boys in Manchester. But I've jobs for you two, too.

"On Thursday evening, you will come here," he said pointing at Blade. "And you," he said, turning to Hemp, "Will coordinate the buyers. And after the last debacle, you will be very, very careful. Very careful indeed. This is your last chance Bernie. Fuck up again, and you're dead. There's been too much filth hanging around your neck recently, Bernie. I will soon know who was responsible for your recent disaster. I pay good money for that kind of information." He broke off and shouted at Lambesi where he was fixing the drinks. "Tony, get Nolan on the phone. Don't worry about Bernie's drink. He won't be needing it." He turned back to Hemp. "Watch yourself, Bernie. It must never happen again. See that it doesn't. Now go." They both stood and prepared to leave. "Not you, Croaker. You stay here."

As Hemp exited, Lambesi connected the call. Richardson sat back down and picked up the receiver from one of the several phones on his desk. "Have you got it?" he said. Blade pretended to occupy himself in examining the gilt-framed artwork on Frankie's walls, while Frankie was busy with his phone call. "Look here, you little piece of Irish shit, I pay you well. You just do your job. Understand?" There was another pause, longer this time. Evidently, Jim Nolan was being creative with his excuses, thought Blade. Frankie was staring at him. It was disconcerting. "Okay, Jimmy. That's fine." He put the phone down.

Blade knew not to speak until he was spoken to. "This Jack Priestley, Croaker. Friend of yours?"

Blade stayed cool "I throw him tit-bits, Frankie." He knew that denying he'd ever spoken to Priestley would only cause him grief he certainly didn't need. It looked as though his position was precarious. "How do you think I learned about the undercover?"

He waited. Frankie was slow in responding. Finally he said, "What's he like, this Priestley?"

"One hard bastard, Frankie," he said. "But he's a wanker. And he trusts me, Frankie."

"He's been making too many noises around and about recently, Croaker. It wasn't easy getting Bernie and his boys off the hook for this last caper."

Blade shook his head. "I don't think you need to worry about Priestley, Frankie. He doesn't know his arse from his elbow."

"He's taken twenty-five grand."

"Probably thinks you'll give him more if he keeps on agitating."

Frankie smiled and Blade fought to conceal his relief as he said, "Okay, Croaker. I'll trust you on this one. But keep an eye on him. He's a troublemaker." A wave of Richardson's hand signalled the end of the audience and Blade left, unscathed, although in the end he'd never been given that drink.

* * * * *

Priestley leant on the wooden railing and watched the water passing underneath the bridge while he tried to work everything out. He was more frightened than ever. He'd tried to contact David Greswolde but every time he rang he got the same reply. "He's in a meeting. Please leave a message or try again later." Well, he'd left messages and he'd tried again later. But nothing. His calls were not returned and Greswolde was never available to come to the phone. He felt abandoned and alone. He felt he was starting to lose his grip on reality. He stood and slowly made his way back towards where he'd parked the car, his mind trying to analyse everything which had brought him this far. And where was that? Where had those incidents and snippets of information brought him?

Sonia Hall was told by a client of a conspiracy to cover up the murders of known informants. Informants who had been identified by bent law. A kid, who had topped himself in the nick, had told Steve Blade about a bookshop, Dale End Books, that was a front for video nasties. He'd spent hours sitting outside the place with nothing to show for it, except the occasional glimpse of that sleezeball, Paul Meade. He'd probably gone in to buy a book on local government reform. Not once had he seen John Briskett, the man reputed to be selling the informants' details. And apart from that there was Nolan, Boyle and Jones. All guilty as hell he was sure. But after months of investigation he still had no real proof. Meanwhile, there was Frankie Richardson, the godfather of them all, or so he suspected. The man pulling everyone's strings. Certainly he was the man pulling Nesbitt's strings, Hemp's strings and now Steve Blade's as well. He'd made a big error of judgement there. Once a con, always a con. There was no such thing as a reformed convict.

He continued walking, on past the spot where he'd left his car. Absorbed in his thoughts. The operation the other day had been a success in the end. Except that he couldn't get a single charge to stick. Frank Newhart had told him to drop it. So now he suspected Newhart was in it as well. It was one fucking big conspiracy. And he felt like he was the only one who cared. The only one who was trying to do anything about it. Why wouldn't bloody Greswolde return his calls? What more could he do without help? The path he'd been following came to an abrupt dead end. Simultaneously, he realised he'd reached the end of the investigation. He had nowhere else to take it. At the same time, he decided he'd give Dale End Books one more go. Why not? He had nothing to loose. Nothing at all.

* * * * *

Dale End Books looked the same as it had every other time he'd parked outside it. In all respects it looked like an innocent bookshop. Quite a successful one, too. Ordinary-looking people wandered in and out all day, going in empty-handed and coming out with a book or two in their hands. For two days now, Priestley had been wondering why he was bothering. He fidgeted in his seat. It was pointless. He looked at his watch. Three thirty. Two more hours until the shop would close to the public. In a few minutes, his favourite newspaper reporter would take over from him. He considered cancelling her. They weren't going to see anything. Why not just admit defeat and get on with life? But Priestley knew, with a kind of fatalistic certainty, that the moment they stopped watching the shop something would happen. He didn't really know what he was looking for. Perhaps a string of young schoolgirls going in to be filmed? Or Frankie Richardson rolling up with an entourage of bodyguards. Or, perhaps one of his own colleagues. The last person he expected was Harry Nesbitt. Instinctively, he slipped down in his seat, anxious not to be seen, as he watched the little man enter.

Hardly daring to breathe, he watched and waited. Within two minutes, Nesbitt was out of the shop again. But this customer didn't have a book in his hand. He paused on the doorstep, just long enough to slip an envelope into the inside pocket of his jacket. Then he walked briskly away in the direction from which he'd come.

Watching him go, Priestley couldn't believe it. Nesbitt! Perfect. His thoughts were interrupted by the sound of tapping at the passenger window. Carol Guardia, come to take her turn at surveillance. Priestley grinned. "Not tonight, sweetheart," he said. "Tonight's cancelled you'll be glad to know."

37

The little man looked as if he would shit himself when he saw the warrant card. "How can I help you Mr ..." he stammered, squinting as he tried to make out the name.

Priestley helped him out. "Priestley," he said. "Detective Chief Inspector Priestley." He knew that this was going to be his last throw of the dice and had decided to go in as though his life depended upon it. "I've come about the protection money you're paying Harry Nesbitt."

That did it. The guess was right. Chrissie Dean staggered and could only hold himself upright by gripping the edge of the desk which supported the old-fashioned manual till. The type of thing Priestley hadn't seen since he was a kid. He hadn't been in a shop which had a proper brass bell attached to the door since then either. "What?" Dean stuttered. "I don't know what you're talking about, but ..."

"But what, Mr Dean?" asked Priestley, pleasantly. "I don't want to hear any bollocks off you, Chrissie. Let's go and see what you've got in your back room shall we." Priestley stepped back to the shop door and slid the bolt across the top, one eye remaining on the lump of jelly that quivered away behind the till.

At last the bookseller managed to splutter something. Most of it was incoherent, except for the final word: "... warrant?"

Priestley got the gist. "Don't need one," he replied. "Under the Police and Criminal Evidence Act, I don't need a warrant to make an arrest for a criminal offence, sunshine."

"Arrest?" said jelly-on-legs. "I'm being arrested?" He couldn't believe it.

Priestley smiled. After all he'd been through recently, he was enjoying this. "Not yet. But you soon will be if you don't hurry up and open that fucking door."

Seconds later, Priestley and Dean were standing in Dean's back sitting room. Carefully labelled video tapes lined all four walls, floor to ceiling. Thousands of them. In the centre of the room was a table upon which a television stood. There was a video tape lying beside it. Priestley picked it up and read the label on the spine. His eyebrows shot off his face. It said, Meade. That rang a bit of a bell. He handed it to Dean. "Play it," he said. But Dean's shaking was now so bad that he couldn't slot the tape into the machine. Priestley snatched it from him. "I'll do it, idiot. The least you can do is switch on the telly for me, Chrissie."

A few seconds later the bare white arse of none other than the ex-leader of the council was bouncing all over the screen on top of some thirty-five-year-old schoolgirl. It wasn't long before Priestley had seen enough and he stopped the tape. This kind of crap made his skin crawl. "Do you know who that man is?" he asked.

But Dean was still unable to talk. Plus his head was shaking just as much as the rest of his body, so Priestley couldn't be certain whether that was providing his answer. Time to shake a leg though, thought Priestley, and get on with it. He hadn't got all day to wait for Dean to pull himself together. He ejected the tape and waved it at the gibbering man. This time he shouted, "Do you know who this is?" That did the trick. The shaking immediately switched to more obvious and comprehensible nodding. "Blackmail?" he said. Dean nodded some more.

Christ, thought Priestley. What a piece of luck. This was like walking into a gold mine. No wonder Dean was paying for protection. He wondered what else he'd find. "Sit down, Chrissie," he said sharply. Dean collapsed onto the sofa underneath the blacked-out window. "Now," he said. "Who else have you got in your collection, Chrissie?"

"I want a ... a ... I want a ..." Chrissie Dean was incapable of making any sense. Priestley had never seen anything like it. The man was wretched with fear. Christ. What did he think he was going to do to him?

"Chrissie," he repeated slowly. "Who else do you have in your collection?" Priestley was beginning to lose his patience. Fortunately, Dean decided to be sensible, and pointed towards a partially hidden drawer in the table. Priestley recovered three more videos from it. Bingo. The labels said: Newhart, Nolan, and Briskett, respectively. Wow, thought Priestley. This must be a gift from God. Each of the tapes showed the man in question in various states of nudity, executing acts in various degrees of sexual perversion. Priestley didn't care to look too closely at the details, but the image of John Briskett's lily-white arse bouncing up and down like Zeberdee would remain with him for a long time. And amuse him in times of difficulty. When he'd seen enough, which didn't take long, he really didn't have the stomach for this kind of thing, he pressed the button on his mobile. "Okay, Chris," he said. "You can bring in the cavalry." Then addressing Dean he explained what was about to happen. "In a matter of seconds, three hundred mounted men are going to ride straight through these premises and find everything you've got."

The little man nodded. In fact he hadn't stopped nodding since Priestley had accused him of blackmail. "Now, to save them breaking the place up completely, I want you to give me the lists you've taken off Mr Briskett. All of them."

He couldn't believe it. Immediately, the bowl of jelly rose from the sofa, walked over to the crumpled-looking mat that lay in front of the fireplace, lifted it, and pulled out a number of loose pages. He handed them to Priestley, who, in his excitement, found the shakes were contagious. They were official intelligence logs containing lists of names, addresses, and payments made to each individual. As Priestley heard the front door being hammered he spotted two of the names he'd deliberately looked for. Kenny Mulch and Annette Colby. He raised his eyes from the evidence and met Dean's. "You'd best answer the door," he said.

* * * * *

"The pages recovered from the bookshop contained eighteen names," reported Barton, later that day. "Five are now dead, and another eight have been the victims of some kind of violent attack or other brutality."

"And the other five?" asked Priestley, his face grey with tiredness. He hadn't been sleeping properly recently. This investigation was making him ill.

"They seem to have been the lucky ones, Boss. Or perhaps they're still on the waiting list."

"Perhaps," Priestley replied. "Well done, Chris. You've done a great job. Thank you. Just remember to keep the lid on it and continue gathering as much information as you can. It won't be long before people start to find out what we've got, and the longer it takes them, the better."

* * * * *

Having pulled off such a stunning coup at Dale End Books, Priestley was now almost ready to take his evidence to the chief constable. He felt he had a few more knots to tie, however. A few more strings to pull. But if, by the end of his investigations, he hadn't quite managed to complete the whole jigsaw, there was sufficient in his dossier for higher authorities to take over and fill in the gaps. The greatest danger he now faced was from his own people. Those trusted detectives who weren't fully aware of the implications of what they were being asked to do for their DCI. They were doing the foot work and providing him with the information he needed to complete the picture.

One word out of place. One hint about what they were doing. One small fragment of intelligence leaked. And all would be lost. As he got closer there wasn't a single hour that passed when he didn't remind them of the need for secrecy. The gentlemen involved had no idea that Priestley now had the tapes Dean was using to bribe them. And it was crucial that it stayed that way. But, best of all, one of the final pieces of the jigsaw, and the piece that would otherwise have eluded Priestley, had now been slotted into place. What Priestley had always suspected might be the case had turned out to be true. Dean worked for Frankie. He wondered if Dean knew that Harry Nesbitt did too? Probably not. Frankie was perfectly capable of manipulating his people and keeping them neatly pigeon-holed. But all that made it doubly urgent that Priestley proceeded with all haste. If word got back to Frankie that Dean had been busted, then the shit would hit the fan.

38

The same day that Priestley busted Dean, Blade was with Frankie. It was Thursday. The day the big shipment, or palette as Frankie liked to call it, was coming in. And Frankie wanted Blade with him to keep him company while he waited for the good news to come down the wire. Frankie always found these big delivery days a bit hard to handle. Everything was out of his control. In the hands of his people. And you could never be certain. Never be absolutely certain, that they wouldn't screw up. On recent performance they probably would. But Nesbitt was a safer pair of hands he hoped. Safer than that idiot Hemp anyway.

While he waited, Frankie was amusing himself by lecturing Blade. He was rather enjoying himself. "You see, Croaker, in this business you can only trust two people. One's the man who saves your life, because you are indebted to him for the remainder of it. And that's you, Croaker," he said, looking at Blade significantly. "And the other's your mother." Frankie chuckled. Blade prayed it wouldn't develop into serious laughter. He didn't think he could stand another bellowing. This time he was lucky though. It didn't.

The big man got up and heaved his corpulent frame over to a teak cabinet in one corner of the room. He made a great ceremony of unlocking it, using a key which he kept on a gold chain around his neck. He removed a large, leather-bound book and brought it back to his desk to show Blade. "See this. And this. And this." His finger darted across one of the pages of the open book. "Each entry is a record of every payment I've ever made. How much and to whom," he said. "Do you know why?"

"Taxman?" Blade guessed, knowing he was wrong. But that did it. The bellows started up again and Frankie nearly fell off his chair in his amusement and delight. Christ, thought Blade. It wasn't that funny. The noise was so loud, Tony Lambesi even risked his boss's wrath by poking his startled face around the door to see what was going on. The wave of Frankie's hand ensured his hasty retreat and Frankie slowly composed himself, to an accompaniment of coughing and spluttering.

"No, Croaker. Blackmail." Blade wondered why Frankie was telling him this. "If any of them step out of line, boom!" The desk shook as Big Frankie's heavy fist fell on top of the ledger.

"Couldn't you just take them for a swim, Frankie?" said Blade, more careful now. The last thing he wanted was to induce a heart attack.

"No, Croaker. You see that's where I'm smart and you're …" The big man hesitated as he searched for a word that wouldn't hurt Blade's feelings. He liked Croaker. He'd become his mascot, ever since he'd put that undercover cop onto him. It was unlikely that Blade would ever have better proof that he'd made it with Frankie. Christ, the guy was bothering to be considerate. That was unheard of. Finally, Frankie settled on "… you're inexperienced." Nice solution, Frankie. "These are all payments made to businessmen and filth," he finished.

Blade took a closer look at the book, but it didn't make much sense to him. Frankie had used a code to make each entry. Frankie sat back in his chair and chuckled in happy self-satisfaction at his own smart-arse methods. Then, one of his phones rang. He picked it up but said nothing. "Good," he said eventually and hung up. He looked at Blade. "The delivery's in." Blade nodded in relief.

*   *   *   *   *

Frankie's office was on the top floor of the building. Only electronic listening devices could have picked up the sound of the nylon rope dropping down the outside of the building from the roof. It took just three seconds for the silent visitor, dressed in black from head to toe, to slide down it and reach the window. As he expected, the room was in total darkness. It took another five seconds for the alarm to be disconnected. Penetrating gas helped to slide the window back more easily. It also had the benefit of keeping things quiet. Less than a minute after leaving the roof, the intruder was standing in Frankie's office. The beam of a powerful flashlight was flicked on and streaked around the room until it came to rest on the teak cabinet in the corner. For the professional it was only a matter of seconds before it was open, so that he could remove the large, leather-bound ledger. Seconds later he was gone. Back on the roof the burglar looked at his watch and noted that the whole operation had been accomplished in less than three minutes.

39

"Jack, wake up. There's somebody at the door." Sonia made sure he heard what she was saying by digging an elbow into his ribs.

"Christ," he muttered, dragging himself out of sleep. "It's the middle of the fucking night."

"I know," Sonia whispered. "But listen. They're going to bang the door down. I think you should go and find out what they want." Priestley groaned. He was exhausted. Groggy from the sleeping pills he'd started using to help him sleep. He winced at the clock. Five thirty. Fucking hell. The banging was becoming more insistent. He dragged himself off the bed and staggered around searching for his dressing gown. A picture of three or four heavies carrying violin cases, sprang into his mind. Christ, he muttered again. He hoped this wasn't trouble come knocking at his door.

He was right. There were three of them. But minus the violins. Thank God. They were law. "Chief Inspector Priestley?" the first one said, brightly. One cheerful Charlie with his hands in his overcoat pockets.

"That's me," he said. "Who's asking?"

"Detective Superintendent Martin. Special Branch. Mind if we come in? Bit parky out here."

Special Branch? "Cards, gents?" he queried. Each one flashed a warrant card and he made sure he examined them all carefully. They were all Metropolitan Police. What the hell were they doing here? He stepped back and let them in.

Detective Superintendent Martin wasn't in any hurry. Once inside the house, he spent the first couple of minutes checking it out. "Very nice, too," he commented.

Priestley was beginning to become impatient. "How can I help you, gentlemen?" he said.

"We are making some inquiries into a criminal organisation and I'm afraid we've come to arrest you on suspicion of involvement."

Jack was taken so much by surprise that he didn't hear any of the caution that followed. They asked him to get dressed, then escorted him out to their car. He remained silent throughout the journey to London. Now he knew how it felt to be in custody. He felt powerless. But he also understood that until he knew what all this crap was about it was pointless asking questions, however many may be cramming his mind. Luckily for Priestley, the effects of the sleeping pill hadn't yet worn off, and the gentle rocking of the car as it sped down the empty motorway soon lulled him back to sleep. Like he hadn't a care in the world.

* * * * *

At least he hadn't been told to sit and wait in the formidable atmosphere of an interview room. Instead, they'd put him in somebody's office. And the room was extraordinary. It had a large ornamental fireplace with a Louis XV clock sitting on the mantel. The fireplace was flanked by two large red leather armchairs. In one corner of the room stood an imposing mahogany desk, and in the other a large conference table, also mahogany. This was where he had chosen to sit as he examined the unusual room. Unusual, because the office was on the tenth floor of the New Scotland Yard building, which, after all, is only a modern office block. It certainly wasn't the elegant gentlemen's club this room had pretensions to be. The only real reminder that the start of the twenty-first century was fast approaching was an open laptop computer that sat on the other end of the conference table.

After a while, he stood and walked slowly over to the window. He could see St Paul's Cathedral in the distance, set against a cloudless winter sky. As he looked across at the impressive dome, he wondered what on earth was going on. Probably his investigation had at last touched a nerve within his own organisation. And this is how they'd chosen to deal with him. He wondered what kind of false and devious tricks were going to be produced from the Pandora's Box they would have prepared for him. He was watching a flight of pigeons wheeling across the sky when the door opened and in walked the cheerful Charlie with a bundle of papers tucked under his arm.

"Take a seat, Jack," he suggested, pointing in the direction of the chair Priestley had vacated only moments ago. Priestley did as he was told. They were joined by another Special Branch man and they sat one on either side of him. Martin started to fumble through the buff coloured folders he'd placed on the table. Eventually, he found what he was looking for and placed a black and white photograph in front of Priestley. "Does this ring a bell, Jack?"

He looked at it. It was a recent picture and showed himself and that double-eyed git, Blade, standing together outside a public house. Big deal, thought Jack. They could have a thousand photos of him and Blade together. They probably did have. But they didn't prove anything. "Do I get to see a solicitor before I answer your questions?"

"I'm afraid not," declared Martin. "You see these inquiries are of an extremely sensitive nature and it wouldn't be in the nation's interests for you to have legal representation at this point in time." Bollocks to the nation, thought Jack. What about me? This was all getting a bit too serious. He knew that if he couldn't satisfy their thirst for answers, he could end up being in their company for another seven days. Held under the Prevention of Terrorism Act for fucks sake. Christ. What in heaven's name was going on?

Martin tapped the photograph with his finger, so Priestley forced his attention back to it. The faster he answered the questions, the sooner he'd be out of here. "Yes," he said. "That's me and a geezer called Steve Blade. We're just ..."

"And who is this Steve Blade?"

"I suppose you could describe him as an informant. Not a very ..."

"And where were you when this photograph was taken?"

"You'd better ask the cameraman," joked Priestley. But nobody laughed. He was starting to get frightened. He must be careful. No more glib comments. Just who exactly did these people think they were? And who did they think he was? Well that much was clear. They thought he was bent. No better than the people he'd spent half a lifetime battling to put behind bars.

Martin repeated the question. "Where was the picture taken, Chief Inspector?"

Priestley sighed and looked again. "It must have been outside the Carpenters Arms. That's the only pub I ever met him in."

"And where's that?"

"Near the city centre."

"Birmingham?"

"Yes."

* * * * *

Colin Boyle was talking into his mobile phone as he stood on the steps of the Central Library building. He felt a hand rest upon on his shoulder and a young student snatched the phone away from him. He thought he'd seen the scruffy looking geezer somewhere before, but he wasn't sure. There were two suits standing behind the long-haired git.

"DS Boyle?" the young man said.

The police officer didn't bother to answer, still aghast at what the cheeky little bastard had done with his phone. But a warrant card was flashed before him. "Special Branch," the student said. "I'm arresting you on suspicion of attempted murder and conspiracy to supply illegal drugs."

*   *   *   *   *

"And where was this picture taken?" A second photograph appeared from one of the folders. It was similar to the first, outside the same building, but this time there was a third person. An Asian or an Arab. Standing immediately behind Blade, as though in their company. But Jack knew he wasn't, or hadn't been. He'd never seen the man before in his life.

"Same place, I presume," he said.

"Who are the people?"

"Blade again. I don't know who the other guy is."

"You sure about that, Mr Priestley?"

"You deaf?" They were starting to rattle him. "I've told you. I don't know the man."

*   *   *   *   *

The Mercedes came slowly up the drive towards the large detached house, the front of which was covered in ivy. Its brickwork was stained with age and was noticeably worn away in places. A man was standing at the front door, searching for his house keys. His expression was crestfallen when he realised the door had not been opened for him by his wife.

"Mr Paul Meade?" There were two of them. One was tall and dark. The other short and fair. Both were dressed in white shirts and dark blue suits and ties.

"Yes." Meade was taken aback and his knees almost gave way when they produced their warrant cards.

"I'm Inspector Rogers," said the dark one. "And this is Sergeant Gaunt. We're from Special Branch. I'm arresting you on suspicion of attempting to pervert the course of justice."

* * * * *

This was the tenth photograph Priestley had been asked to look at. They had all been more-or-less the same. Pictures of himself and Blade, either leaving the Carpenters Arms or crossing the car park. And Priestley was starting to get bored. He felt it was time for him to start asking the questions. "What's going on here? I haven't done anything wrong. Quite the reverse. Would you like to tell me what I'm accused of?" Priestley was on his feet, trying to make an impression. Trying to clear the air. Trying to make some sense out of this load of crap. His finger pointed at Martin. "You start answering my questions now, mister, or ..." Or what, he thought? There wasn't much he could do except sit here and allow whoever was sticking pins in his effigy to continue. But who was the smart arse holding the doll? "I want to know exactly what this is all about, before I answer any more questions, or look at any more of your frigging photographs," he declared. Another photograph was placed in front of him.

* * * * *

Nolan first noticed the two men standing in the far corner of the car park as he walked towards his own vehicle. They were staring at him. He nodded at them as he placed the key in the driver's door, but they remained motionless. He opened the door. "Mr Nolan?" one of them shouted. He looked up, but didn't answer. He felt his stomach turning over although he didn't know why. They approached him, and the older of the two introduced himself. "Deputy Commissioner Falstaff," he said. "Special Branch."

Nolan looked at him. "What can I do for you, Mr Deputy Commissioner?"

"We'd like a word, if you please." Nolan re-locked his car and turned to walk back across the car park to his office. "No. Not here, Mr Nolan," the man said. "We'd like you to come with us."

"Where to?"

"London."

"You can piss off."

"Very well, Mr Nolan. In that case, I'm arresting you on suspicion of conspiring to import drugs and conspiring to pervert the course of justice." Nolan gulped as the second Special Branch man pulled out a pair of handcuffs.

* * * * *

This was too much. Frustrated, Priestley leapt from his chair and began pacing around the room. "I need to know what all this is about," he insisted. The phone rang and Martin picked it up. Priestley realised that it must be his office they were in. Martin put the phone back down. He hadn't said a word. "I've asked enough times," Priestley continued.

"Very well, Jack," Martin conceded. He leant back in his chair, hands twisted together to support the back of his head. But he didn't say any more. He just sat there grinning like an idiot.

"Well?" Jack shouted from the middle of the room.

* * * * *

John Briskett carried his well-built frame across the narrow street. His out-of-fashion trilby and gabardine mackintosh went with the bonfire blazing away in his pipe bowl. He'd parked his car almost opposite the bookshop, in virtually the same spot as Priestley had been using over the past few days. Briskett was carrying a small bundle of papers which he'd taken off the back seat and he approached the shop as if he hadn't a care in the world. But as he reached for the door handle, the door swung open and two men barred his way. A warrant card flashed before his eyes and he just managed to see the words 'Metropolitan Police' written across the top. They introduced themselves and John Briskett's world collapsed.

*　*　*　*　*

"My, my, Jack. Aren't you all over-excited," said a quiet voice behind him. Jack recognised it immediately and swung around to see David Greswolde standing in the doorway. With that bastard Blade behind him.

*　*　*　*　*

Tony Lambesi didn't have a care in the world. He was only employed as a gofer by Big Frankie and wasn't impressed at all by the muzzle stuck behind his right ear. "Some men to see you, Frankie."

For once, his boss didn't have much to say as another two Magnums were pointed in his direction. "How can I help you gentlemen?" he asked. One of the faces behind one of the Magnums told him his rights.

40

"So you see, Jack, we had to get you out of the way before we could introduce the final phase of our operation," explained Greswolde. "Well, it was your operation really." He nodded towards Blade who had joined them at the table and he placed Big Frankie's ledger in front of Priestley. "Steve came aboard early on. Right after you came to see me. And after gaining Richardson's confidence we managed to acquire this book from him last night. This is the evidence that we so desperately needed if we were to be successful. It proves conclusively everything you've uncovered."

Priestley was looking through the ledger as Greswolde talked. "But all the names are in code," he said.

Greswolde nodded. "That's right. But it only took the code crackers a few seconds to decipher it. It's a very simple system. Mr VG Hirpy in the ledger, for example, is John Briskett. John Briskett, by the way, has admitted everything on tape. This morning. Apparently, Dean got sufficient to blackmail him with on the video tape you hid away in your garage yesterday."

Priestley's mouth dropped open. "You screwed my garage?"

"This morning. We had to, Jack, to get the thing back." A wry smile came onto Greswolde's face. "Your DI Barton is a very astute man. You need to encourage him more."

He paused while Priestley struggled to take it all in. "Anyway, whatever Briskett provided, Dean passed onto

Richardson. Frankie wanted to know the names of the informants who'd been responsible for putting in his drugs jobs and Dean got them for him. You know the rest as far as that's concerned."

"So you got the Meade tape from my garage as well?"

Greswolde nodded again. "Yep. And Newhart's and Nolan's. Whenever Richardson wanted to embark on some property development, such as buying land to build a nightclub or whatever, he served notice on Meade and the councillor looked after it for him. Similarly, Newhart and Nolan looked after any issues that arose with the police."

"Blackmail?"

"Yes. Through Chrissie Dean."

"Why didn't they just knock off Dean and get the tapes back?"

"Simple, Jack. Richardson. Nobody knew whether he had copies, and, in any case, anybody bumping off little Chrissie would have been dealt with by Richardson."

It was all fitting into place. Greswolde laughed at him. "You'll find Nolan in Richardson's book under the name of Mr WB Yiz. He totalled more than seventy grand last year."

"And Boyle?"

"Boyle drew the top shelf. More than a hundred big ones. According to the book."

"Well, the dirty little scumbag."

"They've all been arrested this morning. Big Frankie included. He must be screaming blue murder by now. He'll have discovered that we also busted his delivery last night. So we've got Hemp and Nesbitt in custody too."

At last, Priestley turned to Blade, "And you, you little bastard. You knew about this all the time."

Blade shrugged. What could he say? "I'm looking for a knighthood, Jack!"

"We couldn't have done this without Steve, Jack," explained Greswolde. "We couldn't have done it without either of you."

"But you put Curtis onto Richardson." Priestley told Blade.

"I had to, Jack. To get the kind of credibility I needed to get into Frankie's inner sanctum. I knew they wouldn't top him, Jack. And if it had gone pear-shaped, I was right outside the snooker hall. So that if it did go down, I could pull them both out."

Priestley turned back to Greswolde. "Why the Met?"

"Well, we thought a covert operation by another force would make sense. And when you approached Jamie Bunting that settled it for us.

"And all that crap about looking at photographs, in here, earlier?"

"Just to keep you out of the way while we wound up the operation. You would have wanted a piece of the action and the slightest sighting of you would have blown it all."

"So it was a case of me following them and you lot following me?"

Greswolde nodded and smiled. "And meanwhile your chief constable is patiently awaiting your arrival back in your own force, Superintendent."

"Superintendent?"

"Wouldn't be at all surprised." Greswolde winked.

"He knows about this, David?"

"Since you visited me, Jack. Sorry about that, but we both agreed not to interfere with what you were doing." Greswolde smiled broadly. He had one more comment to make. "Turn to page twelve in the ledger, Jack. Who do you think Mr Kirbogh is?" Priestley looked. Mr Kirbogh had been paid twenty-five grand in a single payment. "Mr Priestley, Jack. Mr Jack Priestley." Now Jack joined in the laughter.

* * * * *

Priestley and Blade sat in silence for the first part of the journey home. The policeman was slowly beginning to get over the shock and take in what had happened. He couldn't

242

help but feel a little miffed by what had taken place. After all, he'd been duped into believing nothing was being done. He'd been the one to run around like a mad monkey. Carrying the full burden of frustration and worry. And he was also the only one being kept in the dark. Deliberately. He felt like he'd been used. Like a puppet having his strings tugged by others who were well out of the firing line. He turned to Blade. "You know, I feel like a complete prat. I must have been the only person in the set up who hadn't a clue what was happening." He was really pissed off now he came to think about it. But there was no response from Blade.

After a while, Blade turned away from the window and looked towards Priestley. "I've just done four hard years, Jack," he reminded him. "During which time, I laughed, cried and felt pain in every part of my body." He held up his hand, cutting off Jack's inevitable interruption. "I know I'm responsible for putting myself there. I know I wasn't forced to knock off that post office van. You've told me plenty of times. But consider this, Jack Priestley. What will you get out of this little caper that you didn't know anything about?" The hint of anger in Blade's voice was growing. "It sounds like another rank from what I've heard. And all you can do is sit there moaning like a fat man's armchair." He was right, thought Priestley. He began to feel a little ashamed. Blade must have risked a lot to help out on this one. "What do you think I'll get out of it, Jack? For all my efforts. A promotion? A medal? No. It'll just be a quick, 'Bye, bye Mr Blade and, by the way, thanks for being an honest, upstanding citizen.'"

Blade turned away again. He was right and Jack Priestley knew it. He not only felt ashamed, he felt extremely humble. He offered up his hand. Blade glanced at it out of the corner of his eye, but otherwise ignored it. Seconds passed slowly by. Blade glanced back. The hand was still there. He looked into Priestley's face. It had I'm-so-sorry written all over it. The anger inside Blade dissolved and he grabbed his old friend's hand in his own.

HOUSE OF STRATUS

These, or any other books from the extensive House of Stratus range, can be obtained by:

- Visiting any good Book Store

- Calling the Sales Hotline on 0800 169 1780 (UK only)
  or +44 (0) 1845 527700 (International)

- Faxing The House of Stratus on +44 (0) 1845 527711

- Visiting our website at: www.hosbooks.com

- Emailing: sales@hosbooks.com

- Writing to: Stratus Holdings plc
  Lumley Close
  Thirsk Industrial Park
  Thirsk
  North Yorkshire
  YO7 3BX
  UK

The House of Stratus publishes many other titles in the fiction crime and suspense series including books by **Freeman Wills Crofts** and **Erle Stanley Gardner**.